Praise for the novels of Debra Webb

"A hot hand with action, suspense and last, but not least, a steamy relationship."
—*New York Times* bestselling author Linda Howard

"Debra Webb's name says it all."
—*New York Times* bestselling author Karen Rose

"Compelling main characters and chilling villains elevate Debra Webb's Faces of Evil series to the realm of high-intensity thrillers that readers won't be able to resist."
—*New York Times* bestselling author CJ Lyons

"A well-crafted, and engrossing thriller. Debra Webb has crafted a fine, twisting thriller to be savored and enjoyed."
—*New York Times* bestselling author Heather Graham on *Traceless*

"A steamy, provocative novel with deep, deadly secrets guaranteed to be worthy of your time."
—*Fresh Fiction* on *Traceless*

"Debra Webb's best work yet. The gritty, edge-of-your-seat, white-knuckled thriller is peopled with tough, credible characters and a brilliant plot that will keep you guessing until the very end."
—*New York Times* bestselling author Cindy Gerard on *Obsession*

"Interspersed with fine-tuned suspense...the cliffhanger conclusion will leave readers eagerly anticipating future installments."
—*Publishers Weekly* on *Obsession*

"Webb reaches into our deepest nightmares and pulls out a horrifying scenario. She delivers the ultimate villain."
—*RT Book Reviews* on *Dying to Play*

Also by Debra Webb

The Blackest Crimson
No Darker Place
A Deeper Grave

Look for Debra Webb's next novel
THE LONGEST SILENCE

available soon from MIRA Books.

For additional books by
USA TODAY bestselling author Debra Webb,
visit her website at www.debrawebb.com.

DEBRA WEBB

THE COLDEST FEAR

mira

First Published 2017
First Australian Paperback Edition 2017
ISBN 978 1 489 24341 6

THE COLDEST FEAR © 2017 by Debra Webb
Philippine Copyright 2017
Australian Copyright 2017
New Zealand Copyright 2017

This is a work of fiction. Names, characters, places, and incidents are either the
product of the author's imagination or are used fictitiously, and any resemblance to
actual persons, living or dead, business establishments, events, or locales is entirely
coincidental.

MIX
Paper from
responsible sources
FSC® C001695
www.fsc.org

Published by
Harlequin Mira
An imprint of Harlequin Enterprises (Aust) Pty Ltd.
Level 13, 201 Elizabeth Street
SYDNEY 2000
AUSTRALIA

Cover art used by arrangement with Harlequin Books S.A.. All rights reserved.

Printed and bound in Australia by McPherson's Printing Group

As a parent, I can think of few things more terrifying and heartbreaking than having my child in pain or suffering with a serious illness. In fact, I try particularly hard not to think of those other things—the death of a child or having a child go missing. So very many children go missing each year and far too many are never found. This book is dedicated to all those who know this unspeakable fear. My prayers are always with you.

Enjoy!
Dale

"Always do what you are afraid to do."

—Ralph Waldo Emerson

One

Savannah, Georgia
Tuesday, October 25, 5:20 p.m.

Life had been difficult for Allison Cortland, particularly the past thirty-two years.

She stepped, one by one, out of her shoes. The grass was cold even with the setting sun doing all within its power to extend a little lingering warmth and light as it dropped behind the trees on this late October day. The task was an impossible one. There would never be enough light to chase away the cold, cold darkness encompassing Allison's small world.

Shouldering out of her jacket, she let it fall to the ground as she stared out over the still water. Her father-in-law had given Allison and her husband this lake house forty years ago as a wedding present. He claimed he had lost the desire to visit this special place after his wife died. Allison hadn't understood at the time. The water, the dense woods and the lovely cottage-style home were so peaceful, how could anyone not feel happy and serene here?

In time she had learned the harsh, painful truth that some losses could not be healed by anything in this big wide world.

The crisp breeze sent goose bumps spilling over her skin as she tossed her elegant silk blouse to the ground and reached for the side zipper of her trousers. Her husband often teased her about her obsession with beautiful clothes. Edward showered her with exquisite jewelry and she had always appreciated his generosity, yet there was something cold about jewels. Give her silk and cashmere any day.

But nothing—absolutely nothing—took that deep chill from her bones. Not once in these past thirty-two years had she felt truly warm. She lifted first one foot and then the other from the legs of her pants, leaving the light gray wool twisted on the grass. Reaching behind her, she unfastened her bra and let it fall. Her panties followed that same path. Her nipples stiffened in the cold air. Not even the many lovers she had discreetly taken over the years had been able to warm her.

On this night thirty-two years ago Allison Hall Cortland's life had drained from her body, no matter that her traitorous heart had continued to beat. She dipped a toe into the icy water. Closing her eyes she put one foot in front of the other, stepping into the water.

All these years, no matter how much alcohol she consumed, no matter the various prescription medications she tried, nothing ever expelled the aching nothingness that had invaded her very soul. For any parent there existed no greater agony, no more devastating blow than losing a child. It was unquestionably the coldest fear that haunted every mother's heart.

The chilly water rose above her chest, washed over her shoulders and lapped at her chin. All these years she had muddled through this cold, empty life for *him*. Her husband needed her. They had faced the horror, as best they could, *together*. They had survived *together*. Despite the ways in which each of them had privately struggled to conquer their pain, they had slogged through the months and years…*together*.

As if Fate was determined to land one last, shocking blow, two weeks ago the handsome young man to whom she had said "I do" forty years ago was diagnosed with terminal cancer. The numerous specialists could do nothing more. Her husband had a month to live, possibly more, probably less.

Allison sucked in one last breath of crisp night air before the water engulfed her face. If only the bastard had possessed the courage to take his vile secret with him to his grave.

But no. He'd had to confess his sins…he'd had to plead for her forgiveness.

She wasn't like the others. She couldn't go on knowing this awful thing and she damned sure could not forgive him. The idea of muddling through another single day with this new weight on her heart was unimaginable.

He had stolen the only reason she had bothered to go on at all.

Allison stopped holding her breath and welcomed the rush of death.

Two

The simple definition of *fear* according to Merriam-Webster: "an unpleasant emotion caused by being aware of danger; a feeling of being afraid." Bobbie Gentry hadn't felt that emotion for her personal safety in 309 days. It wasn't that she no longer sensed danger or felt afraid, she did. The sense of danger that haunted her was always for the welfare of others.

As a detective with the Montgomery Police Department she encountered plenty of opportunities to fear for her well-being. Cops felt the cold, hard edge of fear on a daily basis. But it was difficult to fear death when all that mattered most in life was gone and the small steps she had dared take toward building a new one had been derailed.

A psychopathic serial killer known as the Storyteller had murdered her husband and caused the deaths of her child and the partner she loved like a father. Nearly a year later she had learned to some degree to live with the unthinkable reality and, wouldn't you know, along came another crushing blow. A second serial killer had devastated her life all over again. A fellow cop she dared to keep close was brutally murdered a mere two days ago. His killer had left a message for her: *This one's just for you, Bobbie.* The same killer almost succeeded in taking the life of her uncle, the chief of police.

Bobbie sucked in a deep breath. How did she muster the strength to keep going? Revenge? Justice? She'd gotten both. The world was free of two more heinous killers and still it wasn't enough. The expected relief and satisfaction came but the hollow feeling, the emptiness, remained her constant companion. *But* there was the tiniest glimmer of hope. A fragile bond had formed between her and the man who'd helped her stop the two monsters who had destroyed so many lives, including hers. The development was completely unexpected, but surprisingly not unwelcome.

Nick Shade had given her something she'd been certain she would never again feel: the desire to live for more than revenge…for more than merely clipping on her badge each morning. Now he needed her help—whether he would admit as much or not.

Those who knew of his existence called him the serial killer hunter. Nick was unlike any man Bobbie had known. Brooding, intense, impossible to read and yet deeply caring and self-sacrificing. At twenty-one he had discovered his father, Randolph Weller, was a depraved serial killer with forty-two murders to his credit. Since ensuring his father was brought to justice, Nick had dedicated his life to finding and stopping the vicious serial killers no one else seemed able to catch. Like Bobbie, he'd stopped feeling much of anything beyond that driving need for justice a very long time ago. Maybe that was the bond that had initially connected them—the thin, brittle ties of utter desolation and desperation. Two broken people urgently attempting to make a difference that neither of them could completely define nor hope to quantify.

Yet they'd found something together. Something that felt real.

Whatever they'd found had gone up in smoke three days ago when Randolph Weller escaped the Atlanta hospital treating him for an alleged heart condition. Nick was determined to do whatever necessary to find him—including risk his life. Since Bobbie refused to give up on him or that tenuous bond that had developed between them, she had to find a way to give him the backup he needed.

Her search had brought her well beyond her jurisdiction in the middle of the night to the one person who might know how to find Randolph Weller. Her chief as well as her lieutenant were not happy about her decision.

Sometimes you have to do what you have to do no matter the cost to career and relationships.

Bobbie stared up at the big house perched on a hillside well above the street. Towering trees blocked the moonlight, casting long shadows across the lush landscape. She chugged the last swallow of cold coffee, her third cup since leaving Montgomery, squared her shoulders and tucked the empty container back into the slot on the console. She reached down and checked the backup piece strapped just above her ankle. The truth was it really didn't matter how far out of her jurisdiction she'd come since she wasn't in the Peach State in an official capacity.

In fact, there was a strong possibility she would no longer have a place in the department after the actions she'd taken in the past six hours. She'd barely reached the Montgomery city limits when the blue lights in her rearview mirror forced her to pull over. The chief had sent two uniforms chasing after her with orders for Bobbie to report in ASAP or face suspension. There hadn't been time to convince her overprotective uncle that she had no choice. So she'd offered her police issue Glock and her detective's shield to the officer who'd pulled her over and told him to consider her on suspension. The officer had refused to take her weapon or her badge, but she felt confident the message had been adequately relayed to the chief.

Bobbie wasn't backing down until this was done. She would do all within her power to hunt down Weller, the killer who had orchestrated five murders as well as the attack on the chief himself in the past seven days, with or without the department's blessing.

A caffeine burst shuddered through her system. *No more wasting time.* She'd wasted too much already. Judging by the home's dark windows the attorney she'd come to Atlanta to see was either gone or in bed. A smart man would have disappeared the moment he heard the news of his client's stunning escape.

Bobbie grabbed her Glock from the passenger seat and climbed out of the car. She tucked the weapon into the waistband at the small of her back and took care to close the car door quietly. She'd long ago set the interior lights so they didn't come on when a door was opened. Just another one of those cop things. Right now she was counting on the decade of cop experience she'd built with MPD to keep her instincts sharp despite the lack of sleep and the utter desperation clawing at her.

Lawrence Zacharias was the one person on earth who knew most, if not all, of Randolph Weller's secrets. He lived in this multimillion-dollar mansion in one of Atlanta's most affluent neighborhoods, Ansley Park. The community was listed on the National Register of Historic Places and was filled with overpriced homes from charming century-old bungalows to newer, mega mansions like this one. Bobbie hadn't been surprised Zacharias lived so lavishly. She gazed up at the two-story brick. The tasteful landscape lighting ensured that, no matter the hour, passersby would never miss the full impact of the luxurious estate. More than a dozen limestone steps glowed a ghostly white in the moonlight, providing an eerie path to the towering double front doors that appeared better suited to a small castle.

Zacharias was without doubt Atlanta's most well-known attorney. Fourteen years ago his representation of serial killer Dr. Randolph Weller had put him on the map. If anyone had the slightest inkling where Weller would go after his escape, it would be his trusted attorney. Bobbie intended to get from the man what the FBI and local police apparently could not.

According to the many text messages she'd received from her chief, she wasn't thinking straight, which might be true to some degree. She hadn't slept more than a minute here and there in better than forty-eight hours until she'd pulled over on Interstate 85 at ten-thirty last night. Recognizing that the safety of everyone else she encountered on the road was greatly compromised by her need for sleep, she'd parked at a truck stop with the intention of catching a twenty- or thirty-minute nap. She'd awakened two hours later to the sound of a semi's air horn. She'd cursed herself the rest of the drive for losing so much time, but she'd done the right thing. Like soldiers, cops fully comprehended the risks of going too long without sleep. Concentration and focus went first. Cognitive impairment only worsened as the hours passed. Even after the extended nap, she was running on empty. But it couldn't be helped. Stopping wasn't an option.

She pressed the doorbell and listened as the classic chime echoed through the house. No lights came on. No swishes or clatters of the owner stirring. She glanced back down at the street where she'd parked her Challenger. Nothing moved in the near darkness. Not even the distant sound of interstate traffic that wound around the city detracted from the atmosphere of beauty and wealth cocooning the elegant homes. A soft breeze kicked up, sending a handful of autumn leaves scattering across the cobblestoned porch, the deep russets and browns reminding her of all the shed blood she'd seen this week.

So much blood.

After another stab of the doorbell garnered no response, Bobbie reached up to give the door a firm knock. As soon as her knuckles hit the solid slab of wood, the right side of the looming entrance swung inward. Her Glock was in her hand before she'd mentally ticked off all the reasons the door might have been unlocked and ajar. She eased closer and listened. Quiet. Dark, except for the moonlight filtering over her shoulder and through the open doorway.

Taking a deep breath and then holding it to ensure she didn't miss the slightest sound, she stepped inside, weapon held at the ready. In the last house she'd entered under similar circumstances she'd discovered a rotting corpse. She barred thoughts of Steven Devine, the cop who'd fooled her and everyone else for an entire month. As hard as she tried to tamp down the memory of his hand on her breast…of him ripping open her jeans, she couldn't quite accomplish the feat. Sorry bastard. Weller had commissioned Devine to do his dirty work. He'd murdered one of the few remaining people who'd owned a piece of Bobbie's fractured heart.

If she somehow managed to live through what was coming next, her shrink would no doubt insist she return to weekly therapy sessions. After all, someone as broken as Bobbie Sue Gentry, who'd lost her husband and her child not even a year ago and her partner of seven years just two months back, couldn't hope to rebound so quickly. Nearly being raped and having a dear friend murdered all within the past forty-eight hours was more than any human should have to bear. She would need months, maybe years of counseling. Or maybe all the loss and devastation had piled so high on the shattered pieces of her heart that she was beyond the point of no return.

Her gut clenched. Could she trust her instincts at this point?

This wasn't the time for second-guessing. *Focus on what you came here to do.*

Bobbie closed the massive door and put her back against it. *Take a breath. Another.* No metallic odor of blood. No lingering scents of a dinner the owner may have had hours ago. Did Zacharias have his evening meal prepared in the kitchen by a personal chef? Or did he eat out?

The oppressive silence sent another shot of adrenaline into her blood. Did any member of Zacharias's household staff live in the residence? His wife had divorced him years ago and his children had grown up and moved across the country, no doubt to separate themselves from images of bloody, mutilated corpses arranged in grotesque venues for a depraved mind to capture on a painter's canvas.

She wondered if his money brought Zacharias much comfort when he turned out the lights all alone each night.

Alone...exactly the way you do, Bobbie.

The sound of Nick's voice whispered across her senses reminding her that for just a little while she hadn't been alone.

Survey the scene, Bobbie. This was not the time to be distracted.

Why wasn't Zacharias's security system singing a warning about the open door? Bobbie glanced at the dark keypad on the wall not three feet away. Evidently he'd left in a big hurry and hadn't bothered setting the alarm or checking the door.

Or had someone gotten here ahead of her? Someone who wanted more than to ask a few questions?

The extravagant lock on the door appeared undamaged. As for visitors, the feds as well as the local police had questioned him in the past forty-eight hours.

Did you take off right after that, Zacharias?

Seemed strange that a surveillance detail hadn't been assigned to keep an eye on their one potential lead to finding Weller. She shook her head. Maybe the problem was that the FBI and the task force created to recapture Weller were far too focused on proving Nick was somehow involved with his father's escape. No matter that he'd been debriefed by the feds scarcely twelve hours ago and cleared of any wrongdoing in Devine's death by Montgomery PD, the suspicion about his connection to Weller lingered. In part because Nick had spent most of his adult life living in the shadows, finding the killers no one else could. Even trained and experienced members of law enforcement at times feared what they didn't understand. Nick Shade was innocent of his father's crimes. He had turned his back on Randolph Weller years ago after finding him in the process of creating art from his two most recent kills. Worse, he'd discovered that Weller had murdered his mother when she learned her husband's despicable secret. Nick's entire life up to that point had been a lie.

As true as it was that both Bobbie and Nick had suffered some seriously fucked-up heartbreak, the big difference between them was that she'd at least had a real family who cared about her. Nick had never had anything real. The people who should have taken care of him had let him down.

I will not let you down, Nick.

Bobbie forced her full attention to the here and now. "Where the hell are you, Zacharias?"

There was always the possibility that the feds had been watching the attorney and were even now following him to see if he would lead them to Weller.

The truth was she hadn't driven all this way simply to see Zacharias. She didn't even care if he'd taken his millions and fled. Speaking to him wasn't actually necessary. All she wanted was to find any files on Weller that Zacharias might have in his home office before those files and any other notes were confiscated by the task force on his trail. Zacharias was a brilliant attorney. He had endless connections in Fulton County. The man would know all the ways, including attorney-client privilege, to challenge any attempts to seize his files or warrants to pilfer through his home or his phone records.

"But you can't outmaneuver the feds forever," Bobbie murmured. Which was exactly why the man would disappear very soon if he hadn't already.

She glanced around the cavernous entry hall. She was here, the door was unlocked and the place appeared deserted—might as well have a look around. Zacharias had called her to Atlanta less than two weeks ago. No one could prove she hadn't been in his house previously if her prints were found.

There could be security cameras.

After bumping three switches with her elbow, the giant chandelier spilled light over the marble floors. The cool gray paint on the walls spread out to meet the gleaming white trim and lent a cold feel to the space. A massive painting of Zacharias and his family, obviously commissioned a dozen or more years ago, served as the focal point. A round table of mirrored glass sat in the center of the hall, directly beneath the chandelier. The large vase stationed there was filled with cut flowers. The once lush and richly colored petals had browned and now littered the tabletop. A man of means living in a house like this one would certainly have a cleaning staff.

Had he sent them all away before he took his own leave?

Bobbie surveyed the room again. No sign of cameras. In Zacharias's shoes she would have been far better prepared with a surveillance camera in every damned room as well as around the perimeter of the house. On the other hand, an attorney willing to interact with such depraved murderers probably harbored a serious God complex and didn't want any electronic documentation of his movements or those of his visitors. With his most notorious monster no longer in chains behind those drab prison walls, Zacharias might not be feeling so high and mighty now.

"Mr. Zacharias? Are you home?"

Bobbie moved from the entry hall with its elegant curving staircase leading up to the second floor to the parlor on the right. She rubbed her arm against her side, pushing the sleeve of her sweatshirt down over her fingers before reaching under the nearest lampshade to switch on the light. The expected sophisticated furnishings were gathered around an equally stylish stone fireplace that spanned the full height of the room—at least twelve feet. She listened again before progressing across the entry hall to the next room, a library. Floor-to-ceiling rows of bookshelves stood where the fireplace would be and distinguished the room from its near mirror image across the hall. No sign of a struggle or that anyone had combed through the space. Other than the open front door, all appeared to be in order.

One by one Bobbie advanced through room after room, calling the owner's name and bumping a light on with her elbow in each one. *Clear.*

Since she'd found no sign of foul play or of the homeowner so far, Bobbie suspected Zacharias had in fact gotten the hell out of Dodge. His statement about Weller's escape had played over and over on every available media outlet the past forty-eight or so hours.

I am shocked and saddened by this turn of events. No one will be safe until Randolph Weller is caught.

"That includes you, Zacharias."

Bobbie imagined he was well aware of the imminent danger. Under the circumstances, she had known finding him was a long shot but she'd had to try. He hadn't been answering his phone. No-damned-body had been answering their phones—*including you, Bobbie*. Her calls to Nick as well as to Special Agent Anthony LeDoux had gone unanswered. Her instincts told her LeDoux was in one way or another up to his eyeballs in this, too.

As much as she wanted to trust LeDoux after what they'd been through together, she couldn't. The secret the two of them shared was like an open, festering wound deep below the surface where no one else could see. Like cancer, eating them up one inch at a time and at the same time making them dangerously reckless.

Like not calling backup in a situation like this one.

Exiling the warning voice honed by years of investigating homicides, she moved deeper into the house. Just off the kitchen and tucked beyond the family room, she found the attorney's study. Bookshelves lined one wall. Framed photographs of the family that had abandoned him sat in a neat arrangement on one corner of the desk. The blotter was a clean, crisp expanse of white marred only by the fallen blooms from the floral arrangement that sat next to it, a smaller version of the one in the entry hall. To the right of the desk was a set of French doors.

Open French doors.

Shit. Bobbie's fingers tightened on her Glock. She executed a three-sixty, scanning the room.

No movement. No sound.

For a moment she considered calling it in, but she had crossed the line coming into the house. There had been no true exigent circumstances. Knowing her chief, he'd put out a BOLO on her and the Atlanta PD would be on the lookout for her already.

Check the files in the study and get the hell out.

Zacharias could very well be on a private jet headed for some tropical island whose laws didn't include an extradition treaty with the US.

Or Weller had taken him.

With the second set of doors left open, foul play was the more likely of the scenarios. No way two doors in this mansion had faulty locks. Even if Zacharias had been in a hell of a hurry, why leave *both* doors unlocked and open?

Hold on. She hadn't been upstairs. Was someone up there stealing his Rolexes and platinum cuff links at this very moment? Zacharias could very well be dead in his bedroom. It was the middle of the night after all. Bobbie braced her back against the nearest wall to ensure no one came up behind her. *Too quiet.* A thief would have heard her calling out to Zacharias.

A spot on the floor near the desk snagged her attention, then another spot and another. Red wine maybe? Not so lucky.

Blood.

She visually traced the pattern of splatters, a

stark crimson on the champagne-colored rug. The blood trail led around the large mahogany desk.

Adrenaline stinging her senses, she followed the path her gaze had taken, glancing over her shoulder repeatedly and taking care not to step in the blood. The amount of blood increased exponentially as she drew closer to the other side of the desk, as if the bleeder had lingered there. At this point the urge to fish out her cell and call 911 was fierce, but she ignored it.

Not yet.

Behind the desk the trail of blood became a series of small puddles. The phone that had been blocked from her view by the floral arrangement had been dragged to the edge of the desk, the handset dangling from its curly cord. Blood was smeared on the keypad; crimson fingerprints encircled the handset.

Holding her breath in an attempt to slow the pounding in her chest, she listened for the slightest noise as her eyes traced the path of blood that continued beyond the desk and out the open French doors.

"I repeat, this is nine-one-one, what is the nature of your emergency?"

Bobbie's attention snapped back to the phone. What the hell?

"If you can hear me…"

She reached for the handset.

"…we're sending—"

The dispatcher's voice silenced mid-sentence.

Bobbie twisted and leveled her Glock on whoever had entered the room.

"What the hell are you doing, Bobbie?"

Special Agent Anthony LeDoux. His fingers still rested on the switch hook in the phone's cradle, severing the connection.

"What the hell are *you* doing, LeDoux?"

Better question, how the hell had he sneaked up on her like that? *Sleep deprivation is making you sloppy, Bobbie.*

The agent held up his hands. "How about you put your weapon away and we'll talk about the reason we're both here?"

She glanced at the open doors. "We should be looking for whoever all that blood belongs to, not debating our respective motives for breaking and entering."

"I've already looked around inside and out," LeDoux said. "No one's here. I'd be gone, too, except as I headed for the back door I heard someone come inside. I hid in the pantry you walked right past. You're losing your edge, Detective."

Anger and frustration seared through Bobbie. "Fuck you. Where's Zacharias?"

"I can tell you that the illustrious task force assembled to find Weller doesn't have him." He shook his head, his face tightening with distaste or something on that order. "I can't believe the son of a bitch wasn't under surveillance."

Bobbie glanced at the open doors again before shifting her attention back to LeDoux, only then realizing her Glock was still aimed at his chest. Deciding she wasn't ready to surrender the upper hand, she held her bead on the FBI agent. His story was a little too pat for her comfort. He just happened to be going out of the house as she was coming in? The only time she had witnessed timing that perfect was at a Broadway play she and her husband, James, had attended when they'd gone to New York City for Christmas the year before Jamie was born.

LeDoux was lying.

So she asked him again, "If Zacharias is gone, who bled all over the carpet? The blood's not even dry." Though she hadn't touched it, she had seen enough to know the dull, blackness of blood that had been spilled and then sat there for a while. Her gaze narrowed. "Who made that 911 call?"

LeDoux laughed. "I got no idea where the blood came from. As for the call, that was me. The phone was already off the hook, I just selected line one and entered the numbers. I figured it was the least I could do."

A couple of scenarios elbowed their way into her thoughts, neither of which included his story. She restrained the urge to bombard him with the questions pounding in her brain. "You have no idea where Zacharias would go?"

"If I had a fucking clue where he or Weller might be, we wouldn't be having this *friendly* conversation." He sent a pointed look at her weapon.

Judging by the dark circles under his eyes, he'd

had about as much sleep as she. His jeans and sweater were rumpled as if he'd been wearing them a couple of days. He hadn't shaved recently and those bloodshot eyes provided considerable insight into the sustenance he'd chosen for survival lately.

"Have you heard from Nick?" Jesus Christ, the blood could be Nick's. Fear spread through Bobbie's chest like fire through a drought-stricken forest. Nick would no doubt have come to Zacharias looking for answers.

Don't you dare die on me, Nick Shade. Too many had died already, damn it.

"Not a word." LeDoux hitched his head toward the open door. "We should get the hell out of here. Now."

This didn't feel right. Bobbie split her attention between the French doors and the agent she didn't completely trust. "What we should do is have another look around. The bleeder can't have gotten far without help."

"You'd better rethink that strategy." LeDoux nodded toward the phone. The dial tone had turned into a recorded warning: *If you'd like to make a call, please hang up and try your call again.* "Atlanta PD will be rolling by now."

"We'll need to give a statement," she countered. The bloody handprint on the handset, the red smudges on the keypad held her attention for an extra beat. What was she missing here? Her focus swung back to LeDoux. He stood a mere three feet away without a visible speck of blood on his pale gray sweater and faded jeans. No way he'd carried or dragged a bleeding victim out of this house.

"They'll be looking for someone to blame for whatever happened here," LeDoux countered. "We both want to find Weller. And we both want to help your friend Shade." He gestured to the bloody mess. "The questions and the investigation will keep us on-site for hours if not days, and time is our enemy."

Five then ten seconds elapsed while she weighed her options. He was right that the 911 operator would have already dispatched the police. Standard operating procedure for 911 hang-ups. Bottom line, LeDoux had a valid point about the other, as well. She couldn't afford the delay.

"Fine." She lowered her weapon. "We'll do this your way, but if you're lying to me, LeDoux—"

"I wouldn't lie to you, Bobbie. Not when it counts." He held her gaze a moment, then headed for the door.

Maybe she was a fool, but she followed him.

Outside, the blood trail was lost to the darkness. "My car's parked on the street in front of the house," she said. "I'll follow you. Where're we going?"

LeDoux headed toward the street. "I'll hitch a ride with you," he called over his shoulder. "I took a cab."

Bobbie watched his retreating back until he'd disappeared into the darkness beyond the landscape lighting. There were only two or three logical explanations for taking a cab anywhere. You either didn't have personal transportation or you were too inebriated to drive. Since LeDoux didn't fall into either of those categories at the moment there was only one plausible explanation for his actions.

He didn't want any potential witnesses able to ID his vehicle.

LeDoux had good reason for wanting to find the monster Zacharias had represented, just as Bobbie did. She thought about the blood on the floor in the study. Whether or not LeDoux had killed Zacharias in an attempt to extract information was the real question. His erratic behavior the past week or so provided sufficient reason for her to doubt his trustworthiness…but could she really see him as a murderer?

Either way, he was right about her not having time to be waylaid by the investigation to find out or to be cleared of suspicion.

Without looking back, Bobbie turned off the instincts screaming at her and followed LeDoux.

He was the closest thing to a lead she had.

Three

Coventry Court, Norcross, Georgia
3:00 a.m.

"We've been friends for a very long time, Randolph. I've carried out your every request—even the ones I should have categorically denied. I have kept your secrets just as you requested."

Randolph Weller set his unfinished cup of tea aside. It had grown cold anyway. "I find your pathetic pleas to be quite tedious, Lawrence."

Lawrence Zacharias's face paled. "Just tell me what you want me to do and I'll do it. Anything. Anything at all. There's no need to resort to this barbaric behavior."

Poor, poor Lawrence. The injury to his forearm had stopped bleeding hours ago, yet one would think he'd suffered a fatal stab wound. The bloody mess left in his study had been the man's own doing. He'd hoped to send the authorities on a hunt for a killer rather than a fleeing attorney. Frankly, Randolph had expected far more from his old friend. There really was little the man could do now. He was tied to his chair. He could scarcely breathe much less move with the rope wound tightly around his arms, legs and chest. Randolph sighed. Such a waste of true brilliance.

"I fear it's far too late for posturing and gestures now." Randolph cocked his head and studied his old friend. "You see, after I spoke to Lucille, I decided to watch you, Lawrence. The courier you hired is in the other room. He told me about the package. Did you know it was intercepted by Special Agent LeDoux?"

When the other man only stared at him with utter defeat in his eyes, Randolph went on, "I'm certain you didn't. When I learned the addressee, I understood exactly what you'd done. You see, Lawrence, when you decide to betray a man like me, there are certain steps you should not trust to anyone save yourself. If you had personally handled the package, you might very well have made your flight to Maracaibo." He shook his head. "Too bad. I understand the governor himself had selected a luxury villa for you. I'm certain you would have been quite happy spending your twilight years there."

"No one knows where you are—you still have time to disappear," Lawrence said quickly as if he'd gained his second wind in the race against certain death. "No one knows *anything*."

The former was true. Randolph should be well on his way to Morocco. Lawrence had purchased the small desert palace for him years ago. Randolph had always planned to slip away one day. He'd cultivated the perfect pawns to facilitate the move. His son's obsession with Detective Bobbie Gentry had provided the classic opportunity. Randolph had dreamed of rich, mahogany-skinned men and delicious domestic maids catering to his every whim, including serving as inspiration for his beloved art.

But then a loose end he should have clipped long ago unraveled his well-laid plans and, unfortunately, Lawrence was wrong about the latter of his claims. Someone *did* know something and now Randolph had no choice but to tidy up that annoying thread before disappearing. If there was anything in this world he wanted as much as the freedom to create his art, it was revenge. It was a rather base instinct but, despite popular belief, Randolph was only human. Where Nicholas was concerned, the absolute best revenge was to ensure he remained steadfast on his current path. Nothing would make Randolph happier than knowing his son would forever remain alone and in the shadows, afraid of who and what he might become. The quintessential tragedy.

"There are two people who know my deepest, darkest secret, Lawrence." Randolph stood. He unbuttoned the light wool suit jacket. He had to give his old friend credit—he'd had everything Randolph needed waiting for him in that Huntsville, Alabama, storage locker, including transportation.

He removed the jacket and placed it carefully on the back of the chair he'd vacated.

"I made a mistake," Lawrence urged. "I can take care of it. Now. This minute. Let me...let me help you, Randolph." His words had begun to slur.

Ah, the timing was flawless. The high-powered muscle relaxer would render Lawrence quite helpless. Randolph crossed the room and opened the liquor cabinet. He'd stored the items he would need there, including the half-empty bottle of Scotch he'd laced. The moment was, admittedly, gratifying. Randolph had been in prison for fourteen years, three months and six days, and he still hadn't lost his touch.

"Dear God," Lawrence muttered thickly.

Randolph chuckled. "God can't help you now, Lawrence." He removed the carefully folded white sheet from the shelf below the whiskey tumblers and spread it on the floor. "You see—" he walked toward his old friend "—God holds no dominion over me."

Randolph released the knot and unwound the rope. Lawrence slumped forward, tried to move but his body failed him. Still, he grunted and gnashed his teeth.

"Now, now, Lawrence, you know there's nothing you can do. Why put on this pathetic display?"

Randolph reached under the drugged man's shoulders and lifted him, then dragged him to the middle of the room. He arranged him, arms stretched out to his sides, legs spread eagle.

"It's such a shame I won't have time to capture this momentous occasion on canvas." He smiled down at his old friend. "You know I've always fancied myself quite the artist." He sighed. "Before Nicholas turned against me I had my own studio. I miss those days."

A wet spot appeared on the crotch of Lawrence's trousers.

"Really," Randolph chastised, "I would have thought you far braver than this."

The man on the floor groaned pitifully.

Randolph returned to the liquor cabinet and retrieved the final tool he'd stashed behind it.

He approached his old friend once more. "I will miss you, Lawrence."

Tears poured from the other man's eyes. The pulse at the base of his throat fluttered wildly.

How very sad and yet intensely titillating.

"See you in hell, old friend." Randolph hefted the ax. The first blow shattered the elbow as the blade cut through bone and tendon, leaving the forearm detached and hemorrhaging on the floor. The second swing sent blood splattering across Randolph's face. Muscles and ligaments splayed open at the shoulder like the freshly severed parts of a hog. The humerus easily popped out of the glenoid socket and Lawrence's body twitched and shuddered. A feeble scream croaked out of his sagging jowls.

Randolph sighed with pleasure as the hot blood

slid down his skin. His own blood pulsing with sheer bliss, he raised the ax again.

Thumping and grunting echoed from the other room. Randolph hesitated and glanced toward the wall that separated the two men who would die this day.

He smiled. "Don't worry, dear boy, you're next."

Four

Bobbie had barely reached the end of the block when she spotted the cruiser in her rearview mirror. The Atlanta PD official vehicle rocked to a stop in the spot she'd vacated mere seconds before. Unable to help herself she'd sat a moment at the intersection and watched the two uniformed officers rush up the steps toward the house. LeDoux hadn't said a word but she'd felt the tension vibrating from him.

Eighteen minutes later she pulled into the parking lot of the Country Inn and Suites where LeDoux had a room. Definitely a step down from the luxurious four- and five-star hotels the agent typically called home when on assignment. Just another indication of how much LeDoux had changed over the past year. He didn't wear his scars on his skin the way she did, but they were there nonetheless.

"You'll need a jacket or something," he said. "Unless you're planning to leave your weapon in the trunk."

Maybe it was the sleep deprivation or the burden of so many murders so close together but her mind felt as if her head were under water. Every thought, every reaction was far slower than it should be. Agreeing to come to this hotel with LeDoux was likely another sleep-deprived decision she would regret.

He works for the FBI, Bobbie. He used you once...

Considering she didn't have a better plan, she popped the trunk and climbed from the driver's seat. She glanced at LeDoux as she grabbed her overnight duffel bag from the back seat. There were a lot of people she'd let down. Her son, her husband, her partner, her friend, the chief. Special Agent LeDoux was guilty of that egregious sin the same as she was—all the more reason she shouldn't trust him, except he had certain connections she didn't.

She moved around to the trunk and dug out the windbreaker she kept there for emergencies. Dragging on the jacket, she reluctantly admitted to herself that whatever LeDoux had or hadn't done, she owed him. He had protected her that once when there was no one else—*when it counted*. He had allowed the monster to take him instead. His screams echoed deep in her soul. Bobbie shook off the haunting memories.

"We have to go through the lobby to get to the room," LeDoux explained as if the silence or her lack of a response had gotten to him and he needed to speak just to make sure they were both still alive.

The two of them were like the walking dead—ghosts. Mere shadows of their former selves moving among the living. The breeze she'd noticed earlier felt colder now. She zipped the jacket and secured the car. "How long have you been in Atlanta?"

She hadn't seen LeDoux since late Tuesday night, some fifty hours ago, when they'd met at a crime scene in Athens, Alabama. Weller's latest victim had been chopped into pieces and then displayed like a broken doll that had been reassembled by a two-year-old. Had LeDoux come straight to Atlanta after that to question Zacharias?

"About twenty-four hours."

So what had he been doing between Tuesday night and yesterday? At some point this past week she'd gotten the distinct impression he was on thin ice with his superiors. Something else they had in common.

When he reached for the entrance door, she asked, "Are you on the Weller task force?"

He hesitated, his gaze settling on hers. "Not officially."

Before she could ask the next question poised on the tip of her tongue, LeDoux headed through the lobby. The clerk, young and female, smiled as they passed. LeDoux gave her a nod. The clerk grinned, checked out Bobbie and then looked away. Whatever else he was, LeDoux was an attractive man with plenty of charm when he chose to use it. When he and Bobbie worked together the first time, he'd had a wife. She'd had a husband and a child. Ten months and a couple of vicious serial killers had changed everything.

Without speaking, they took the stairs to the second floor. LeDoux stopped at room 216 and swiped his keycard, then held the door open for her. Bobbie stepped inside, tossed her bag on the floor and surveyed the room. Window on the far side. Drapes pulled tight. Desk, chair. Small sofa. King bed.

One king bed.

"You take the bed," he said, noting her gaze there as he locked the door. He crossed the room and rummaged in the mini fridge, found a bottle of beer and collapsed on the sofa.

"If you're not *officially* on the task force, then you're tracking Weller on your own."

He shrugged. "Aren't you doing the same thing?"

Rather than answer him, she pitched another question at him. "You've watched Zacharias since you arrived?"

Her real question was pretty clear. *How did he get away or get himself injured and maybe dead with you watching?* God she needed a shower. And sleep. It was three-thirty in the morning. She couldn't think clearly anymore. Maybe she hadn't been thinking clearly in a long time.

Rather than answer her question, he opened the beer and chugged a long swallow. When the need for oxygen overrode his desire for alcohol, he lowered the bottle and wiped his mouth with the back of his other hand.

Finally he said, "The local cops interviewed Zacharias on Wednesday, as did the Bureau. I tried to question him this morning—" he glanced at the clock by the bed "—technically yesterday morning, round eight. He wouldn't talk to me. Just before dark, five-thirty maybe, a local courier service picked up a small package at his front door. I followed the guy to see where the package was going. By the time I got back to Zacharias's house he was long gone or he appeared to be." He shrugged. "I took advantage of the unoccupied house for sale across the street. I've been watching his place since, waiting for him to come back or for the right opportunity to get inside. At some point I guess I fell asleep. When I woke up I saw your car and decided to find out what you were up to."

"So you lied to me earlier," she accused, "when you said you were already in the house when I arrived."

He waved off her charge. "There wasn't time to explain all the nuances involved so I ad-libbed."

Bobbie let his lie go for the moment. The way he referred to the Bureau—as if his decisions and theirs were mutually exclusive—reiterated her feeling that Agent LeDoux's career was like hers, teetering on the brink of disaster. Bobbie crouched down and dug through her bag for the clean underwear she'd packed.

"So you never saw Zacharias when the courier went to the door?"

"I did not. I suppose anyone could have given the guy the package." He downed another long swallow of beer. "But I never saw anyone else go in or come out of the house."

She tucked the panties into her back pocket and got to her feet. "Who was the package addressed to?"

He lifted his shoulders in another listless shrug. "Who knows? The courier refused to tell me the name."

"You stopped him?" Jesus Christ. LeDoux really was flirting with the edge.

"I followed him to the service center parking lot, showed him my credentials and told him I needed to see the package. He told me to get a warrant."

"Did you inform the agent in charge of the task force?" The package could be headed to wherever Weller was hiding. Anticipation had her pulse pounding. "This might be a major lead in finding Weller."

Rather than answer, LeDoux finished his beer and went for another. Images of Weller's numerous victims filtered one after the other through her mind like flipping the pages of a macabre family album. Randolph Weller, aka the Picasso Killer, wasn't just another serial killer. He'd spent most of his adult life as a celebrated, highly respected psychiatrist whose secret hobby was mutilating the corpses of his victims and then painting macabre scenes of the carnage. More shocking, the sick son of a bitch had served as a consultant to the FBI's Behavioral Analysis Unit—still did, or at least he had until he escaped. Weller was also a father. Images of Nick flashed through her mind. Unlike his father, Nick had spent his adult life stopping the most ruthless serial killers, the ones no one else appeared able to find. He'd found the one who'd stolen Bobbie's life. *The Storyteller.* She flinched. Hoped LeDoux hadn't noticed.

"The Bureau has no fucking idea where he is." LeDoux grunted. "They've torn Atlanta apart. Can't find him." He shook his head and downed more of his beer. "Zacharias gave them zip. He's sticking by his attorney-client-privilege bullshit."

"What about the package, LeDoux?" she repeated, impatience swelling inside her.

He lifted a bleary gaze to hers and exhaled a big breath. "He wouldn't tell me who the recipient was, but—" the hint of a smile tugged at his lips "—for a hundred bucks he gave me the address."

"Where?"

The smile made a full appearance. "The same place I'm headed after a few hours' sleep. Savannah. I would've left already but I guess I was actually waiting for you. I knew you'd show up eventually."

"Savannah?" She ignored the remark about him waiting for her. Why would Weller risk staying in the state of Georgia? Savannah was only three or four hours away. "That makes no sense."

"Who knows? But I'm damned sure going to find out." LeDoux laughed, the sound as weary as she felt. "That's why I brought my car back here and took a cab to Zacharias's house. In case the courier grew a conscience and decided to report me."

At least that cleared up her question about how he'd followed the courier and why he didn't have a rental car.

"You're here," he went on, "we have a lead. You going with me?" He tipped up his second bottle of beer and finished it off.

Either LeDoux had gone rogue or his new assignment was to keep her off track. Considering his apparent need to inhale those beers, maybe if she nudged him enough he'd slip up and reveal his true objective.

She chose her words carefully. "The FBI is still suspicious of Nick?"

Just saying the words out loud had anger stirring inside her. Bobbie had no idea exactly how many killers Nick had stopped in the past decade but the FBI wanted to label him a vigilante. The man was anything but. He hadn't taken a single life…until just over twenty-four hours ago. Montgomery PD had cleared him of any wrongdoing in Steven Devine's death. If Nick hadn't stopped the bastard who had used being a cop as a cover for what he really was—a cold-blooded murderer—he would have killed both of them. Devine had already taken five lives, including a fellow cop she'd loved like a brother.

Bobbie pushed the memories of Asher Bauer away. *No looking back until this is done.*

"There are those who want to take him down," LeDoux acknowledged, "but they have no proof. All they can do is watch and wait for him to fuck up. They got nothing on Shade and nothing on Weller. You and I are the only ones with a lead."

She wanted to rant about the injustice of it all. Nick was a hero. "Then I guess we'll be working together again." At least as long as it benefited her goal of helping Nick. She didn't wait for LeDoux to respond. She picked up her cell and headed for the bathroom.

He grabbed her arm as she passed. "We want the same thing, Bobbie. But I'm not sure we can win this." His thumb rubbed across the scar on her wrist.

"That won't keep me from trying." She tugged free of his hold and shut herself up in the bathroom. She placed her clothes, her Glock, the ankle holster with her .22 and her cell on the closed toilet lid and then sagged against the door. She squeezed her eyes shut to block the memories that tried to intrude. The long scars on her wrist burned as if LeDoux had dashed lighter fluid on her skin and lit a match rather than simply touched her there.

The first cut had been long and deep. She hadn't been able to hold the knife well enough to slash the other wrist so she'd taken the handle between her teeth and sliced as hard and deep as she could. Blood had flowed like a river. The knife had dropped to the floor and she'd slumped against her little boy's bed and waited for the relief of death.

Only it hadn't come.

Bobbie opened her weary eyes. Now, despite that horror, she had something more than revenge or just the job to live for. "Where the hell are you, Nick?"

He had no right closing her out like this. He thought he was protecting her, but he was wrong. Forcing herself to move, she turned on the water in the shower and placed a towel over the curtain rod. She watched herself in the mirror as she methodically undressed. Stripping off her sweatshirt first, she dropped it on the floor. Reaching behind her she unfastened her bra, pitched it on the pile. She shucked her jeans and underwear next.

For a long moment she stood staring at her reflection. She made herself inventory the ugly journey she'd taken ten months ago. Every step was carved onto her flesh. The thin line around her throat where a plastic surgeon had repaired the deep groove left behind by the noose she'd worn like a too-tight dog collar for weeks. The marks on her breasts where the monster in her nightmare had cut around her nipples and then sewed them back on like a demented surgeon. The slashes and gouges that had healed into grotesque ridges and shallow craters. The unsightly ridges from the surgery to repair her right leg. The small bulges that gave away the location of the screws and pins that held it together. The things he had done to her on the inside couldn't be seen, but they were there... always would be.

It was the words tattooed on her back that told the real story. The words she chose not to remove. The words that spilled across her skin in broad black strokes like a tragic monument to all she'd lost.

She had left the story the bastard started on her back to remind her of what she'd done.

Bobbie had chosen to risk her life, but she hadn't realized until it was too late that she'd put her family at risk, too.

The hot steamy air clouded the mirror, hiding the things she didn't want to look at. She shook off the pity session and climbed into the shower. As she scrubbed her body and washed the sour smell of worry and desperation from her skin and hair, she considered that the Atlanta PD's forensic unit would be lifting her prints from Zacharias's front door. If he was dead she would be a person of interest in the investigation no matter her explanation. Her chief would not take it well.

As much as she didn't want to hurt him, she couldn't call in yet. She'd known Chief Theodore Peterson her whole life. He was her godfather. He'd been her father's best friend, the best man at his wedding. The two had played football together in college, had married the same year, and she'd grown up calling him uncle. Bobbie had to do this and the chief didn't agree. He wanted her clear of whatever fallout was coming related to Weller's escape and the inevitable federal investigation into Nick's actions.

Bobbie shut off the spray of water and climbed out of the shower. As soon as she'd dried off, she checked her cell. Still nothing from Nick. Another missed call from the chief, of course. A text from her sergeant and another from her lieutenant. Both ordered her to return to Montgomery.

Not yet.

She dressed and tucked the phone into her back pocket. Strapped the .22 back to her ankle and nestled her Glock into her waistband. With a deep breath she opened the door and the cooler air made her shiver. Rather than deal with the noise of the hair dryer she took the towel with her to continue rubbing at her damp hair. LeDoux had crashed on the sofa. Four empty beer bottles and an empty bottle of vodka she hadn't noticed before lay on the floor next to his abandoned loafers.

Bobbie sat down on the end of the bed and watched him sleep as she squeezed the dampness from her hair. LeDoux wasn't much older than her. She'd turned thirty-two this year; he was thirty-six. His beard-shadowed jaw and the tousled light brown hair that was almost blond added believability to the idea that he was as desperate as she was. The weary man lying only a few feet away was not the hard-ass agent she'd first met last December.

She laughed, a dry sound. Like she was the same

naive, ambitious detective she'd been back then. Bobbie tossed the towel aside and went in search of her phone charger. She found it in the bottom of her bag. After scooting aside the night table she was able to unplug the lamp and plug the charger into that slot. Out of habit she checked the lock on the door and turned out the other lights before climbing under the covers. She tucked the Glock under her pillow and kept her cell phone next to her so she could feel it if it vibrated. Maybe she was being paranoid, but if she received a call or a text from Nick—which was highly unlikely but she could hope—she didn't want LeDoux to know.

Forcing her eyes closed and her mind to quiet, she thought of D-Boy, the dog she had adopted from her negligent neighbor. She missed him. As an adult she'd never had a pet to worry about. She and James, her late husband, had been too busy for a pet and then she'd learned she was pregnant. James had taken up her slack with Jamie, their little boy, during the extra-long hours she dedicated to the job. She missed them both so much. It had taken her a very long time to allow another living creature close. Now she had D-Boy. When she'd decided to come after Nick, she had panicked at first. Who would take care of D-Boy? She couldn't just leave him locked up in the house, even with plenty of food and water and a doggie door providing access to the backyard. There was no way to calculate how long she would be gone.

She'd called Andy Keller, a lab tech in Montgomery. He was a friend. He'd been only too happy to come pick up D-Boy. He had a pit bull of his own. D-Boy would be fine with Andy.

Bobbie allowed her eyes to close and stopped fighting the need to shut down.

Five

Nick Shade pulled on a pair of gloves and knocked on the door. The small brick house was the last in a cul-de-sac, with a yard bordered by trees on three sides. The two neighboring houses were empty, faded for-sale signs leaned precariously in the neglected yards. The driveway of his destination was empty and there was no garage. Overall, the condition of the house was poor at best. The only light or sound inside was a television set to the early-morning news broadcast from an Atlanta station.

If Lawrence Zacharias was in hiding, he'd picked a damned good place for camouflage. No one would look for the affluent, high-powered attorney in these living conditions.

Nick rapped on the door again. Their meeting had been scheduled for six. Either Zacharias was still en route or he wasn't coming.

Fury twisted in Nick's chest. Zacharias had ignored his calls and then, around midnight, he'd called to say they needed to meet in person. Zacharias had insisted he must pass along in person information imperative to Nick's future. If the son of a bitch had ditched him, Nick would hunt him down no matter where he tried to hide. And when he found him, there would be no forgiveness.

If this was a distraction to keep Nick from catching up with Weller, Zacharias would pay for that misstep, as well.

One way or the other, he would end this cat-and-mouse game with Weller.

Nick made his way around to the rear entrance of the house. A small covered deck surrounded by the trees that grew denser behind the house allowed for a reasonable amount of privacy. When the door opened with nothing more than a twist of the knob, a new kind of tension filtered through Nick. He used the flashlight on his phone to confirm the lock had not been tampered with. Not just any lock either. Nick frowned. The door was secured with a state-of-the-art deadbolt set—only it was unlocked.

Inside the meteorologist on the newscast was giving a rundown of the day's weather. Nick closed the door behind him and listened. No sound beyond the television. He inhaled a deep breath and analyzed the scents permeating the space.

Blood. Human waste. Both smelled fresh.

Defeat nudged him. No matter that he'd arrived on time for the meeting, he was too late.

He scanned the room with the flashlight app. No blood or evidence of foul play in the kitchen. As ramshackle as the house looked outside, the inside was clean with generous amenities. The fixtures were high-end. Nick wondered if Zacharias had used this place as a getaway during the more notorious days in his career.

He had a bad feeling the attorney's career and likely his life were over.

He moved into the main room and there on a white sheet in the center of the room was Lawrence Zacharias. Weller had gotten here first. He'd taken Zacharias apart as he did all his victims. Nick's jaw tightened with hatred. Weller started with an arm or a leg. All four limbs were separated at the joints, elbows and knees. Then, the stubs were chopped from the body at the main joint. The torso was divided in half and, finally, he removed the head. Before his incarceration, Weller had only taken victims to use in his art projects. He mutilated their bodies and spread the parts on a white sheet in some grotesque manner and then he painted the scene on a painter's canvas.

Nick hesitated. One of Weller's victims hadn't been an art project. His wife—Nick's mother— had discovered the kind of monster her husband was. Weller had murdered her and buried her in the backyard when Nick was only ten years old. For the next decade or so he had believed his mother had deserted him…that she hadn't loved him enough to take him with her.

Just another reason to hate Weller.

Nick searched the house, knowing full well he would find nothing to help in his hunt for the bastard. Weller would have taken anything relevant with him. The only bedroom revealed another victim. This one a younger man. The younger victim's shirt had survived mostly intact as his body had been chopped into pieces. The previously white polo shirt sported the logo of a well-known courier service.

Moving through the house a second time, Nick found nothing other than the smattering of possessions that apparently made Zacharias feel at home whenever he visited this place. A framed photo of his family sat on a table. Now the family that had deserted him was rid of the scourge on their name.

Nick slipped out the back door and into the darkness. The darkness had always been his closest ally. It was the one thing he could count on. He reached the car he'd parked three blocks away and climbed inside. His only recourse now was to attempt picking up Weller's trail again. The murders were barely a couple of hours old. He wouldn't have gotten far.

Several hours ago Bobbie had arrived in Atlanta. She'd gone to Zacharias's home. The tracking software Nick had installed on her phone gave him her exact location every minute of every day. It wasn't the same as being near her, but it made him feel better to know where she was and, to some degree, what she was doing.

If she steered clear of him maybe she would stay safe. Bobbie deserved a real life. He could never give her that.

His cell vibrated and Nick checked the screen. *Dwight Jessup.*

Jessup was Nick's resource within the FBI. Their relationship was a tenuous one, but Jessup had not let him down in the six years since they literally ran into each other on an investigation in Minnesota. Nick had been watching his target for weeks when Jessup showed up and accidentally plowed into the house where Nick had set up surveillance. An icy road had been the culprit. Jessup had also facilitated Nick's way into Bobbie's life.

He had no business being a part of her life now.

"You have something for me?" Nick asked, going straight to the point.

"The Atlanta field office is about to bring in Anthony LeDoux. The word is they think he has knowledge of your or Weller's whereabouts. I thought you might want to know."

Nick had suspected LeDoux was on the edge. The agent was almost as obsessed with stopping Weller as Nick.

"LeDoux is in Atlanta?" If he was here, he had a lead. Nick didn't know why he was surprised— LeDoux was damned good at his job. At least he had been before almost losing his life to the Storyteller.

"Hold on and I'll give you his exact location. I just saw the alert."

Nick slid behind the wheel of the Buick he'd bought in Chattanooga in the middle of the night.

"Here we go," Jessup said. "He's at the Country Inn & Suites."

Nick knew where LeDoux was before Jessup provided the physical address.

Bobbie was there, too.

Six

Something shuddered against her. Bobbie stirred, tried to open her eyes. Too tired. Again that vibrating sensation nudged her. Somehow she pried her eyes open. It was dark. Her heart galloped during the three or four seconds it took for her brain to register where she was.

Hotel. LeDoux.

How would she ever find Nick?

That damned shuddering again.

Phone.

She felt under the cover for her cell. The sound of the shower drew her gaze first to the empty sofa and then in the direction of the bathroom. Light peeked from the crack around the door. LeDoux was in the shower.

What time was it? According to the digital clock on the bedside table it was 6:40 a.m.

Focus, Bobbie. Check your phone.

Text message.

Do not trust LeDoux.

Bobbie blinked and reread the message. Her breath trapped in her throat when her sluggish brain registered the sender's name.

Nick.

Get away from him! Now!

Bobbie threw back the covers and sat up. She pushed her feet into her sneakers and tucked her cell into her back pocket. She shoved her Glock into her waistband, snatched the charger from the wall, tossed it into her bag and headed for the door. Before walking out she glanced back at the bathroom. The water was still running. The urge to kick the door in and make LeDoux tell her the truth about his intentions assaulted her.

Now! Nick had urged her to hurry.

Bobbie unlocked the door and slipped out.

As badly as she wanted to run she forced herself to walk through the lobby and across the parking lot. She tossed her bag into the back seat of her Challenger, climbed behind the wheel and slipped her Glock into the holster she kept between the seat and the console. At some point she might need to resort to a different vehicle. Her Challenger would be too easy to track. Her chest tightened. The smell of Bauer's blood still lingered inside it. *I'm so sorry.*

Taking her time, she rolled out of the parking lot. Instead of heading for the interstate, she drove across the street and pulled into the adjacent parking lot. She chose a spot behind a row of crepe myrtles. She shut off the engine and waited. It was just past seven, still dark.

She stared at her phone and waited for another message from Nick, but nothing came.

Where are you?

She hit Send and held her breath.

Seconds turned into minutes and no response came.

Fingers cold, she placed the phone on the console. Twisting around to dig in her bag, she found the small purse she'd tucked her driver's license and insurance card into. She pushed it aside and fished through the clothes until she found her hairbrush and a hair tie. It took a minute to untangle her hair and corral it into a ponytail after going to bed with it still damp. Once she'd shoved the brush back into her bag, she relaxed into the seat and watched the street.

Another five minutes passed and then the trouble Nick had warned her about arrived. No blue lights or sirens came. Just the dark, nondescript sedans the FBI preferred along with two Atlanta PD cruisers.

"You son of a bitch."

Had LeDoux set her up? If she found out he'd killed Zacharias and had relevant insights he was keeping from her, she would make sure he regretted it.

Bobbie scanned the parking lot around her and then the street just to be sure she was still alone. She had a perfect view of the hotel entrance and the official vehicles that had descended on the parking area. LeDoux would be dressed and looking for her by now. If he was the one who'd called in the troops, she would know soon enough.

She waited, the seconds and minutes ticking off like tiny explosions in her brain. *7:31 a.m.* Still no movement across the street. Anticipation had her foot stretching toward the accelerator. She should just drive away, but she had to know for sure if LeDoux had betrayed her. If she left now she might never know.

Two months ago when they were both being held hostage by the Storyteller, LeDoux had drawn the danger from her, sacrificing himself to protect her in that run-down cabin in the woods. Why would he suddenly turn on her now? It didn't make sense.

She glanced at her cell phone. Nick had not responded to her question. He didn't want her to know where he was. He didn't want her to get involved. Bobbie shook her head. Of all people, he should understand by now that she was inextricably intertwined in this. As much as he didn't want her coming to his aid, Nick would never lie to her. For whatever reason, he believed LeDoux was up to something that was not in her best interest.

Bobbie trusted Nick completely.

The entrance doors of the hotel flew open and two of the suits who'd gone in earlier marched out,

LeDoux between them. He wasn't wearing hand-cuffs but it was obvious he was being escorted out of the building. Halfway to the first of the official vehicles LeDoux stopped and turned to the agent trailing behind him. Bobbie leaned forward to get a better look at the agent. Female. Blond hair tucked into an updo. There was no way to know what she was saying to LeDoux, but it was clear from the body language that the two were arguing.

For a few beats they stared at each other in what appeared to be some sort of standoff. Finally the female agent glaring at LeDoux reached into her jacket pocket and withdrew something. A cell phone, maybe? She offered whatever it was and LeDoux snatched it from her hand. After walking a few yards away, LeDoux held the device to his ear. Definitely a cell phone.

Bobbie's cell rattled on the console. She jumped. She picked up the device and stared at the screen. *LeDoux.*

For the space of another round of urgent vibrating Bobbie split her attention between the phone in her hand and the man across the street. Finally, she accepted the call. "What do you want?"

"Listen carefully," he said. "I don't know how you got the heads-up that I'd been located, but for what it's worth, I'm glad one of us is still out there."

"Are you saying you didn't know they were coming?"

He glanced over his shoulder. The agents waited,

watching his every move. "What I'm saying is this is my one phone call."

"Are you under arrest?" Had Nick received bad information? Or was this LeDoux's way of keeping her trust? Wait. That wasn't likely. He had no way of knowing she was watching, and those FBI agents damned sure didn't appear to be playing.

"Go to 162 East River Street in Savannah."

Another call beeped in her ear. Bobbie checked the screen. Didn't recognize the number. "What's in Savannah?" she demanded. How could LeDoux be sure the package the courier had picked up from the attorney's house had anything to do with Weller or Nick?

There was a hesitation on the other end of the line. The female shouted at LeDoux, warning him that it was time to go. As Bobbie watched, she moved toward him.

LeDoux turned his back to the woman. "I lied to you, Bobbie. The courier sold me the package for a hundred bucks. Find Amelia Potter. You have the address."

"Who's Amelia Potter? Is she a distant relative of—?"

"Just go." His free hand went up stop-sign fashion to halt the agent's approach. "When I finish speaking to my attorney, you can have my phone back and I'm all yours," LeDoux snapped at the woman.

The agent backed off but they were clearly running out of time. Bobbie cut to the chase. "What was in the package?"

"Only one item," LeDoux said, turning his back to the agent once more. "A recent photo of Nick Shade."

While Bobbie absorbed that information, LeDoux dropped his phone on the asphalt and crushed it with the heel of his shoe. The female agent grabbed him by the arm and pointed to the damaged cell phone, her face twisted in anger. Another of the agents gathered the pieces of the broken phone from the ground.

The suits loaded up, LeDoux in tow, and drove away. Atlanta PD followed. Why would Zacharias send a photo of Nick to someone in Savannah? Was this Amelia Potter a distant relative or the front for a hit man or maybe another serial killer? Bobbie's phone vibrated and she dragged her attention to the screen. Voice mail. Expecting to find another lecture from the chief or someone from her major crimes team, she tapped the screen and listened to the voice mail.

"Detective Gentry, this is Lieutenant Troy Durham from the Savannah Chatham Metropolitan Police Department. We've reopened a cold case and we found your name in the detective's notes." Durham exhaled a big breath. "Frankly, we're hoping you can help." He hesitated for a moment before going on. "If you could give me a call I'd really appreciate it. I've never seen anything like this."

The call ended. Bobbie stared at the screen. She

couldn't imagine why her name would be in the notes of a cold case in Savannah, but the call and the address LeDoux had given her couldn't be co-incidence.

Something was happening in Savannah and somehow it involved Nick.

And her.

Seven

Tony stared at the nameplate on the desk. *Janet Kessler.*

Supervisory Special Agent Janet Kessler.

LeDoux shook his head then remembered the hellacious headache he'd awakened with. Beer didn't usually give him a hangover but he'd added the vodka. Apparently the lack of sleep and food along with dehydration and the quantity of alcohol had set a new precedent.

He'd been questioned about any contact he'd had with Zacharias and interrogated about Weller's and Zacharias's whereabouts. Most of the answers he'd given had been tactical evasions or flat-out lies.

A BOLO had been issued for Zacharias. The blood in his study was presumed to be the missing attorney's. His driver's body had been found in the home's garage, cause of death a nasty blow to the back of the head. The driver's car had been located in the parking lot of the Paces Ferry Road Home Depot. No blood in the car but there was a suitcase and a briefcase, both of which belonged to Zacharias. Cell phone, passport, money, all sorts of goodies were in the briefcase. He'd hired a private jet to take him out of the country. The pilot had been located and questioned. Zacharias hadn't shown up for the flight—yet another indication he was dead. Not so surprising, Zacharias's destination had been Maracaibo, Venezuela. Venezuela had no extradition treaty with the US.

"How cliché," Tony muttered. Weller would be doing the same. If anyone involved in the search expected any different, they were fools.

Except Weller appeared to have something to take care of first. It was that something that would be his downfall...if Tony could figure out what the hell it was quickly enough maybe he could intercept the bastard.

That was the thing, the Bureau had nothing on Weller. Not one damned lead. At least Tony had Savannah.

After the last round of questioning, Tony had been sequestered to this room—to Kessler's office. Nothing he hadn't expected. She was on his short list of insiders who'd given Weller far too much leeway. Some-damned-body in the Bureau had been providing him with reports on his son and all sorts of other classified material. Kessler, Tony felt confident, was nothing more than a pawn—one close enough to keep a close watch on Weller.

Except she'd seriously fucked up.

The door opened and the uptight bitch walked in. Her navy skirt was snugger than it should be, ensuring that anyone who bothered to look noted her taut ass and toned legs. The white blouse showed more cleavage than necessary. The matching navy jacket fit her narrow waist, accentuating her nice tits.

That was the only damned thing nice about her. She wore her blond hair in one of those severe buns that suggested sexual repression, and just enough makeup to demonstrate she had a feminine side even if it was locked down tight to facilitate her climb up the management ladder. According to his research, she would do anything for a promotion. Didn't mean she wasn't damned good at her job, just a cold, calculating bitch who didn't mind stepping over the bodies she left in her wake.

"I spoke at length with your supervisor."

Yay. "Then you know I'm on administrative leave pending an OPR review." No point beating around the bush. Supervisory Special Agent Rodney Pitts of the Behavioral Analysis Unit-2 had no doubt given her a complete rundown on his rogue profiler and his issues with the Office of Professional Responsibility.

The thought had no more flitted through his brain when the man himself entered the room. He closed the door and gave a nod to Kessler.

What the hell? Tony had expected that Pitts would be involved in the task force, after all Weller had been his pet project for more than a decade. In fact, Pitts's rise up the ranks had more to do with Weller's unprecedented cooperation than the man's leadership ability. The first two years of Weller's incarceration he had done little to back up the deal he'd made to lend his powers of analysis to the Bureau. Then suddenly he was all in and Pitts was on the fast track to stardom. The latest rumor was that Pitts would be the next unit chief at BAU. He'd already been offered a lucrative book deal on his work with Weller.

Pitts—above all others—should want Weller back where he belonged. The real question was, what had Pitts been giving Weller in exchange for his collaboration all these years? Tony had a feeling he'd provided the monster with whatever he'd wanted short of his freedom. All Tony had to do was prove it before the quest to uncover that truth cost him his career.

Kessler settled behind her desk and studied her notes while Pitts pulled a chair around so that he faced Tony. Pitts wasn't that much older than him, late forties. His dark hair had started to gray at his temples but he hadn't slowed down. A strict workout regimen kept him in shape and his expensive taste in suits ensured he always looked the part of a power player. His team—discounting Tony's recent fall from grace—was the best in BAU. He had a smoking-hot wife and two perfect kids, despite spending sixteen hours a day at work.

Tony hated him on so many levels.

"It doesn't look good for you, LeDoux," Pitts announced. "You've had a stellar career with the Bureau until the past year. I've done all I can to save your ass, but this latest move may very well be the straw that broke the camel's back."

Tony shrugged. "What do you want me to say?"

Kessler braced her forearms across her desk and leaned forward a bit. "You could start by telling us the truth."

Though Pitts was ultimately the one who set the rules where Weller's interactions with the Bureau were concerned, Kessler was the boots on the ground, so to speak, in Atlanta. She took care of any special needs Weller had on a day-to-day basis. Sometimes Tony wondered if she was the reason the sick piece of shit had always seemed completely satisfied with his accommodations— at least until recently.

"I've already told you everything I know. Zacharias wouldn't talk to me and I haven't heard from Nick Shade. That's all I got." Tony turned up his hands. "I'm mostly hanging around to see the fireworks when the real shit hits the fan."

A showdown was coming and not just the one between Shade and Weller.

"You are to return to Virginia immediately and stay put until the review into your recent actions is complete," Pitts announced. "Your travel arrangements have been made and two of Kessler's agents will escort you to Hartsfield and see that you board your flight."

"No problem." Tony readied to stand.

Kessler said, "Why don't I believe you, Agent LeDoux?"

"No idea." He collapsed in his seat once more. Damn he needed aspirin or, better yet, a couple of beers. If he'd required any additional proof that Kessler was Pitts's puppet, he had it now.

"The task force is doing everything possible to find Dr. Weller," Kessler reiterated as if Tony might not understand the situation. "I, for one, am convinced that the combined effort of the Southeast Regional Task Force of the US Marshals Service and the Bureau will locate him. Soon."

Pitts nodded his agreement. "We will not allow him to get away. Whatever your misgivings, LeDoux, trust me on that one."

"I can't tell you how reassuring those words are, sir." Tony had thrown that statement around himself on numerous occasions with no intention of backing it up. *Trust* was just a word. A word used to manipulate and appease.

His ire showing now, Pitts demanded, "Is it your intention to destroy your career the same way you did your marriage, Agent LeDoux?"

As hard as he tried to restrain his anger, Pitts had pushed his buttons with that one. "In case you've forgotten, my best friend destroyed my marriage when he decided to fuck my too-willing wife. At the moment, I haven't made up my mind who's working the hardest to destroy my career, me or *you.*"

When Pitts said nothing else, Tony stood. He turned his back and headed for the door.

"Just so we're clear, LeDoux," Kessler warned, her voice razor sharp. "Weller is mine. He escaped under my watch and I will see that he is captured."

Tony hesitated and faced her once more. "Don't worry, I got the message." He glanced at his superior. "I'm out."

He should have let it go at that, but some part of him couldn't resist a final dig. He hesitated at the door and glanced back at the two he suspected were ultimately as instrumental in Weller's escape as the prison nurse the bastard had chopped into nearly a dozen pieces. "Trust me on that."

In the corridor, two agents waited for Tony. Without a word they escorted him to the first floor and out of the building. When they reached a waiting sedan, he said, "I'm starving. Any chance we can stop for lunch before we reach the airport?"

The two glanced at each other and then the taller one shrugged. "Why not? All you've got now is time, LeDoux."

He flashed a fake smile. "Lucky me."

Tony would get back to Virginia eventually, but right now he needed to be in Savannah.

Eight

Bobbie parked on the street. She'd spent almost as much time watching her rearview mirror as she had the highway during the nearly four-hour drive from Atlanta. She'd tried returning Lieutenant Durham's call but she'd gotten his voice mail. Since she had no idea what the call was about or the actual identity of the caller, she'd opted not to leave a message. In fact, she'd decided to drive directly to Savannah-Chatham Metro headquarters and make sure Durham was actually who he claimed to be. The address LeDoux had given her would have to wait until she made a decision as to whether or not she was walking into a trap. At this point she didn't trust anyone except Nick.

Climbing out of her Challenger, she surveyed the headquarters. The building was a collage of the new and the old, the newer part of the three-story brick building's facade being a deeper red like the

Georgia clay for which the state was known. A wide sidewalk led from the street to the steps and created a border around flowering shrubs and sago palms. Majestic oaks draped with moss blocked the afternoon sun. Bobbie climbed the half a dozen steps that rose to the main entrance. The glass doors were decorated with orange pumpkin cut-outs and ghosts. Inside a wide counter cut through the center of the lobby, a statue of a big black cat waited on the counter, back arched in fury. On the entrance side of the counter the usual bulletin board loaded with notices and dispatches hung on the wall to the left. Beneath it stood a table covered with informative and instructional brochures. Four chairs lined the wall to the right. Typical police headquarters lobby. Straightforward and practical.

A receptionist looked up from her desk behind the counter. She adjusted her reading glasses. "May I help you?"

Bobbie held up her badge. "I'm Detective Gentry. I received a call from a Lieutenant Durham."

The sixtyish woman—Delores Waldrop, according to the nameplate on the desk—smiled. "Oh yes. Troy asked me to be on the lookout for your call. I guess you decided coming in person was better. Montgomery, right?"

Bobbie nodded. "That's right."

Delores removed her reading glasses and let them fall against her chest, a strand of pearls serving as the neck strap that held them in place. She shook her head. "Sorry. I was under the impression you were a man."

Bobbie produced a smile. "It happens. Is the lieutenant available?"

The woman's expression turned somber. "Since you're here in person, I'll send you straight on over to his location." She drew in a heavy breath. "We've had quite a startling day. It started just after midnight."

Deciding it was better not to mention that she didn't have a clue what was going on, Bobbie nodded as if she understood completely.

Delores stood and moved toward the counter. "You spend your whole life thinking you know someone and then you discover you never knew them at all." She shook her head as she reached for a tourist-type map of the city from the neat stack next to the sign-in sheet. "All right." She circled a spot on the map. "This is where we are. You'll go right on East Jones." She traced the route and then handed the map to Bobbie. "It's just a little piece off Skidaway Road. Look for the Happy Pets Veterinary Clinic. If you get to the cemetery on Bonaventure, you've gone too far. It'll take you about ten minutes to get there from here."

Bobbie thanked her and walked out of the building the same way she'd entered. As she settled behind the wheel, she considered that the sweatshirt and jeans she wore weren't exactly proper work attire, but hopefully her excuse that she was on vacation would fly. Maybe she could gain some insight as to what was going on and why someone had inserted her name into the situation before the locals figured out her sticky situation. One call to her chief and she would probably be escorted back to the interstate.

She itched to drive by the address LeDoux had given her but she had to do this first. The more time Durham had before she spoke to him, the more opportunity he had to reach out to Montgomery PD for additional information. Whatever she could learn before that happened might help find Weller. She'd spent most of the drive trying to recall a case where a detective from Savannah had called her or Newt—Howard Newton—her former partner. Newt had died two months ago after a run-in with the Storyteller. The hurt sliced through her chest afresh.

Miss you.

Since she couldn't call Newt and checking in with Sergeant Lynette Holt, her immediate supervisor back in Montgomery, was out of the question, Bobbie had to rely on her memory and so far she hadn't recalled ever assisting a Savannah detective on any sort of case. If Newt had taken a call from this department he wouldn't have given her name as a point of contact without telling her.

Although both cities were positioned next to a river, Savannah and Montgomery had little else in common. The many manicured parks and the ornate antebellum architecture made Savannah a definite tourist destination. The city's label as one of the most haunted places in the world didn't hurt tourism either. Savannah had a slow, genteel feel about it, far more so than Montgomery. The politics of being a state capitol gave Montgomery a not always pleasant underlying intensity Savannah didn't suffer. She and James had spent a few days here before Jamie was born—a *babymoon*, her husband had called it.

Like the receptionist said, the drive scarcely took ten minutes. The half dozen official vehicles and the crime scene tape were visible as soon as Bobbie hit the intersection before her final turn. Two news vans had been pushed back a block from the scene. As she stopped for the uniform at the perimeter, she noted a coroner's van. Definitely a homicide. Not surprising. For a city so laid-back and steeped in history and tourism, Savannah had an inordinately higher than average violent crime rate.

Bobbie showed her badge to the officer. "Lieutenant Durham is expecting me."

The uniform stationed at the outer perimeter nodded and pointed to the side of the road beyond the house and the more modern clinic where all the official vehicles were gathered. "Park anywhere over there."

Bobbie rolled forward, easing off the road and onto the grass. The veterinary clinic had been built next to an older craftsman bungalow, probably historic, much like the ones back home. The typical oak trees dripping with moss surrounded it. The house appeared well maintained and the lawn was nicely manicured. The same was true of the clinic. Pumpkins sat near the doors while witches and ghosts hung from a couple of trees. A sign advertising a church trunk-or-treat was posted in the front yard of the house. She showed her badge again as she approached the inner perimeter of yellow tape that draped around the property. The uniform gave her a nod and lifted the tape.

Since the activity was focused in the grassy area slightly beyond the clinic, Bobbie bypassed the sidewalk that forked, one side going toward the clinic and the other toward the house, and followed the stepping stones around the corner of the clinic. The yard was larger than expected. Dogs yapped in the fenced-in kennels behind the clinic. Between the clinic and the woods was a small park. Wait, no. As she moved closer she recognized head-stones. Not a park, a cemetery. The small cem-etery could have been any one of the thousands of family cemeteries that dotted the Old South. An old-fashioned iron fence surrounded the space. More of those big old trees with low-hanging limbs shaded the slumbering residents. Bobbie surveyed the first of the small headstones she encountered. Except this cemetery was for pets. The statue of an angel partially covered in moss watched over the rows of markers. Yellow crime scene tape wrapped around the iron fence, the breeze making the plas-tic flop back and forth against the metal.

Two guys in suits, detectives she suspected, as well as a couple of forensic techs dressed in full protective gear stood around a grouping of small statues in the center of the cemetery. Another man, this one wearing protective clothing, as well, knelt next to a broken statue. Now that Bobbie looked more closely, all the statues were damaged in some way. An arm broken off, the head missing. The statues ranged in size from three to five feet— *children.* The intricately detailed pigtails and wide skirt of a little girl as if she were skipping along. A perfectly formed baseball cap on a little boy with bat in hand. The sculptor certainly showed a talent for capturing the essence of children at play.

She hadn't spotted a body but there had to be one around here somewhere. As if she'd said as much aloud, a man turned and looked at her. His cowboy boots, jeans and button-down shirt told her little, but the weapon in the shoulder holster, the shield clipped at his waist and the weary look on his face said plenty. This was Lieutenant Troy Durham. The cell phone he held at his ear was likely the reason he had turned from the activity. Maybe to hear better or maybe because he'd received a call to say Bobbie was headed his way.

He tucked the phone into his back pocket and walked toward Bobbie, meeting her a few yards from the ongoing activity. Thrusting out his hand he said, "Troy Durham. Glad you could make it, Detective Gentry." Confusion or something along those lines furrowed his face. "I apologize for staring, but I had you figured for male and a whole lot older."

As tired as she was, Bobbie smiled. "And I was certain you would be a little older yourself and maybe a lot shorter." Durham was probably late thirties. Very tall, blond hair, blue eyes. The way his shirt and jeans fit, it was clear he spent a good deal of his off-duty time at the gym. His current attire made her feel loads better about her own.

He laughed, the sound as fatigued as the lines around his eyes. "I guess I had that one coming."

"So what's going on?" If he felt her driving all this way rather than simply calling until she reached him was odd, he kept it to himself.

He glanced back at the damaged statues. Bobbie watched as a trace sheet was spread on the grass and bones—small bones—were placed one by one onto the sheet by a forensic tech or a coroner. Near the statue with the missing head was another trace sheet with a lone human skull placed on it. *A child's skull.*

A lump formed in Bobbie's throat. *What the hell happened here?*

"Why don't we go inside where we can speak in private?"

Bobbie drew her attention back to the lieutenant and followed him across the yard. The dogs in the kennels yapped even louder as they passed along the backside of the clinic. Durham led the way straight to the back porch of the house that was apparently part of the crime scene. More of that yellow tape adorned the perimeter. Durham tossed his keys to a passing officer and asked him to bring his briefcase inside. As Durham opened the door another forensic tech exited. Inside, the kitchen was clear of bodies and official personnel. No sign of foul play. No coppery smell of blood. The room was clean save for the scattering of dust used for collecting prints. Apparently, all the trouble was outside.

Durham settled his attention on her once more. "I guess I'm a little confused."

"Because I'm a woman or because I'm younger than you expected?" Maybe there was another detective somewhere with the name Bobbie Gentry. But it was her cell phone number Durham had called.

"Have you ever consulted on a case in this jurisdiction?"

Bobbie shook her head. "Never."

Maybe the call from Durham had been sheer coincidence. She thought of the name and address LeDoux had given her. No way. Whoever had given her name and number to Durham wanted her in Savannah as this case broke. But why? Wouldn't be Nick. Weller? He was the most likely possibility. Could be LeDoux, but that option was doubtful. He'd already given her a reason to come to Savannah.

The officer returned with Durham's briefcase and keys. Durham thanked him and placed his briefcase on the floor. He dug out a brown file folder. The edges were dog-eared as if the contents had been rifled through a thousand times.

He spread the folder on the counter and flipped through a collection of photos—photos of children. The children ranged in age from three to five or six. Three boys, two girls. There was no particular consistency to their appearance. Dark hair, light hair, brown, blue, green eyes. With each photo Bobbie's heart rate increased and the lump in her throat expanded.

The photos of the children were stamped with the word *MISSING*. She thought of the broken statues and the bones outside. Not anymore. These children were dead. Their remains were right out that door.

Damn.

A sheen of sweat rose on her skin.

"See here." Durham pointed to a handwritten note in the file. "Detective Mike Rhodes, the detective in charge of this case back when the kids went missing, mentioned you in his notes."

Sure enough, there was Bobbie's name and cell phone number at the bottom of one of the detective's reports. Her mouth dropped open when she read the date. Thirty-two years ago. Bobbie laughed. "I'm certain you don't need me to point out that this report is dated three months before I was born. How many people had cell phones back then?"

Durham shrugged, his expression warning he was as stumped as she was. "Honestly, whether this was a cell number or a landline didn't occur to me."

"May I?" She indicated the note.

"Be my guest."

Bobbie gingerly picked up the report and studied the handwriting in the upper portions and then her name and phone number. Whoever had added her contact info had taken great care to match the handwriting.

"This is a copy." She placed the report back on the folder. "If we had the original we could prove my information was added more recently." *Like yesterday.* She examined the pile of documents in the folder. Most appeared to be originals. Why was this one a copy?

"Yeah, I noticed that, too." Durham considered her for a moment. "Why would anyone want me to call you about this case?"

Where to begin? "Well, Lieutenant, I'm afraid the only explanation I can give you will take some time and it's complicated. Worse, I can't guarantee you it's the right one."

Durham closed the file and tucked it back into his briefcase. "You had a long drive. Did you have a chance to stop for lunch?"

Food was the last thing on her mind. "I didn't, but I'm good."

"Well, I'm not. There's a hole-in-the-wall café a few blocks from here. Why don't you fill me in over lunch and my unit will take care of things here for half an hour or so."

Bobbie would prefer to be out there determining how many sets of remains had been discovered and what they could possibly have to do with

Weller, but this was Durham's case and his town. "Just one question. Is the person who lives here or runs the clinic somehow involved in what's happening in the pet cemetery?"

"Unfortunately that's what it looks like." Durham hitched his head toward the other room. "See for yourself."

She followed the lieutenant into the living room and then down a narrow hall. At the first door on the left he gestured for her to go in ahead of him. Bobbie stalled in the open doorway. An adult male victim was on his knees in front of the toilet, his body was nude and his head was deep in the bowl. Bobbie leaned nearer to make sure she was seeing what she thought she was. A grayish powder was splattered on the white vinyl floor. Urine had trickled from between the vic's legs and joined the powdery substance. As she leaned closer still, her eyebrows went up. The toilet bowl had been filled with what appeared to be concrete and the vic's head had been shoved into the mixture and held there until it hardened.

Bobbie glanced back at Durham. "Homeowner?"

Durham nodded. "Dr. Bill Sanders. He's lived in Savannah his whole life. He built the veterinary clinic next door. His motto was to never turn away a sick animal whether the owner could pay or not. He was a highly respected member of his church. The first to volunteer whenever help was needed. We're all in shock."

"Does he live here alone?" Her mind instantly ran down the possibilities of how this man, Sanders, could be connected to Weller.

"The wife's down the hall, in the other bathroom. They just got the body out of the tub. The coroner is having a look at her. We called in both coroners for this one."

Bobbie was surprised they had two coroners. Montgomery was lucky to have one part-time coroner.

"Nancy Sanders was a retired elementary school teacher. No children. Everybody always said the animals were their kids," Durham went on. "Neither of them ever had so much as a parking ticket. Their killer didn't seem to be interested in anything of value in the house. Her jewelry is on the dresser. A couple hundred bucks in cash was left in his wallet. Credit cards. As best we can tell, nothing's missing."

Like the scene at Zacharias's home...except with bodies and the remains.

Durham showed Bobbie the way past a small bedroom to the end of the hall where what had likely once been two bedrooms had been remodeled into a master suite. Two men, one carrying a portable jackhammer and the other armed with a large crowbar, filed out of the room. A trace sheet had been placed on the floor near the bed. The female vic, early- to mid-sixties, was stretched out there. Most of her nude body was covered in bits and pieces of gravel-like fragments. The grayish film and fragments coated her hair and face.

"They had to jackhammer the concrete from around her. She was submerged up to her eyes."

Gruesome way to go. Had the victims, including the children, still been alive when they were encased in that concrete? Suppressing a shudder, Bobbie shifted her attention back to the lieutenant. "Have you spoken to the original detective in charge of the case?"

"He died five years ago. Both the primary detectives who investigated those missing kids back when the case was active are gone now. Last year we started a new Cold Case Unit but they hadn't gotten around to this one yet."

"Were the Sanderses persons of interest thirty-two years ago?"

Durham shook his head. "According to the file, they were instrumental in organizing community search parties and raising awareness of what folks should be doing to keep their children safe."

"Obviously they were instrumental in a whole lot more."

"Obviously."

"The remains found in those statues are the children you showed me?"

"We haven't started the official ID process but we have reason to believe they are, yes."

"Why were the statues here—in a pet cemetery?" Bobbie assumed the statues had been some sort of tribute to the missing children but it seemed an odd place for a memorial. Besides, the cemetery appeared far older than the clinic.

"The way I always heard it Dr. Sanders insisted he was concerned the community would forget about the children so he created a memorial to them. Three of the five kids who went missing brought their pets to his clinic. That pet cemetery had been in his family for generations." He glanced at the dead woman on the floor. "This is completely crazy."

Murder was always heinous, but when it involved a child it was unspeakable. What did this decades-old case have to do with Weller? Or Nick? Or her, for that matter? There had to be a connection, otherwise Bobbie would not have been drawn into the investigation. "Lieutenant, I'm guessing you know who Dr. Randolph Weller is and that he recently escaped the federal prison in Atlanta."

"I don't know what that has to do with this." He shrugged, glanced around as if to ensure no one was listening, then added, "But I damned well intend to find out. You ready for that lunch now?"

"Sure."

Bobbie assumed he had his reasons for wanting to keep their discussion off the record. Durham claimed his briefcase, informed another detective that he needed to take a break and then he ushered Bobbie to his vehicle, a silver Chevy Tahoe.

The barking dogs had her glancing back at the kennels.

"We fed all the animals this morning," Durham explained as he opened the passenger-side door for her. "As soon as we've removed the bodies and the…remains, we'll contact the owners to pick up their pets."

When they'd driven a couple of minutes, Bobbie recognized they weren't heading back toward town. Instead he drove to the Bonaventure Cemetery and parked.

"I hope you meant it when you said you weren't interested in lunch because I couldn't eat right now if my life depended upon it."

Bobbie considered the man. "Is there someone in your unit you don't trust?" She glanced around. "I'm sure you didn't bring me here to show off one of your famous tourist spots."

He shook his head. "The detectives in my homicide unit are the best. This case has haunted Savannah for a long time. The idea that those missing children were right under our noses all these years is hard to swallow. Jesus. Bill Sanders sculpted those statues and dedicated them to the children." He looked away. "How sick is that?"

"People show you the face they want you to see." She had learned that lesson the hard way. "Sometimes it's very different from who they really are."

Durham exhaled a heavy breath. "Right now my main objective is to keep the whole thing quiet until we understand what the hell happened."

Bobbie had a feeling that keeping this investigation quiet would not be in any way easy. She imagined most of his department was composed of locals who had known those kids or who knew their families.

"And frankly," Durham added, "I'm struggling with who may have tampered with this file. No offense, but what could you or this Randolph Weller possibly have to do with my case?"

Where to begin? *Keep it simple and to the point.* "Nearly a year ago I worked with the FBI on a joint task force to stop the Storyteller. Heard of him?"

Durham nodded. "He was—oh hell. You're the victim who survived."

Bobbie cleared her throat of the lump still lodged there. "That's me." The image of those small bones back there flashed over and over in her head. "He murdered my husband. He was the reason my little boy and my partner died."

"I'm sorry." Durham shook his head. "I'm even sorrier you had to see what we found in that cemetery."

Bobbie stared out the windshield at the headstones of the famous cemetery standing tall beneath the moss-draped oaks. "I'm a cop. We see things." She turned to him. "The Storyteller's dead, but what happened with him drew another serial killer's attention my way."

And Nick's. He was the primary reason she had survived.

"Weller?"

She nodded. "In addition to more than forty murders in the past, he orchestrated several murders in Montgomery during the past eight days. I believe Weller is attempting to lure me into some twisted game he's determined to play out in your backyard. If I'm right, then he may have been responsible for the murders of your two newest victims. I don't know about the children. None of this is his usual MO but I've learned recently that isn't always relevant." She took a breath. "I'm not sure I could possibly find the right words to convey to you the depth of Weller's knowledge and insights into other killers—or the depraved acts he's capable of carrying out."

"I read the report on him that hit the wires Tuesday night." He shook his head. "That's the first I'd heard of him."

"Do you know if he ever consulted on any cases in Savannah? Before your time, maybe? Prior to being outed as a serial killer himself, he often consulted with the police and the FBI on difficult cases."

"I have no idea." Durham blew out a disgusted breath. "I left Savannah right after high school. I only returned three years ago. I'm still catching up on the past sixteen years. Hell, I got the call about the Sanderses just after midnight. A noise disturbance was reported around eleven-thirty. When uniforms showed up the front door was open and the television was blaring. If one of my uniforms hadn't needed to take a piss and literally stumbled over one of the damaged statues with bones falling out of it, we probably wouldn't have noticed the remains until daylight. By four this morning I was digging out this damned cold case file. Sometime around my tenth cup of coffee I found the reference to you. My head has been spinning ever since."

"Was the 911 caller male or female?"

"Male." He rubbed at his temple. "One of the neighbors. He's been interviewed, but he didn't see anything. The noise woke him up and he called it in."

Bobbie digested the information for a moment. "I wish I could give you more. What I've told you is my best assessment based on what you have so far."

She decided not to mention Nick or the woman LeDoux told her about. Durham seemed like a nice guy, but right now it was best not to be too trusting even with kind strangers who were cops. She'd trusted Steven Devine. After a decade in Birmingham PD, he'd transferred to Montgomery PD a month ago to replace her partner. Fury tightened her gut.

"If someone in my department added your name to the case file," Durham said, drawing her attention back to him, "I need to figure out who the hell he or she is. I'll get the Records Section working on that ASAP." He stared out over the cemetery. "If this Weller character is the one who wants you involved in this case, there must be a reason. You think your department will have a problem with your sticking around in an advisory capacity for a few days?"

Bobbie laughed. "That's another complicated

story, but the abbreviated answer is no. I'll bring my chief and my lieutenant up to speed as soon as I have a better handle on what's going on."

Durham shifted back into Drive. "Well, let's get started then. The sooner we figure out this mess, the sooner we can stop it."

Five dead children.

Bobbie closed her eyes as they headed back to the crime scene.

What the hell are you trying to show me, Weller?

He'd warned her that every ounce of courage and tenacity she possessed would be required to survive what was coming.

Bobbie glanced at the man behind the wheel. If Weller had started this, Durham had no idea just how bad things were going to get.

Nine

"How're you today, Ms. Balfour?" Amelia Potter smiled as her oldest client settled at the table. The elderly woman refused to allow anyone to assist her into or out of a chair. She contended that she was perfectly capable of taking care of herself.

"I'm just peachy." Ninety-four-year-old Camille Balfour propped her umbrella against her chair and then loosened her scarf to let it drop from her head to her shoulders. "Every morning I wake up is a blessing."

"A blessing, indeed." Amelia had already washed her hands so she picked up her deck. The worn cards felt like an extension of her. She'd found this deck twenty-five years ago and she'd used it since. A good deck of tarot cards was like an old, dependable friend. Part of the magic was in the relationship. "I hear those great-grandchildren came to see you this past weekend."

Camille's smile chased away the ravages of age, lifted her sagging jowls and brightened her eyes. "You better believe it. Lauren graduated from medical school back in May and Gwyneth will graduate next spring. She's going to be an attorney. Two smart girls."

"Just like their great-grandma."

Camille reached across the table with one hand gnarled by the progression of rheumatoid arthritis and clasped Amelia's. "I'm having visions again." She exhaled a shaky breath. "I've been worrying about you all week."

Camille had never been a reader of the tarot. She'd never traded her knowing for money the way Amelia did, but not all were blessed with family money. The truth was until Camille had confided in Amelia that she felt things, she'd never before confessed aloud her abilities for fear of reprisal from her late husband, from his family and the community. She had held firm to her station in life and never permitted the slightest impropriety. It was the way of things with her generation.

Amelia set her cards aside and patted the dear woman's hand. "Why in the world would you be worrying about me?"

Camille chuckled. "You know I've always had a soft spot for you, Mia."

No one called her Mia except Camille. Amelia's parents had kicked her out of their home outside Atlanta when she was sixteen. She didn't hold it against them. She'd allowed herself to get involved with drugs and the wrong people. Three years of dealing with her issues had worn down her parents. It was a miracle she had survived her own recklessness. A sad smile tugged at her lips. If she hadn't come to Savannah and ended up pregnant, she might have lost her life to those damned drugs.

Her little boy had saved her. Her heart squeezed painfully. If only…

Cold fingers tightened on her hand. "Mia, someone is coming and whoever it is she won't let me sleep. I keep seeing her running through the woods with you. The trouble is right behind the two of you and I…" She shook her head, her rheumy eyes shining with emotion. "I'm terrified for you, Mia."

Amelia smiled at her old friend. "For thirty-seven years you've helped me. Whether it was a safe bed to sleep in or a hot meal in my belly, you watched out for me until I could watch out for myself." She didn't mention how Camille had ensured Amelia was accepted at one of the best private rehab facilities in Georgia all those years ago or how she'd cosigned with her at the bank when she purchased this shop. Her friend was well aware of all she'd done. "It's time for me to watch out for you. You don't need to worry about me anymore. I'm doing just fine."

The Gentle Palm had a steady clientele. Amelia had paid the final payment on the shop last month. It was hers now. Her little apartment on the second floor was all she would ever need. She didn't own a car but she didn't need one. When she wanted to go somewhere she took the bus or the train, but she rarely left town anyway. Her clients depended on her and she wanted to be available for them. Amelia had all she needed right here in Savannah.

For the past ten years she had been helping Camille with her gardening. Though the Balfours had money to spare and a loyal housekeeping and gardening crew, Camille trusted no one except Amelia with her roses. Her lovely home on Gordon Street faced Monterey Square. The house had been in her family since the day it was built in 1879. It was enormous and beautiful just like the heart of the lady squeezing Amelia's hand so hard right this moment.

"She has hair as dark as night," Camille murmured, "and the bluest eyes. She's come for you, Mia. There are bones all around the two of you." She shook her head and squeezed her eyes shut. "All around you. Then I see the water and the red, red blood." She exhaled a shuddering breath. "I can't make the images go away."

"Come along." Amelia stood. "We should have a cup of tea. We can do your reading later."

Camille didn't argue. She struggled to her feet, somehow weaker now. To Amelia's surprise, the elderly woman leaned on her as they made their way to the kitchenette in the back. Camille prided herself on her independence. Her sudden show of uncertainty and weakness was very much out of character. Amelia's heart clutched with worry.

"A cup of hot tea will do us both some good," Amelia promised.

When Camille was seated at the small table in the back of the shop, Amelia moved to the stove and reached for the kettle. Thankfully it wasn't until her back was fully turned to her friend that the trembling showed in her hands.

Camille was right. Amelia had experienced a similar warning in her dreams. But the stranger wasn't coming…she was already here.

Yet it was what Amelia had read in the newspaper that really terrified her.

Dr. Randolph Weller was still at large.

Ten

A few cardboard file boxes represented the lives of five children. Now two adults—possibly the two who had murdered those children more than three decades ago—had been added.

Bobbie reached for the bottle of water she'd been nursing since Delores had forced both her and Durham to eat a sandwich she'd ordered from the deli down the street. Chicken salad prepared the usual Southern way with mayonnaise, pickles, eggs and celery. Bobbie had realized after the first bite that she'd been starving.

Falling into those old bad habits.

During the long months of recovery after she escaped the Storyteller, she'd forgotten to eat more often than not. Even after she'd returned to work, her partner had to remind her to grab breakfast or lunch.

You gotta eat to stay strong, girlie.

God she missed Newt. Her life had been turned upside down and then shaken. And just when she'd thought she might be able to pull it back together to some degree, a new wave of tragedy had hit like the aftershocks following a major earthquake. Only this time Bobbie wasn't going to fall apart the way she had the last time.

You will not win, Weller.

She and Nick had stopped the Storyteller as well as Steven Devine, a man—no, not a man, a monster—who had posed as a cop for nearly a decade. They would stop Randolph Weller, too. Then Bobbie intended to take her life back—starting with Nick.

Durham walked back into his office and plopped in the chair behind his desk. "The coroner confirmed we only have four sets of remains. No extra pieces, no missing pieces."

Bobbie sat up straighter. "So one of the missing children is unaccounted for."

The entire homicide unit and the forensic squad had spent the past twelve hours searching the pet cemetery and the grounds of the Sanders home as well as the clinic. Tomorrow the FBI agent who'd helped with the case all those years ago, though retired now, was coming to Savannah along with the local field agent currently holding the position he'd vacated. Bobbie hoped the retired agent would recall if Weller had advised on the case or some other case in Savannah during or near that time frame. There was nothing in the three boxes that suggested he had, but Bobbie's name being in that case file didn't make sense otherwise.

She surveyed the case board Durham had built. Alice Cortland, five; Heath Wilson, five; Braden Cotton, four; Noah Potter, three; and Brianne Durham, three, all went missing on the same night, October 25, thirty-two years ago. All but Noah Potter were from wealthy, influential Savannah families.

She shifted her attention to the lieutenant. "How long will it take forensics to determine which child is still out there?"

Durham set his elbows on his desk and scrubbed at his jaw. The man was exhausted. Bobbie knew that place all too well. "Depends on how many had been to the dentist before they went missing. Some folks don't take their kids to the dentist until they're at least school age. Any documented injuries prior to their abductions could potentially help. Which means we have to bring the parents into this before we have enough answers to give them all closure."

Never the best avenue. "Do we have anything new from the lab or the coroner's office?"

Bobbie wished she had said *you* instead of *we*. Durham had invited her to stay and advise, but this was his case.

Durham reached for a folder. "Nada."

"Have you looked into any similar cases during that same time frame, say within a hundred-mile radius?"

If this was a serial killer, it was unlikely these

children were his only victims. There was always the chance the murders were simply a mass killing. The question was why these children? Why that particular day? And why hadn't anyone come forward with information about the killer? Few mass murderers got away clean. Someone usually saw or heard something. The fifteen minutes of fame was typically the mass murderer's objective.

"There were a couple of human sacrifices over in Charleston during that same time frame. Ritual killings. But the kids were older. Rhodes suggested in one of his reports that it was possible these children had suffered that same fate. He and the detective as well as the boys from the GBI who worked the case over in Charleston compared notes." Durham shook his head. "But since the bodies were never found the way those in Charleston were, nothing came of it as far as I can tell."

"Did anything happen during that time that might have caused Sanders to go off the deep end and abduct all these children? Any personal issues with the parents of the children?"

"About three weeks before the children disappeared—" he reached across his desk for another file "—a twelve-year-old girl was raped and murdered." He checked the label on the folder. "Christina Foster."

Bobbie accepted the folder he offered and flipped through the grim contents.

"There was a witness who said she saw Treat Bonner, a local seventeen-year-old, with Christina before she disappeared. Her body was found three days later. A couple weeks after that it was determined he wasn't the rapist, but the folks in the community already had him tried and convicted before he was even charged. Bonner was intellectually challenged, which made him a bit of an outcast. He spent a lot of time walking the streets around his neighborhood. Kids made fun of him and his way of reacting was to try to scare them. People were desperate for a boogie man to blame the girl's murder on and Treat Bonner fit the bill."

"Is he still alive?" Bobbie wasn't sure how he could help, but it was a lead worth following.

Durham shrugged. "No one knows. Before he was cleared of suspicion, he disappeared. Some said his mother sent him away to avoid murder charges and never allowed him to return after he was cleared."

"What do you say?"

"Based on the number of documented times she showed up demanding to know why no one was looking for her son, I'd say she had nothing to do with his disappearance. Both the FBI and the GBI came to the same conclusion."

The Georgia Bureau of Investigation appeared to have worked closely with the FBI and the local cops when the children went missing, but the result was the same: unsolved.

Bobbie asked, "Would the Sanderses have been involved? Maybe they were friends of the Bonner family or the Foster family."

"Rhodes never found a connection beyond Sanders being a local veterinary who treated some of the kids' pets and that he attended the same church as the victims' families."

"So all the children attended the same church?"

"All but the Potter boy."

The Potter boy was the anomaly amid the children who'd gone missing all those years ago. The Cortlands, Wilsons, Cottons and Durhams were all occupants of the same tax bracket in addition to attending the same church. The same could be said of Christina Foster. Noah Potter didn't meet either criteria. Nor did Treat Bonner.

"What about Potter's parents?" Bobbie shouldn't have been surprised when she read Amelia Potter's name in the file. Was her connection to this case the reason Zacharias had sent her a photo of Nick? Did he believe Nick could help her find the killer or killers who'd taken the children? If the Sanderses were the killers, who killed them? Could the identity of their killer be somehow connected to Nick?

Another theory hit Bobbie hard. Bill and Nancy Sanders had been murdered. Was the photo being sent to Potter some way of connecting Nick to those murders? Would the FBI find the intercepted package among LeDoux's belongings and use it against Nick?

"There's only Amelia," Durham said. "The boy's father died before he was born. The two were never married so the child was given his mother's name."

Bobbie decided to keep the information LeDoux

had given her about Potter to herself. At this point she could see no reason why Durham needed that potentially detrimental information.

"What about the Bonners?" she asked. "Are either of the parents still alive?"

"The Bonners are still around, yeah. They don't get out much. The father was injured in a construction accident just before Treat was born. A few years later he had a stroke. He's bedridden. Can't do anything for himself or even speak. Mrs. Bonner's had it pretty rough. Treat was their only child."

"The Fosters?"

"Christina was an only child, too. A heart attack took the father years ago. The mother is still alive. She's in an assisted living facility over in Macon but she has advanced Alzheimer's."

"No trouble or disputes between the Sanderses and the Fosters or the Bonners?"

"None we've found or that were listed in the case file." Durham shook his head. "The neighbors and family friends we interviewed this morning insisted the Sanderses were kind, honest, salt-of-the-earth folks. 'Course we didn't reveal what we'd found in that pet cemetery." He ran his hand through his hair and exhaled a big burst of frustration. "There's even a special prayer meeting tonight at the church. The members are all torn up because two such fine Christians and neighbors have been murdered. Several of their most prominent friends have already been nudging the mayor to get this case solved." He laughed a frustrated sound. "None of it makes a lick of sense. How could two God-fearing folks have murdered those children?"

Bobbie had recently learned unexpected surprises about people she had known her entire life—her parents in particular. Nick had warned her that everyone had secrets, even the people who brought you into this world and raised you.

Even you, Bobbie.

"Everyone has secrets, Lieutenant. I have mine, you have yours. Some are just more shocking than others."

Durham grunted. "No kidding."

Dr. Sanders had made all the headstones and statues in the pet cemetery. One neighbor had stated that Sanders occasionally made animal statues for those who wanted a memorial for a family pet to keep in their own yard. Bobbie hoped like hell the Potter boy's remains weren't out there in a statue in someone else's landscape.

She asked, "There's no way to track down all the statues Sanders created that didn't end up in his cemetery?"

"We could ask for anyone who has one to come forward." Durham shrugged. "Sanders didn't keep any records about how many pieces he'd done or where they were all located."

"No other unsolved missing children cases in the area?"

"Not one."

If a serial killer abruptly stopped killing, there

had to be a compelling reason. Usually it was because they were deceased or in prison. That wasn't the case with Sanders. He could be the rare killer who simply stopped, but Bobbie's instincts weren't settling for that answer. Was he even a serial killer? Five children in one event. No question the more reasonable conclusion was that Sanders was a mass murderer. What was his motive? Every killer had a motive. Why make the big kill and then keep it to himself?

Moving on for the moment, Bobbie ventured, "Brianne Durham, was she your sister?"

She had wanted to ask him about the child for the past two hours. She'd seen the parents' names but most of the reports related to the Durham girl were not in the file, which suggested the answer was yes. Typically cops were the only people who had direct access to case files. Then again, someone had added Bobbie's name and phone number to this one.

If Weller had a contact in this department…no if about it. There simply was no other explanation. Somehow Weller had reached into this department in the past twenty-four hours or so and maybe thirty-odd years ago, as well.

"She was." Durham reached into a desk drawer and withdrew a folder. "This is what you're looking for. I pulled all the reports related to Brianne from the file when the case was turned over to the Cold Case Unit. I guess I didn't want anyone reading about my personal hell. I figured if they uncovered who took the other children, we'd know who took Brianne. No need to keep questioning my family." When Bobbie would have spoken he held up a hand. "I know, I know. I shouldn't have, but I did. It wasn't like they were taking a second look at the case right now. They have hundreds of others."

"Do you want to talk about it?" Bobbie understood how it felt to be the object of scrutiny in a situation like this one. How many times had she asked herself if she had done something differently would her son still be alive? "You were what, five or six years old?"

He nodded. "Six. I was supposed to be watching her. It was the fall festival at the elementary school I attended. My folks were volunteering in the cafeteria, helping raise money for a new playground, and it was my job to take care of Brianne. But I was only interested in playing the "shoot a duck out of the water" game. I wasn't worried about my baby sister."

Bobbie could imagine the hurt and suffering he'd endured every day since. She doubted anyone had blamed him more than he blamed himself.

"We should speak to any cops or detectives who were in the department back then—they could have useful insights. Beyond finding the missing set of remains," Bobbie went on, "it's imperative that we learn any changes in marital or financial status among the players around the time the children disappeared or shortly after. We're looking for intersections."

"Intersections?" He leaned back in his chair.

Bobbie nodded. "The places where aspects of each family's life intersected with another player involved. So far, we have attendance at the same church and tax bracket. The only one who doesn't intersect in those two places is Potter. For now, we'll leave Christina Foster and Treat Bonner out of the equation since there's no evidence of an actual link between the cases."

"I wouldn't call my family wealthy—not like the Cortlands or the others anyway." He hesitated a moment. "I suppose they were closer to the Cortlands than to Potter."

"Exactly," Bobbie explained. "Position in the community is something else the Cortlands, Wilsons, Cottons and Durhams have in common over Potter. Thirty-two years ago that likely didn't feel relevant. They say hindsight is twenty-twenty for a reason. Looking back, it may be easier to see what no one could see beyond the haze of emotions at the time."

"There were plenty of high emotions. Everyone took sides. Those involved suspected each other. My old man had to break up more than one heated argument at the church."

"I can imagine."

Durham braced his forearms on his desk and studied her. "While you were reading through my case files, I did a little reading myself." He looked away a moment before meeting her gaze once more. "I don't know how you get up every morning and go on with your life. What you survived is unthinkable. I can't imagine adding to that the incredible loss you suffered. There were a lot of years I couldn't look myself in the mirror, it's still difficult."

Bobbie had expected him to do his research. "We do what we have to do."

He shrugged. "Guess so."

"Your parents are still alive?" Shifting the conversation while staying on subject was a maneuver she'd mastered during the past year.

He nodded. "Luke and Heather Durham. I have dinner with them on Sundays. My mother proclaimed that edict as soon as I moved back to town. Ironically, like me, my father was the homicide unit lieutenant before he retired ten years ago. He and I don't talk much."

"Have you given anymore thought to who in the department may have tampered with the file?" Bobbie disliked bringing up the subject, but Durham couldn't let that part of this investigation slide.

"I have." He searched her eyes, his hopeful. "Don't take offense, but that's something I need to do on my own."

Bobbie held up her hands. "I completely understand. It's difficult enough to deal with this kind of issue; you don't need an outsider poking through department business. I only ask because things are likely to get even more complicated when the FBI and the GBI show up. Following up on that issue might get lost in the frenzy."

"Point taken." He reached for his cell. "Durham."

Bobbie surveyed the photos on the case board. All those smiling faces. The preliminary exam by the coroners hadn't noted any visible cause of death. However those children died, she hoped like hell it had been in their sleep. *Don't let him have tortured those babies.*

"Thanks. We're headed that way."

Troy stood as he tucked his phone away. Bobbie followed his cue.

"Dr. Weston has an update for us."

"You're lucky to have a real coroner's office." Montgomery's part-time coroner worked out of her small family-practice clinic. She was a damned good one, but if an autopsy was required the body had to be sent to the state lab. There was never enough money for the needed facilities or a full-time staff.

"I'm not sure luck has anything to do with it." He grabbed his keys from his desk. "Supply and demand, Detective. Supply and demand."

East Sixty-Seventh Street
5:50 p.m.

Four cold steel tables draped with trace sheets lined one side of the room. The two coroners, Weston and Mather, had painstakingly reconstructed the remains. A picture had been placed near the skull of the three they had identified.

"Alice Cortland, Braden Cotton and Heath Wilson," Carol Mather indicated each table in turn. Mather looked to be around forty. She wore glasses and kept her brown hair in a meticulous knot on top of her head. "Cortland and Wilson had dental X-rays available which made identification reasonably easy."

"Braden Cotton," Lloyd Weston said, "didn't have dental records but his right humerus as well as his clavicle were fractured in a fall from the back deck of their home when he was three. His pediatrician hand delivered the X-rays. We studied them at length and we're as sure as we can be this one is the Cotton boy."

Weston couldn't be far from retirement age, Bobbie decided. His gray hair had thinned on top. He stood about the same height as Mather, around five-nine. Both were trim and wore running shoes. Beneath the white lab coat Weston wore a white shirt and gray tie that matched his gray trousers. Mather, on the other hand, wore a colorful paisley print blouse with a tan skirt that hit a couple of inches below the knee. She imagined both had been their respective class nerds back in school.

"What about this one?" Durham indicated the final table. "Is it the Potter boy or...is it Brianne?" The agony in his voice was palpable. Everyone in the room felt his pain.

"We can deduce certain things," Weston said.

"Based on the age of the child at the time of death and the size of the bones, we do believe this is Brianne but, let me be very clear, we cannot confirm that conclusion. At such a young age it's difficult if not impossible to make that call primarily because the bones in the pelvic region that would generally tell us the gender of a set of remains aren't developed enough to be conclusive."

"If we had a documented injury or dental X-rays for comparison that would help," Mather offered, "but according to the files there are none. We're hoping the lab will find some trace element that will help us with identification."

Bobbie asked, "What about DNA?" DNA could be extracted from bones centuries old, surely they could find something in those only a few decades old.

"We will certainly try that avenue, as well," Weston explained. "As soon as we've done all we can here, we'll send the bones to the lab in hopes of finding enough DNA for a comparison." He surveyed the small sets of remains. "Unfortunately, that process takes time."

"We've waited thirty-two years," Durham noted.

The two coroners gave somber nods.

The children's clothing appeared to have been removed before they were encased in the concrete. Hair and other small fragments found with the remains were being prepared for shipment to the lab. Bobbie hoped some bit of trace evidence would be discovered that could provide speedy closure.

"I appreciate your hard work. Both of you have gone above and beyond today. Anything on cause of death?"

Weston shook his head. "Not the slightest fracture beyond the Cotton boy's previously documented injuries. The bodies appear to have been intact when they were entombed."

Durham rubbed a hand over his jaw and muttered into his hand. "Son of a bitch."

"And the Sanderses?" Bobbie asked, shifting the discussion away from the children for a moment. "Were they alive when they were submerged into the concrete mixture?"

"No indication of a struggle on either body," Mather said. "It's too early for the lab results, but I suspect they were immobilized or rendered unconscious by one drug or another. Both had small amounts of the concrete mixture in their nasal passages and throats. With the husband, some amount may have entered those passages when his head was forced into the mixture—which likely included a fast-setting ingredient to speed up the hardening process. The wife, on the other hand, was submerged in a different manner. The amount in her throat and nasal passages definitely suggests she attempted to breathe after submersion."

Durham set his hands on his hips. "It's hard to find any sympathy under the circumstances."

Bobbie doubted anyone in the room would argue with him.

"I should let the families know and then I

guess it's time to have a press conference." Durham glanced at Bobbie. "We've been dodging the media all morning."

Bobbie had to give him credit, Troy Durham was very good at fielding questions and giving evasive answers without angering the media. The reporters they had encountered so far appeared to adore the homicide unit commander. Bobbie had stayed in his shadow as much as possible. Any connection made to her would only shift the focus of the investigation. Never a good thing.

Durham thanked the coroners again and Bobbie followed him out of the building. For a moment he hesitated. "Maybe we'll get lucky with some of that trace evidence. I suppose any kind of confirmation is better than none."

"It'll take some time." Time was never a friend in a case like this. Bobbie sympathized with how desperately he and his family as well as the others needed closure.

He opened the passenger-side door the same way he had every other time they'd gone anywhere together. He scanned the street. "Even after all these years I'm not sure this is the ending anyone expected."

It never was.

When he'd settled behind the wheel, he said, "Damn, I really dread giving the news to Mr. Cortland." He shook his head. "His wife drowned at their lake house on Tuesday."

"It's pretty damned cold to be swimming." Bobbie had intended to mention her thoughts on the woman's death earlier. It wasn't as cold as it could be for the time of year, but it was damned well too cold to go skinny-dipping.

"Yeah. With Tuesday being the anniversary of the abductions and her husband having been diagnosed with terminal cancer a couple weeks before that, I figure she had no intention of making it back to shore. She took off her clothes on the bank and, as best we can tell, just walked out into the water. When she didn't come home that night, a friend took Mr. Cortland looking for her. The scene was pretty clear-cut. The coroner found no indication of foul play."

"That will be a hard notification to make," Bobbie agreed. "Does he have any other family?"

Durham started the SUV. "The Cortlands had no other children. Mr. Cortland's only sibling, a brother, was killed in an accident when he was about forty. There's a nephew, Justin Cortland, a few years younger than me. He came down from St. Louis to help Cortland with his wife's final arrangements."

Bobbie didn't envy the task in front of Durham. "I should keep going through the case files while you do what you need to do." She felt confident the families wouldn't appreciate a stranger showing up to help deliver this painful news.

"Delores will give you whatever you need. Once I make the notifications and give a statement to the press, I'm going home and getting drunk."

Bobbie tried to laugh but the weary sound fell considerably short. "I can't say as I blame you."

His gaze lingered on her a moment before he spoke. "You're welcome to join me."

She mustered up a smile. "I appreciate the offer, but I still have to find a place to stay and I should check in with my LT." The latter was something she seriously dreaded, but she couldn't keep Lieutenant Owens in the dark any longer. The chief would be worried even though she sent him a text letting him know she was fine. Sergeant Holt, the only other surviving member of their small major crimes unit, probably didn't give a damn if she ever heard from Bobbie again.

Not fair, Bobbie. Holt was hurting right now. Bauer had been her partner for many years. She was grieving the same way Bobbie had when Newt died. Like Newt's, Bauer's death sat squarely on Bobbie's shoulders.

"I'll give my aunt Lou Ella a call." Durham's voice interrupted Bobbie's self-pity session. "She runs a bed-and-breakfast over on Hull Street. She'll set you up and charge it to the department."

"You don't have to go to all that trouble," Bobbie argued. She preferred to find a place a little more off the grid. Besides, when Durham learned the full circumstances of her appearance in his jurisdiction, he might not be so excited about the department paying for her stay.

"No trouble." He sent her a smile, the first real

one she'd seen since her arrival. "Just so you know, the place is supposed to be haunted."

"The story of my life, Lieutenant."

"Troy," he corrected her. "My friends call me Troy, you should, too."

"All right, Troy." She nodded. "Then you should call me Bobbie."

He flashed her another smile. "When I was a kid, my momma used to listen to that singer you're named after." He belted out a line from one of Gentry's most famous songs.

Bobbie laughed and shook her head. She decided not to bother explaining that Gentry was her married name. "I get that a lot."

He braked for a traffic light and turned to her. "I can see how you would."

Bobbie recognized that look. He'd spent a lifetime hoping his baby sister would be found alive and living with the guilt that her abduction was his fault. Now, with the knowledge that she was in all probability dead, he desperately needed the escape of alcohol and the comfort of sex. Oddly, after losing her family she hadn't wanted either...she'd felt too numb beyond the overwhelming desire for revenge. She had focused solely on her work and had done all within her power to close out everything else. Eventually Troy Durham would learn as she had that there was no escape. There was only the learning to live with a new reality.

Maybe he'd get lucky and find someone who would show him the way, like Nick showed her.

When the light changed Troy rolled forward and Bobbie checked her cell, grateful the moment had passed. She wished she would hear from Nick or even Weller.

The same questions nudged at her. Why this place and why all these children?

Dead children.

God, she hated Randolph Weller.

Eleven

Nick had followed Bobbie to the police headquarters, to the coroner's office and then back to the headquarters before returning to the cemetery. Once there, he had watched until the last of the official vehicles except one left the scene. The kenneled animals at the clinic had all been taken away by their owners. A surveillance detail remained parked on the street in front of the veterinary clinic to protect the scene.

Finding a local resource, a maintenance worker at the police headquarters, had been easy enough. So far the information wasn't that much, but hopefully he would have more soon. Two bodies and several sets of remains had been discovered at the scene. He wasn't sure how Bobbie had been drawn into the investigation. Whatever her involvement, he suspected Weller would be pulling the strings as he had in Montgomery.

Nick moved through the trees until he reached the backside of the cemetery. Under the circumstances there was little he could do in the way of analyzing or searching the area, but simply being here would provide him with a sense of the place.

In the middle of the cemetery where the remains of broken statues lay scattered about, he sat down on the cold ground and surveyed the area. The likenesses of five children had been standing amid the headstones all these years, concealing the ugly truth. At least four children had been murdered and entombed in this place.

Nick stared up at the larger statue that remained intact. An angel. He wondered where all the angels were when children went missing every hour of every day. No one had been looking out for these children.

No one had looked out for *him*.

He touched a fractured piece of the concrete, felt the grainy texture of its timeworn surface, the sharp, broken edges. Not one of the pet headstones had been damaged. The children's statues had been targeted for the specific purpose of revealing the remains trapped inside.

Nick got to his feet and moved through the darkness to the home that had belonged to Bill and Nancy Sanders. Crime scene tape still cordoned the property. A plastic seal warning the property was a crime scene had been placed on the rear entrance and likely the front entrance of the home.

Nick bypassed the back door and went to one of the first-floor windows along the rear of the house.

Gaining entrance to the home was as easy as lifting the lower sash and climbing inside. The window wasn't locked. He slipped into a bedroom and quickly made his way into the hall. The victims had been found in the bathrooms. In the master suite Nick used his phone's flashlight app to survey the framed photos. He picked up one from the Sanderses' forty-fifth wedding anniversary.

Both victims had been pillars of the community. There was nothing in their pasts that he'd found so far that would point to an event such as this one. He would keep digging for information on the two. Their closest friends would need to be scrutinized, as well.

He studied the older couple's faces. "Who else knew your secret?"

His cell vibrated. Nick set the photo aside and tugged the phone from his pocket. *Unknown Number.*

He accepted the call but didn't speak.

"So sorry I was unable to stay and chat with you during your visit with Lawrence."

Weller.

Nick laughed despite the rage clawing at him. "I'm right behind you, old man."

"So very close, indeed," Weller said. "In fact, I watched you in the cemetery when you first arrived minutes ago."

Nick resisted the urge to rush outside and look

for him. He would be long gone. He would never put himself in a position so close and then make this call.

"I should have allowed you to have pets growing up." Weller sighed. "I'm convinced the bond between boy and dog often translates into better relationships as an adult. Perhaps that's why you can't seem to keep anyone in your life."

Nick would not rise to his bait. "Enjoy your temporary freedom, you piece of shit, because this time I'm going to make sure you never take another life."

"Ah, so you'll take mine." Weller chuckled. "That's my boy."

Fury burst inside Nick despite his best efforts to remain calm.

"Keep your eye on the prize, Nicholas," Weller warned. "Bobbie's need to save everyone but herself may be the death of her this time."

"It's me you want," Nick growled. "Why the games? Every second you choose not to completely disappear is one more you risk being caught. Tell me where you are and we'll finish this now."

"Good luck, Nicholas." Weller laughed. "May the best *killer* win."

Twelve

Bobbie closed the file she'd been reviewing and decided she'd had enough reading for the day. She thought of the address LeDoux had given her. If nothing else she would drive by and see if this Amelia Potter was home before calling it a night. She could show Potter a photo of Nick and ask if she knew him. She could question her about Weller.

Was the photo Zacharias's way of warning Potter somehow? Was she a so-far-unidentified serial killer? If so, maybe she was involved with what happened to the children. Maybe Sanders had been her lover. Or was she connected to Weller some other way? Would Nick be coming for Potter? Or did she need Nick's help? To Bobbie's knowledge, neither Weller nor his attorney had ever directed anyone to Nick for help.

Too many questions and not enough answers.

Delores had gone home hours ago. She'd told Bobbie to exit the headquarters building through the side entrance. The rest of the offices in the building were already locked except Troy's. Bobbie turned out the light in his office and set the knob to lock when she closed the door. She followed the side corridor as the receptionist who, according to Troy, was also his right hand had instructed. Once Bobbie had exited the building, the door locked behind her. A cold rain had fallen while she was huddled over those files. She was thankful for the sweatshirt she wore.

Bobbie climbed into her Challenger. If anyone was watching her, she hadn't spotted the tail. She should call the chief first. He was still in the hospital and she hated the idea of making him worry any more than he already had.

After setting the navigation system to direct her to River Street and muting the audio, she made the call she'd been avoiding all day. Chief Theodore Peterson answered his cell on the first ring.

"I should suspend you right now, Detective."

Bobbie almost smiled despite the fury she heard simmering in his voice. "You can't suspend me, I resigned, remember?"

"I don't recall accepting your resignation," he countered. "Where the hell are you?"

Going for the abridged version, she brought him up to speed on the case.

"You should let the FBI, GBI and the Marshals

Service handle this, Bobbie. You're getting in way over your head. Weller is—"

"You know I can't do that. I was invited into this, I can't just walk away." She'd already provided him with the details of how she'd come to be in Savannah. Most of them, anyway. She hadn't mentioned her encounter with LeDoux.

The chief argued with her a minute more but finally caved after she offered again to turn in her badge. "I need to know you're safe, Bobbie. That's all."

"I'm as safe here as I would be anywhere. I have to finish this…" For Nick. And for Bauer.

As if he'd read her mind, he asked, "You aren't coming back for Bauer's funeral?"

His question echoed inside her well after the call ended. How could she go back until she had stopped Weller? She was the reason Weller came to Montgomery, in a manner of speaking. How could she put aside what she had to do, drive all the way back to Montgomery for the funeral and face the people who knew he had been murdered because of her? She couldn't face those people until she brought down the evil primarily responsible for his death. She couldn't. Bauer would have done the same for her.

Every second Weller was out there was a chance someone else would die and the likelihood of catching him dwindled.

As she made the final turn indicated on the nav screen, she wondered if LeDoux was still in custody. She also wondered again if he'd killed Zacharias and hidden his body. What the hell else had he done to have the very Bureau to which he had dedicated his life coming down on him?

Maybe she didn't want to know the answer to that last question.

Bobbie cleared her head and surveyed River Street. The area was home to mostly retail shops. Many appeared to have apartments on the second and, in some cases, third floors. All the shops were decorated for fall with pumpkins and pots of mums; some included cornstalks and bales of hay while others sported the usual Halloween ghouls and goblins. Finally, on the corner, she spotted the number she'd been looking for. The sign on the plate-glass window read The Gentle Palm. Bobbie pulled over to the curb opposite the small shop. Amelia Potter was a palm reader? Why would Zacharias send a picture of Nick to her? Was he that desperate for help?

Yeah, right, Bobbie. A man as intelligent and cunning as Zacharias would have a good reason for every step he made. Especially when his life was going to hell in a handbasket.

The downstairs portion of the shop was dark. Light glowed from the windows upstairs. Rather than driving away since it was so late, Bobbie decided to watch for a while. Eventually a woman appeared at the French doors that exited out onto a small second-story balcony. She wandered out onto the outdoor space, a steaming mug in her hand.

She gazed up at the sky. Her hair looked blond or gray. She was tall and thin. According to the information in the case file, Potter was fifty-four. The woman she presumed to be Potter went back inside and closed the doors. Drapes slid across the French doors. Bobbie started the car and pulled away from the curb. No point waiting around out here in the dark. Sleep would do her a world of good and then she would be fresh in the morning.

A few blocks later she found her destination. The bed-and-breakfast was actually a historic home that had been meticulously restored from what she could see and transitioned into an inn. Bobbie parked on the street. She grabbed her bag and locked the car. The damp night air was thick with the pungent scents of the nearby river and the heavy moss hanging from the trees. She climbed the steps that were lined with pumpkins and mums to the front entrance. Inside the lobby that had been a parlor in a former life, she stepped up to the antique counter and rang the bell. The sound had barely stopped vibrating the air when a pleasant-faced woman of sixty or so appeared behind the counter. She wore a pink sweater that complemented her fair complexion. Her brown hair was peppered with gray and fashioned into a long braid that hung over one shoulder.

She grinned. "You must be Bobbie. I'm Lou Ella." She thrust her hand across the counter. "Troy told me you were coming."

Bobbie gave her hand a shake. "Thanks for taking care of me on such short notice."

The innkeeper snagged a key from an old-fashioned row of wooden boxes. "We're thrilled to have you. In fact, you're getting the best room in the house for your stay, sweetheart."

"Don't go to too much trouble," Bobbie urged. "I'm not sure how long I'll be here."

"No trouble at all." Lou Ella bounced up the stairs like a woman half her age. "We're usually full up this time of year—you know Halloween is just a couple of days away—but we had a last-minute cancellation. So you're in luck."

Lou Ella spent the rest of the climb to the third floor and on to the end of the hall telling Bobbie about Troy. By the time Lou Ella unlocked the door, Bobbie knew Troy had been married once and then divorced. He had no children and currently wasn't dating anyone.

All things Bobbie certainly needed to know. She wondered if Troy knew his aunt liked playing the part of matchmaker.

"I hope you'll be comfortable here. Pay no mind to the ghosts." Lou Ella grinned. "They're harmless."

Bobbie surveyed the big room with its four-poster bed and antique furnishings. "Thank you." She decided not to mention that she didn't believe in ghosts.

Lou Ella left the key with Bobbie and said goodnight.

When she'd locked the door, Bobbie tossed her bag aside and went to the front windows. Streetlamps gave a preview of the stunning historic architecture along the block. Across the street was Chippewa Square. She and James had walked that park. She closed her eyes against the memories. She should take a shower and get some sleep. Anything could happen before daylight. She thought of the Potter woman. Maybe she would go see Potter in the morning and get a reading. At this point she was just desperate enough. If the woman really had any so-called sight she would recognize Bobbie wasn't just a tourist.

Bobbie shook off the idea. Something else she didn't believe in.

She plugged the charger into the outlet near the bedside table and set her phone to charge. She found the remote and clicked on the television. She zipped through the channels until she hit a local newscast. When she saw Troy's face in the video clip playing over the anchor's shoulder, she raised the volume.

"Tomorrow," Troy said, "the GBI and the FBI will be joining our investigation. For now we're doing all we can to find closure for the families. They have a right to know how this happened and to see that justice is served."

The broadcast went back to the anchor and Bobbie muted the volume. She toed off her sneakers, tugged off her sweatshirt and shucked off her jeans. A long hot shower was calling her name. She needed time to process all that had occurred in the past twenty or so hours. Had Weller killed the Sanderses or was the killer another of his cronies like Steven Devine had been? Either way, the move seemed damned bold for a man on the run from the feds.

Did those long-missing children have some bearing on whatever he needed to prove to Nick? Or was he only playing more games with their lives? If Nick would stop trying to push her away, they could talk this out. He would build his case map and they would figure out what the hell was going on.

Her cell rang and Bobbie rushed to check the screen, hoping against hope it was Nick.

The boss.

Damn it. She grabbed her phone, jerking it loose from the charger. "Hey, is the chief okay?" She'd spoken to him less than an hour ago.

"He's doing well," Owens assured her. "He may be able to go home tomorrow."

He'd been too busy debating Bobbie's decision about this case to mention he might be released from the hospital soon. The man worried about her far too much. Another stab of guilt elbowed Bobbie. She should have called the chief and Owens already. Lieutenant Eudora Owens was the commander of the Major Crimes Unit in Montgomery. She was also the chief's undisclosed girlfriend. Bobbie had suspected for a while that the two were close but she'd had no idea how close. *Good for you, Uncle Teddy.*

"That's great." Part of her felt ashamed for not being at the chief's side. He'd always been there for her. *You have to do this, Bobbie.*

"Bobbie, I just received a call from Special Agent Hadden."

That couldn't be good. Michael Hadden was the agent assigned to Montgomery's small FBI field office. He'd worked with the task force on the Storyteller case and more recently during the Devine-Weller investigation. Typically when the LT received a call from Hadden, the feds either wanted something or MPD had stepped on their toes somehow.

"Have they found Weller?" Bobbie knew that wasn't likely. It would have been all over the news, but it was better than asking what she had done this time.

"Unfortunately not." Owens's heavy sigh cut through the silence that followed. "Weller's attorney, Lawrence Zacharias, was murdered this morning. They found his body as well as his driver's and that of a courier from a local delivery service a few hours ago."

Shit. Both she and LeDoux had been in the man's house that morning. LeDoux had admitted intercepting the courier. Damn. If LeDoux had lied to her… "Do they believe Weller killed them?"

"The driver was bashed in the head and left in the garage at Zacharias's home, but Zacharias and the courier were left in a rental house in Norcross owned by one of the attorney's LLCs. Their bodies were mutilated the same as all Weller's other victims. Hadden suggested the consensus is that the work is Weller's."

Wow. Somehow Bobbie had hoped the attorney would come forward and help with the hunt for Weller. She should have known they'd never get that lucky. "Have they found anything that might help in the search for Weller?"

"Not that I've been made aware of, but there are three things our friends from the Bureau wanted me to know they considered relevant to their investigation."

Oh hell.

"*Your* fingerprints were found in Zacharias's home."

Bobbie should at least attempt to explain why she had been in Zacharias's house. "I wanted to ask him if he'd heard from Nick or from Weller, but he wasn't home." Without giving Owens time to comment, she asked, "What about Nick's prints?" She didn't want him to be considered a suspect in the attorney's murder. She was certain Zacharias's home was his first stop after leaving her house. It was the only logical step he could have taken.

"His, too."

Damn. Bobbie had hoped that wouldn't be the case.

"But those weren't the only curious finds. Our favorite fed's were there, too. Imagine."

LeDoux. "Of course LeDoux's were there. He probably questioned Zacharias right after Weller escaped." She opted not to mention she'd run into LeDoux. She would get around to sharing that part eventually.

"Except that Agent LeDoux is on administrative leave pending a review by the Office of Professional Responsibility," Owens said. "Hadden wouldn't give me the details but apparently LeDoux has been on thin ice for several weeks now."

Bobbie had suspected the same. "I had a feeling something was going on with him." The events of the past year had cost him dearly. "Are the feds looking for me now?"

"Since you went to Atlanta to see Weller last week," Owens said, "I told Hadden your prints were in the attorney's house because you met with him, as well." The LT sighed. "I don't fully understand what's going on with you right now, Bobbie, but I'm trusting that you're doing what you have to do. Don't make me regret covering your ass."

"I appreciate it." She was more than grateful the LT had backed her up. "Wait, you said three things. What else did Hadden mention?"

The LT's hesitation had adrenaline roaring through Bobbie's veins.

"He made it clear Nick Shade is a person of interest in the facilitation of Weller's disappearance as well as in the deaths of certain serial killers."

A hot mixture of anger and fear on Nick's behalf roiled in Bobbie's gut. "They're wrong. When Nick went to see Weller two months ago, it was the first time he'd seen him since his trial fourteen years ago. He went to Weller about the Storyteller. He was trying to help *me*."

"I'm with you on this, Bobbie," Owens reminded her. "Stay safe and out of trouble."

Bobbie relaxed just a little for the first time in days. "I'll do my best."

"Good, because we need you back here. We're rebuilding this team. Holt and I need you."

"As soon as I'm finished here, I'll be back. You have my word."

With a final warning to take care of herself, Owens ended the call. Bobbie plugged her cell back to the charger. She stared a moment at the black screen of her phone. Considered calling Nick again, but the call would only go unanswered.

Where the hell are you, Nick?

Thirteen

Nick stood on the sidewalk well away from the streetlamp. He watched Bobbie stare out the window, the soft light inside the room like a halo around her long dark hair making him want to reach out and touch her.

He curled his fingers into fists. She shouldn't have come. He closed his eyes and wished he could make her understand the moment they'd shared had come and gone. His place was in the darkness searching for the monsters that haunted the lives of innocents like her. A reluctant smile tugged at his lips. Bobbie would be the first to say any innocence she had ever possessed was tarnished now. Evil had touched her life with a heavy hand. Daring to draw so close to him had pulled her more deeply into the darkness she used that badge of hers to fight every day.

Why won't you go home?

Naively she thought she could help him. Some

foolish part of her dared to believe she could make him the man she wished him to be.

Not possible.

He could never allow her close again. Not once in all these years had he allowed anyone close until Bobbie.

A mistake.

The destiny he had fought against his whole life had come to be. *Killer.*

He had taken a life. No matter that the bastard he had eliminated was a heartless serial killer who would have murdered Bobbie, Nick had ended his life and he had savored the feel of freshly spilled blood on his hands. Nothing could have stopped him from taking Steven Devine's life in that moment. After all the bastard had done, Nick had needed to watch and to *feel* him die.

Weller had warned him.

When it comes, you're completely helpless. You'll see.

On some level Nick refused to accept that reality, but deep inside where no one else could see, he was afraid he would feel that urge again. That he would become the kind of monster he had spent years hunting.

No. He would never be like Weller. He had taken the life of a serial murderer to protect Bobbie. Nick was not a killer.

As if she sensed his presence, she touched the glass.

Nick stepped back, deeper into the darkness.

Somehow he must convince her to leave. Weller was close. Nick had tracked him from the carnage he'd left outside Atlanta only to lose him once more. His call while Nick was in the cemetery confirmed he was in Savannah. The monster wanted him to know just how close he was. Stopping Weller had to be his priority. Nothing and no one else could get in the way.

Not even you, Bobbie.

She moved away from the window and his chest tightened. He remembered well how she had attempted to push him away when he first showed up at her door. Detective Bobbie Gentry had been on a mission to stop the serial killer known as the Storyteller at all costs. No one was going to get in her way.

Aren't you doing the same thing now, Shade?

Nick ignored the mocking voice. How could he choose between focusing solely on finding Weller and protecting Bobbie? She was here because Weller had lured her to Savannah somehow. She would not have known to come otherwise. The son of a bitch wanted Bobbie nearby to serve as a distraction or to play the starring role in some depraved game he had set in motion.

"You will not win, old man."

Nick's resource at the FBI had warned him that LeDoux had been released after several hours of interrogation. He would be headed this way already. He, too, would be an unwelcome distraction. LeDoux had alerted Nick days ago that he suspected someone inside the FBI was facilitating Weller's actions. As far as Nick was concerned, that was the FBI's problem. His singular goal was to stop Weller.

Bobbie had spent most of the day with the homicide commander, Lieutenant Troy Durham. Only a few minutes ago, the local source Nick procured had provided him with a copy of the report that included Bobbie's name and cell phone number. The news left no doubt—Weller had inserted her into this investigation. He had something to say to Nick and those long-dead children were part of the message. Weller was far too much of a coward to face Nick one-on-one. He would put as many innocents as possible between them.

Nick closed his eyes and called to mind his favorite dream. The house where he grew up was burning down and Weller was inside with no way to escape. The flesh would melt from his bones and that insidious brain would be scorched from this earth.

The cold wind kicked up, scooting leaves along the cobblestoned sidewalk. Nick opened his eyes and looked around. For the first time since his arrival just before noon today, he felt eyes on him. He scanned the windows. All dark. Even Bobbie's light had gone out.

He moved quickly across the street and into the alley tucked between the inn and another historic home that was now a business. He'd almost made it to the far end of the alley when he sensed some-one behind him. He darted into a stoop and waited.

Bobbie moved soundlessly past the stoop. Nick stepped out behind her.

She whirled around, eyes wide, Glock palmed. "Nick."

Hearing her voice changed the rhythm of his heart. He cursed himself for the foolish reaction. "Go back to Montgomery, Bobbie. There is nothing you can do here."

"You know that's not going to happen." Her full lips in a tight line, she slipped her Glock back into her waistband and covered it with her sweatshirt. "Hello to you, too."

Arguing with her was pointless. He understood this. He also fully understood the infinite danger and still he wanted her to stay. Instead of walking away, he took her by the arm and pulled her close to his side. "Don't say I didn't warn you."

Neither said a word as they moved through the darkness. The warmth from her body invaded his, making him weak like no one else he had ever encountered. He braced himself against the inva-sion. Her safety depended on his ability to keep his distance.

Three blocks later they reached the room he'd rented. Just about anything could be found and purchased or rented on the internet. The room was one of four above a bakery. The stairs on the side of the building led to a common hall. Nick guided her past the closed doors of the other rooms to the final one at the end of the hall. His was the only room with an original fire escape out the back of the building. The four had likely been one large space before being chopped up into rentable rooms. He opened the door, waited for her to go in ahead of him and quickly locked it behind them.

For one long moment he stood there inhaling the scent of her. If his life was different…but it wasn't. She deserved to spend her life with someone like the lieutenant, Troy Durham. A man who could provide her with a real relationship…a real life and family without the fear of passing on a monster's genes. With the flip of a switch, the room filled with light and frustration nudged aside the other, dangerous tension Nick felt.

"When did you arrive?" She surveyed the small room, her attention settling on the work he'd started on the far wall.

The furnishings were few and simple. A single bed, a three-drawer chest and a sparsely appointed kitchenette. But he hadn't rented the room for its amenities. The location near the police headquarters and the anonymity of a place hardly noticed by passersby were the qualities he had sought. The blank wall she studied was the one necessity he sought when preparing for a hunt.

She moved to his case map and stared at the photos. The face of each child, of their families and of the suspected killers, the Sanderses, were taped to the wall. Fury burned in his gut as his gaze moved over the photo of Weller and then the one of Zacharias, his attorney.

Nick joined her, his attention fixed on the photo of the man who was his father. He felt her watching him. "Weller is close," he warned as he gave up the battle and turned to her.

"I know. He killed Zacharias, his driver and a courier in the last twenty hours." She chewed her bottom lip for a half beat. "The FBI found your prints at Zacharias's house in Atlanta."

"I heard." Jessup had given him a heads-up. "After I left Montgomery—"

"After you left *me*," she corrected, anger laced with frustration colored her voice.

"I called Zacharias," Nick finished without acknowledging her jab. He held her gaze. He never tired of looking into her pale blue eyes. So clear, so full of concern for him. How long had it been since anyone looked at him that way? As if it mattered whether he lived or died. He averted his gaze. "He told me I would find what I was looking for in Savannah. He wouldn't say more on the phone. He wanted to tell me the rest in person so he picked the time and place."

"But he never showed," she guessed. Then her eyes widened. "Weller got to him first."

He nodded and turned his attention back to the case map. "I found their bodies at the location where I was to meet Zacharias but it wasn't his house in Ansley Park. I was especially careful— if my prints were found there, they were planted."

"You have no idea what Zacharias wanted to share with you?"

The surprise in her voice had him searching her eyes once more. "Do you?"

"Maybe." Bobbie touched the photo of one of the younger children, the boy, Noah Potter. "LeDoux told me the courier was sending a photo of you to this child's mother, Amelia Potter."

Evidently someone high up in the Weller task force was keeping aspects of the investigation close to the vest. Jessup had not passed along that one. Nick offered, "Her son was the anomaly in the case of the missing children."

Bobbie nodded and gestured to the other children's photos. "Wealthy parents, members of the same church." She explained about the Foster girl who'd been raped and murdered just three weeks before the children went missing. "Treat Bonner, the young man initially accused of her murder, was the other anomaly."

Nick studied the photos of the dead children's parents. "Is there any connection between Foster's murder and those of the children?" His source hadn't been able to get his hands on the coroner's report on the remains found at the pet cemetery.

"Nothing tangible yet," Bobbie began, "but her violent death may have been a sort of trigger."

"Is that Durham's opinion?" Nick gritted his teeth at the edge in his voice. He had no right to be envious of the time another man spent with her.

"We discussed the possibility." Bobbie searched

his face, attempting to read what he was thinking. "What about Potter? Is it possible Weller had some sort of relationship with her? Or is she connected to him some other way?"

Nick studied the photo of Amelia Potter. "He would have been intrigued by her purported gift. He once wrote a paper on the link between psychic ability, schizophrenia and psychosis." At the time Nick had wondered if he would ever be as brilliant as his father.

What a fool he'd been.

"Lieutenant Owens called," she said, drawing his attention back to her. "She warned me that the FBI still considers you a person of interest in Weller's disappearance as well as the deaths of certain serial killers. You need to be especially diligent about keeping a low profile."

"What the FBI believes or doesn't believe is irrelevant to me. Finding Weller is the only reason I'm here."

She ignored his obvious snub. "We're more likely to stop him if we work together."

Nick refused to meet her gaze this time. "Stopping him is my responsibility. *I* will stop him."

"You believe sending me away will protect me from him, is that it?"

He glared at her then. "I know it won't protect you completely, but the risk is far greater with you close. Walking away will protect you in the future."

She shook her head. "You know, I thought I was the one who couldn't stop looking back long enough to look forward, but I think it's you. You're so afraid of the past, you won't dare reach for the future. You'll avoid it, go around it." She moved in toe-to-toe with him. "You'll keep existing in the shadows…*alone.*"

"That's where I want to be."

"You'll be there because you're a coward."

He flinched. Mentally kicked himself for the reaction.

"That's right. You're a coward." Sadness clouded her eyes. "All this time I thought you were some kind of hero. I guess I was wrong."

She turned her back and walked out.

As much as her words stung, he couldn't let her walk through the night alone.

Keeping his distance, he followed her back to the inn.

When she disappeared inside he drew in a sharp breath and turned away.

Before returning to his room, he made a detour.

The Gentle Palm was dark, as were the living quarters above it.

He thought of the woman in the photo in his room.

Who are you, Amelia Potter?

Fourteen

Amelia dabbed her face dry. The towel dropped from her fingers. When had she grown so old? She traced the lines around her eyes, and the ones that bracketed her too-wide lips. A smile trembled across them as she closed her eyes and remembered kissing her little boy. She had loved him so, so much. More than anything else in the world.

She drew in a sharp breath and stepped away from the sink. Her fingers trailed down to her breasts. She had nursed him with these breasts. Her nipples peaked at the memory. Her belly had swollen with him. Her palm glided over her abdomen. He'd been a big baby but she hadn't cared. The marks her expanded belly had left on her skin were a badge of honor to Amelia. She had been so in love with her little boy.

How had she allowed him to be taken? How had she not seen the evil lurking so close?

Her hands dropped to her sides and she went in search of a nightgown. She'd made a mistake. A terrible, terrible mistake. That mistake had cost her the most precious thing in her life.

How was it that she could warn others of imminent doom while she had been completely unaware?

When the worn thin cotton fell over her skin, she shuffled into the next room and knelt at her prayer bench. She smiled as her fingers traced the sweet face in the framed photo of her little boy. She lit a candle and said the same prayer she had said every single night for thirty-two years.

Please come home to me.

After a minute of meditation she stood and padded to her bed. She burrowed beneath the down covers and turned off the lamp. From the moment Camille left today, Amelia had been in a state. How could Camille have experienced the same dream Amelia had?

The dark-haired woman had visited her dreams. Amelia had felt herself running in the woods. She'd watched her labored breath fog in the cold air. She'd felt the damp leaves beneath her bare feet. Then the water came rushing up to her waist. She and the dark-haired woman were in the water together. The struggle was powerful.

Amelia hadn't seen the bones Camille saw, but now she understood why her old friend had. Troy Durham had stopped by earlier this evening. All afternoon she had sensed tragedy was coming.

The children had been found. All but one.

Troy had explained how all the remains had been positively identified except his little sister's and Noah's. As selfish as it was, she had immediately started to silently pray that her little boy was not among the bones.

Her heart broke for the other parents. Their deepest, coldest fears had been realized.

Their babies were dead.

Dear God, why?

When those precious babies had gone missing not the first piece of evidence had been uncovered. It was as if they had simply vanished into thin air. In the beginning the other parents had come to her and demanded to know why she couldn't use her gift to see their babies the way she had seen the Foster girl with Treat Bonner. Merciful Lord, if only she could have.

Sadly, the glimpse she had gotten of the Foster girl and Treat had led the police in the wrong direction. Had likely cost poor Treat his life. Another burden Amelia lived with every day of her life. She had gone to Lucille, his mother, and explained how she had tried to tell the police that Treat had not hurt Christina Foster, but the damage was done. Lucille had only stared at her. It was too late for apologies.

In all these years Amelia had not once felt the children's presence. Her gift had become a curse and yet it was her only means of survival. For thirty-two long years she had clung to the thread of hope that her little boy would be found. That perhaps he had grown up and would eventually find her in this shop where he had been born.

Only he had not found her, nor had she found him.

Amelia closed her eyes.

Maybe the dark-haired woman would help her see. Or perhaps she had come to end Amelia's misery once and for all.

Fifteen

A six-pack of beer hadn't made a dent in reality.

Troy rummaged in the cabinet under the sink until he found the bottle he was looking for. He blew off the dust and twisted off the top. Not giving himself time to rethink his strategy, he turned up the Jack Daniel's sipping whiskey and drank until he had to breathe.

Bottle in hand, he walked back to the table and collapsed into the chair. The pictures of the children were spread on the table. Other photos from the crime scene in the Sanders house were stacked next to them. He'd shuffled through those damned photos a dozen times and he didn't know one damned thing more now than he had when he first saw the fucked-up scene.

How the hell had he lived in the same town with Bill and Nancy Sanders most of his life and not realized they were killers? That they had encased those babies in concrete and erected the statues in their freaky little pet cemetery like an inside joke that only they knew about?

He'd shown his parents the photos of the bones and explained that they couldn't be sure to which of the three-year-olds they belonged. His mother had cried so hard. His father had only stared at the images. The truth was Troy had killed his parents the same day he killed his baby sister. They hadn't been living these past three decades. They'd existed. Now he'd ripped open that wound all over again. It was as if his entire career in law enforcement had culminated in this one nightmarish act— to reiterate what he had done or failed to do all those years ago.

He should have stayed gone.

Drawing long and deep from the bottle again, he ignored his body's need to breathe until he choked. Whiskey spewed from his mouth.

He'd graduated high school and gone straight into the Marines. He'd done two tours in the Middle East where he'd volunteered for the most dangerous assignments in hopes of getting himself killed while doing something that mattered. When that route failed, he'd become a cop in New Orleans where there would be plenty of opportunities to get his throat cut or his head blown off. During all that time, his mother had written to him faithfully two or three times a month. Once in a while he would call to check on her, always picking a time when he knew his father wouldn't be home. Luke Durham and his retired department buddies had coffee once a month like clockwork and Troy used that time to call on the rare occasions he worked up the nerve.

Most likely he would never have come back, but then three years ago his father had a major heart attack and his mother had called. For the first time in nearly thirty years she'd asked him for help. Troy had transferred to Metro that same week. He and his father rarely spoke beyond hello or goodbye, primarily because he despised Troy for what he'd done.

Tonight had torn another rip in their damaged relationship. When his mother had excused herself to wash her face, he'd asked his father if there was anyone in the department—now or then—who would tamper with the case file. His father had exploded.

It's not bad enough that you nearly destroyed your mother leaving the way you did. Now you want to damage my name and the department's?

No matter what Troy said in an attempt to explain that he hadn't meant his father, the old man wouldn't listen. Troy downed another swig of JD. He scrubbed a hand over his face as the alcohol slowly numbed his mind. Every damned thing he did was wrong in his father's eyes.

"Nothing you don't deserve, dumbass."

He thought of the woman who'd answered his call. *Bobbie Gentry.* The kind of shit she'd suffered through made him feel like a coward. She was as tough as any Marine he had known. He wondered how she had managed to go on with her life. Maybe she merely existed the way he did. The way his parents and the other parents of the children did.

The parents had all asked him the same question today. How did they die? *Cause of death is inconclusive at this time.* Most likely they would never know how the children died and the possibilities would haunt them for the rest of their lives.

He reached for the bottle but stopped himself and then pushed it away. He'd had enough.

Too much.

He folded his arms on the table and laid his forehead there. All these years he had hoped that one day he would find his little sister. He had hired private detectives. He'd even gone to fucking psychics. A waste of time. All these years Brianne had been dead and entombed only a few miles from home.

He hoped she hadn't suffered before she died. The thought hurt like no other pain he'd ever experienced. She must have been terrified. Had she been tied up and forced to lie there and watch the bastards prepare to murder her? Had the other children cried, the sounds making her own tears more desperate?

He should have watched after her, protected her.

The burn of soured whiskey rushed up his throat. Troy shot out of the chair and staggered to the sink. He puked until it felt like his eyeballs would pop out. Then he crumpled to the floor and leaned against the cabinet. When he was sure he wasn't going to puke again, he pulled his knees to his chest and did the thing men weren't supposed to do.

He cried.

Sixteen

Bobbie stacked her empty coffee cup inside the other three filling the slot in her console. Lou Ella had caught her an hour and a half ago as she'd tried to slip out of the inn unnoticed. Despite Bobbie's protests the woman had dragged her to the kitchen for breakfast.

How long had it been since she'd had home-made blueberry muffins? A year, maybe? Bobbie couldn't remember when bacon had tasted so good. Or eggs, for that matter. Until recently most everything had tasted the same, like cardboard or dust. Her shrink had told her that the ability to enjoy the taste of anything was often hampered by trauma and tragedy.

Though she'd started her return to the land of the living around two months ago, there were times when the guilt still piled on at the idea that she was moving on with her life.

One day at a time, Bobbie.

Last night, she'd sensed Nick watching her before she'd glimpsed him disappearing into the shadows. She'd hurried outside and caught up with him. He'd made his feelings on the matter of her involvement in finding Weller crystal clear, but Bobbie didn't care. He was wrong to push her away.

Still, she shouldn't have called him a coward. He had to get it through his head that he didn't have to do this alone. If they stuck together, Weller was far less likely to accomplish his ultimate goal.

If only she knew what that goal was.

The lights came on inside The Gentle Palm. Bobbie sat up a little straighter. She'd been watching Amelia Potter's shop for thirty-four minutes. According to the placard hanging on the door the shop opened at nine.

Troy would be at his office and Bobbie needed to be there, too, but this visit couldn't wait any longer. The shop door opened and Potter retrieved the newspaper lying on the sidewalk. She stared at the headlines—all of which were related to the case—as she went back inside and closed the door. Since one of the missing children had been her son, seeing the news splashed across the pages had to be painful. Noah Potter had been three.

Just like Jamie.

Bobbie didn't have to imagine Potter's pain. She knew it well. The uncertainty must have been agonizing. Thirty-two years of not knowing whether her child was dead or alive was assuredly a fate worse than death. Then again, Potter had likely clung to the remote possibility that he would one day be found.

Those kinds of happy endings rarely happened in real life.

Grabbing her shoulder bag, Bobbie climbed out of the car and hit the fob to lock it. She tucked it into her bag and crossed the damp street. The drizzling rain had stopped right after she woke up this morning. She tugged her jacket closer around her to fight the damp chill. The jeans and sweater she wore today were the only other outfit she'd hastily packed. At some point soon she'd have to grab a few necessary items. She reached for the shop door and hesitated. The sensation of being watched had the fine hair on the back of her neck standing on end. Bobbie turned around and scanned the street. Morning traffic rolled past. A man in a black trench coat hurried toward his destination. Two women, deep in conversation, rushed along on that same side of the street, their heels clicking on the cobblestone.

Nick was likely following her every move in hopes of spotting Weller—which made his determination to keep his distance that much more illogical.

Shaking off the frustration, Bobbie opened the door to the shop and the bell jingled. In Montgomery they had a couple of shops like this. She'd been in one during the course of an investigation. The atmosphere had been dark and mysterious with blackout curtains over the window and all sorts of psychic tools like birth charts, runes and tarot cards for sale. Various teas and books on magic and mysticism had lined the shelves while the scent of sandalwood was thick in the air. The so-called psychic had worn clothes as if she were reliving her 1960s teenage years.

The Gentle Palm was different. The large windows on the front of the shop were free of curtains or blinds. The meager morning sun filled the space. The soft scent of lavender reminded Bobbie of home and the body wash she used. She'd always preferred lavender. Shampoo, candles, air freshener, even laundry detergent. The worn wood floors were bare with nothing more than aged varnish for color. The walls were white. Nothing to draw the eye from the jars, candles and books for sale on the display shelves and counters. I love Savannah T-shirts hung on a clothing tree in one corner. A fair-sized table draped with a white linen cloth sat in the middle of the shop, a chair on either side. Another, smaller table and two chairs sat closer to the rows of shelves. At the back was a small counter with an antique cash register much like the one at the inn.

The woman Bobbie presumed to be Amelia Potter appeared in the cased opening that led into the storeroom or whatever lay beyond the small counter.

She hesitated, then smiled. "Good morning. I'm

not open just yet but feel free to make yourself at home."

Her hair was that soft white gray color that came from being a natural blond. Her eyes were brown. She was as tall as Bobbie. Thin but not fragile. Her strength showed in her eyes.

Bobbie unclipped her badge and held it up for her to see. "I'm Detective Bobbie Gentry. Amelia Potter?"

She nodded. "Yes, I'm Amelia Potter."

Bobbie clipped her badge back on her waistband. "I have some questions for you if you have a few minutes."

"Of course. Would you like a cup of tea?"

"No, thanks." Bobbie reminded herself not to stare. Something about Potter made her want to stare. The curve of her cheek, the shape of her nose seemed familiar though Bobbie was reasonably certain they hadn't met before.

"Please," Potter gestured to the two chairs flanking the smaller table that sat to the side rather than the larger table in the center of the room. "Let's sit. If you'd prefer, I have a private room in the back. Some of my visitors prefer more discretion."

Bobbie shook her head. "This is fine." She couldn't really say her visit was official business, though on some level it was. Troy had asked for her help on his investigation.

Potter moved to the chairs. The oversize cowl neck of the dress she wore skimmed her shoulders, the fabric of the skirt flowed to just below her knees. There was nothing sparkly or fancy about the dress or the fabric but it somehow gave her the look of old Hollywood. There was a quiet elegance in the way she moved.

When they had settled into the chairs, Bobbie opened her mouth to ask her first question but the words eluded her. Strange. She was usually more on her toes than this. The past week was catching up with her way too fast.

"You're working with Troy?"

Bobbie blinked back her surprise. At least one of them wasn't having trouble staying on point. "Yes. I came down from—"

"Montgomery," Potter said. "Troy told me last night. He said you're helping with the children."

Bobbie nodded slowly. "Do you mind answering a few questions about what you recall from the time period the children were abducted?"

"The children," she repeated. "That's what we've always called them. The case was never given one of those names like Black Dahlia or the Angel of Death." She lifted her thin shoulders and let them fall. "Just 'the children.'"

"I'm sure you've told countless officials what happened, but will you share with me what you remember from the night Noah went missing?"

Potter dropped her head and seemed to consider the request. Bobbie suddenly regretted asking. How many times had she been forced to repeat those final moments as she'd pushed her little boy out the front door of her home?

Run, Jamie! Run for help like Mommy showed you!

Bobbie's heart ripped open all over again as those words echoed through her.

"I couldn't have saved him."

Bobbie jerked at the sound of Potter's voice. "What?"

Had Potter said those words or had Bobbie thought them. Newt had told her hundreds of times—everyone had told her. *You couldn't have saved him.* But she should have saved him. He was her little boy. A mother was supposed to protect her child.

"Detective Rhodes told me that so many times. *You couldn't have saved him.*" Potter swiped at her eyes. "I'm sorry. I always cry when I talk about this. You'll have to forgive me."

Bobbie forced her head up and down in a nod. "I read your statement. You had put Noah down for the night. You still had appointments." Bobbie could see the single mother working long hours to keep a roof over her child's head. "The intruder came up the fire escape at the back of the building."

"I'd felt ill at ease all day. As if something were about to happen." She drew in a sharp breath. "But I couldn't see it."

Bobbie gave her a moment then asked, "Was there anyone during that time who paid particular attention to your son or to you?" Any good cop would have asked the same questions she intended to ask, but none of the answers were in the reports—didn't mean they weren't asked. Just meant they weren't documented.

"No one." She shook her head. "I have gone over those days and weeks so many times I could write a script of my life during those final two weeks… *before*. There was nothing unusual. It was October so tourist season was high."

Bobbie swallowed to moisten her throat. "Most of the time when a child is abducted, it's by someone you know. Someone the child knows."

Potter looked away. "The Sanderses weren't exactly friends of mine." A smile trembled across her lips. "Their church, like most others, frowns upon what I do. Considers it a sin."

"Was there ever any trouble between you and the Sanderses or their church?"

"Not at all. That's the true irony." Potter picked at her dress as if she'd spotted a piece of lint. "After Noah was gone, they were the first to show up at my door bearing gifts of food. They even paid my utilities that month. Leon Collins—his wife owns the clothing boutique next door—worked at the utility company. He mentioned at their church that he had been instructed to turn the power off since I hadn't paid my bill. Bill Sanders paid it the very next morning. I didn't know until years later. I was so devastated I could hardly function much less attend to my bills."

Some killers liked to show their softer side by helping those left behind. "Nothing the Sanderses

did or said ever made you feel uneasy? Nothing unusual that you noticed about any of their friends?"

Potter opened her mouth to speak, then closed it.

"Anything at all could be useful," Bobbie assured her.

"They all—the other parents, especially the fathers…" She clasped her hands in her lap and appeared uncomfortable. "Whenever they see me,
they look the other way. If we meet on the sidewalk, they walk around me. I've always thought
that it was their disapproval of my chosen beliefs
and what I do but…"

"But you don't think so."

She pressed her fingers to her lips, then she
looked directly at Bobbie. "No. Last night I was
thinking about the days before Noah was taken. It
was after Troy had stopped by and I couldn't get
my mind to settle down." She shrugged. "It happens sometimes. My mind has a mind of its own,
so to speak."

Bobbie nodded her understanding and waited
for her to go on.

"I had this vivid memory of Shelia Cotton smiling at me. Her son was only a few months older
than Noah. We were in that little shop that used
to be on Thirty-Seventh Street. I could never afford any of the clothes for Noah but I would go in
anyway, just to look. Sometimes—" she laughed
softly "—I would attempt to copy the patterns and
make him little outfits. I was pretty successful a
time or two."

Bobbie smiled. She'd never been very good with a needle and thread. Her domestic skills were hardly her strongest assets. "So Mrs. Cotton was polite to you that day?"

Potter nodded. "I'm sure such a random memory isn't important, it just felt important last night. I guess I needed to feel something besides the pain."

The memory was proof that at least one of the other parents hadn't thought badly of Potter before the children went missing. "During the months before or after the children disappeared, did anything happen that put you at odds with anyone in the community, specifically anyone related to the case?"

Potter nodded, a new sadness etching into her face. "A few weeks before the children went missing, Christina Foster was raped and murdered." She exhaled a heavy breath. "They didn't have a speck of evidence. The whole city was up in arms. Detective Rhodes—his wife was a client of mine—came to me and asked if I would try and see what happened. He brought a shoe the poor girl had been wearing that day. It had fallen off, I guess, when she was trying to escape her...killer." Potter shuddered visibly. "I told Detective Rhodes what I saw. I could see her walking on the road that led to her house. Treat Bonner was walking along that same road. They were talking."

"Did she seem afraid or was there tension between the two of them?"

She shook her head. "That's what's so sad. I

believe with all my heart that Treat was the last person to see her *before* she was murdered, but he did not hurt that girl. I told Detective Rhodes as much. I told them all, but no one would listen. They dragged him through that nightmare like he was the devil himself. Then he disappeared. It wasn't a week later that they found the vile man who had hurt that sweet girl."

Bobbie held her gaze for a moment, trying hard to see what it was that felt so familiar. "Do you believe the girl's family—the Fosters—had anything to do with Treat Bonner's disappearance?"

Potter stared at her hands a moment before meeting Bobbie's gaze. "I don't believe so. His mother, Lucille Bonner, came to me and demanded that I tell her what happened. She blamed me for telling anyone that I saw him with the Foster girl. But I was only telling the truth. I heard rumors later that Christina Foster tried to be Treat's friend. She was always kind to him and stood up for him when others made fun of him. A witness came forward and corroborated what I said about him being innocent. He'd seen the two talking, as well. But it was too late. Treat was already gone." She exhaled a heavy breath. "It was a difficult time for everyone."

"One more question." Bobbie withdrew her cell phone. "I want to show you two photos. I'd like you to tell me if you recognize either man."

"All right." Potter appeared to brace herself.

Bobbie skimmed the saved images in her phone

until she came to a photo of Weller. She showed it to the other woman. "Do you know this man?"

Potter stared at the photo for several seconds before shaking her head. "I don't." She crossed her arms over her chest. "Sorry. No, I don't know him. I've never seen him before."

A simple no would have been sufficient. An apology plus three ways of saying no generally equaled a yes. Bobbie glanced around the shop. "Do you have a television?"

"I don't watch television."

If she didn't watch the news, she might not be aware Weller was on the loose. His face had been plastered all over every imaginable media outlet for days. During the five or so seconds of silence that followed her response Potter kept her gaze averted.

Bobbie studied the image on the screen. "He's a serial killer, but before that he was a psychiatrist. He often worked with the police to help find the very sort of monster he turned out to be."

The other woman's slim shoulders lifted and then fell. "Is he involved in the murders of Bill and Nancy Sanders?"

"We're looking at that possibility since he escaped prison just four days ago." Bobbie thumbed through the images on her phone until she found one of Nick. She turned the screen back to Potter. "What about this man?"

Potter stared at the screen so long Bobbie thought she'd fallen asleep with her eyes open. Finally she reached for the phone, touched the screen, then shook her head. "I don't...recognize him." She drew her hand away and clasped it in the other. "Who is he?"

Bobbie noticed that she hadn't asked who Weller was. "Nick Shade. He advises on cases like this one."

Potter shook her head. "I'm sorry. I don't recognize him, but..."

Bobbie's instincts stirred. "But?"

The other woman bit her lower lip, then took a breath. "He's here." She looked directly at Bobbie then. "He wants to protect you."

Bobbie's heart stumbled at her words. "If I give you my number," she offered, "will you call me if you remember anything else? Any little thing around the time that Noah and the others went missing. And anything since that you feel is relevant."

"Yes." Potter nodded. "I will." She went to the counter and picked up a pad and pen, then returned to the table. "Put your number here and I'll keep it handy."

Bobbie jotted down her name and cell number, then she stood. "Thank you, Ms. Potter."

The other woman stood and held out her hand. "Amelia. Please call me Amelia."

"Thank you, Amelia." Bobbie placed her hand in the other woman's, expecting her to shake it. Instead, Amelia held it tight.

"It's true, Bobbie," she urged, her voice as

well as her gaze insistent as she murmured, "You couldn't have saved him."

For long minutes after she left the shop, Bobbie sat in her Challenger staring forward at the street. No question Amelia Potter could have Googled her. Troy might have mentioned what happened to Bobbie's family.

But what about Nick? Amelia Potter couldn't have known that part.

He wants to protect you.

Habersham Street
9:30 a.m.

Bobbie had made it all the way to Troy's desk when a hand grasped her forearm from behind.

She whirled to face the threat, her free hand moving instinctively toward her Glock. *Troy.* She forced herself to relax. *You're in a police precinct. What the hell is wrong with you?*

Then again, Steven Devine had been a homicide detective. *Sick bastard.*

Troy released her. "I didn't mean to startle you."

"It's okay. I was distracted."

He studied her a moment longer than was comfortable. The lieutenant wasn't entirely sure he believed her. Understandable. If she stopped long enough to really think about what she had asked him to believe, she wasn't sure she believed it herself. How often did one person—cop or not—find themselves the victim of a serial killer and live to tell about it much less to fight back? The concept happened pretty often in the movies, but this was real life and she was asking a lot of this man. So far he hadn't let her down.

"I was headed to the copy machine." He held up a report. "I met with the GBI folks already this morning and the suits from the FBI are here now."

"The retired agent you told me about?" What was his name? Terence something. Bobbie was more interested in what the FBI had to say since they seemed to have been lead on the case all those years ago.

"Yeah, Special Agent Terence Snow, retired. His replacement is here, too. Steve Ellis."

Bobbie looked forward to any insights the two might be able to provide, particularly where Weller was concerned. "Should I wait for you or join the others?"

When Troy shifted his gaze she understood there was more. "Another agent came with them. She's part of the Weller task force." He leaned closer, the gold stubble on his jaw and the bloodshot eyes evidence he'd had a rough night. "You have my word, I never mentioned you were here when I spoke to Snow or to Ellis. She's asked a dozen questions, every one of them about you."

"What's her name?" The memory of the female agent who'd showed up at LeDoux's hotel flickered.

"Janet Kessler. She's the agent in charge of the Atlanta office."

Bobbie didn't recognize the name. "Never heard of her." She remembered Agent Angela Price during the Storyteller investigation. And LeDoux, of course, and Kent Mason—another agent from the BAU.

"Give me a minute." Troy rushed over to a desk and asked the detective there to make his copies.

Owens had said that Hadden had called her. Evidently he hadn't bought her story about how Bobbie's prints ended up in Zacharias's house. No other reason for someone from the Weller task force to show up looking for her...unless Weller had some connection to this case. Bobbie's summons to Savannah made no sense otherwise.

There was always the chance that someone completely unrelated to Weller had murdered Bill and Nancy Sanders. Their murders may have been revenge for what they did to those children thirty-two years ago. The killer obviously knew their secret.

But that wouldn't explain why her name had been inserted into the case. Whether he'd committed or commissioned the murders or not, Weller was somehow involved. Considering he was a fugitive, she could only assume that he had one hell of a motive.

Otherwise, his involvement made no sense either.

Troy moved up beside Bobbie and ushered her toward the corridor leading to his office. "You come up with a lead you wanted to follow up on this morning?"

Bobbie should have known. "You have someone following me?"

He hesitated, his gaze settling on hers. "I didn't have a choice. Your chief called my chief."

Since kicking something wasn't an option, Bobbie laughed resignedly. "Sorry about that. He's my godfather. He worries about me."

Troy smiled, the expression as weary as Bobbie's laugh. "I can't blame him. I made the mistake of not looking out for someone I cared about and...well, you know what happened."

"I guess that makes us members of the same club." If she'd been looking out for her family instead of focusing so completely on the case, things might have turned out differently.

You can't change the past, Bobbie.

He glanced at her as they continued toward his office. "I don't like this club."

"Me either. It sucks," Bobbie agreed. "So I'm stuck with your surveillance detail?"

"Sorry. I'm already in the hot seat. My chief isn't happy I'm on this case for obvious reasons. I couldn't refuse both his demands."

"You made the right choice."

Troy gave her a nod and led the way to a small conference room beyond his office. The woman in the charcoal suit was the same one Bobbie had seen outside LeDoux's hotel. Her blond hair was pulled back into a smooth bun. Early forties. Medium height, lean. She didn't look the least bit friendly. The other active duty agent in the room wore the usual wash-and-wear dark suit. He was younger, mid to late thirties. The man whose position he had assumed was well into his sixties. He wore a flannel shirt and wash-and-wear trousers along with comfortable walking shoes. Deep furrows lined his face. From the years of helping find killers like Weller, Bobbie imagined.

The two men stood when she and Troy entered the room. He took care of the introductions. Though she didn't stand, Kessler held Bobbie's gaze and remarked, "I've looked forward to this meeting since I read your file, Detective." She thrust out her hand. "Janet Kessler."

Bobbie resisted the urge to ask "What file?" and gave her hand a quick shake, then took her seat. She wasn't sure whether the other woman's comment was a compliment or a threat. The FBI would have a file on her as one of the Storyteller's victims. No surprise there, but Bobbie suspected that wasn't the file Kessler meant. She'd know soon enough. "I hope you're here to tell us you've found Weller."

Kessler made a disgusted sound. "Not yet, I'm afraid."

No surprise there either. Weller was out there planning God only knew what and Agent Kessler was wasting time checking up on Bobbie. Now there was an aspect of this case that truly made no sense.

During the half hour that followed, former Special Agent Snow recounted the facts of the abductions to the best of his knowledge. Occasionally the new guy, Ellis, corrected something he said based on the reports Snow had filed at the time. The side notes didn't seem to bother the retired agent. There had been no true suspects during the time frame the five children went missing. The case had gone cold quickly. No additional victims, no persons of interest. Nothing.

"No one close to one of the families died or moved away after the abductions?" Bobbie asked. She and Troy had already been over this scenario, but there was always the chance Agent Snow would remember something the detective on the case had left out of his reports or felt wasn't relevant. The man had certainly left plenty out of his reports.

"There was the young man—Treat Bonner— who disappeared," Snow said. He reviewed the details Bobbie had learned already about the rape and murder of the Foster girl.

"Bonner was cleared," Troy reminded Snow.

Snow nodded. "He was but not before the damage was done, I'm afraid. Before the real rapist and murderer was discovered over in Brunswick, there were all sorts of rumors about the young man. A top psychiatrist came all the way from Atlanta to evaluate him."

Bobbie leaned forward. "Are you talking about Dr. Randolph Weller?"

Snow flipped through his notes, then nodded. "That's the one."

Agent Ellis looked as surprised as Bobbie felt.

Kessler on the other hand said nothing, her face clear of whatever the hell she was thinking.

Snow recited Weller's findings from the report in his notebook. "Bonner had been found to be incapable of planning and executing such a wanton and vile crime. He showed absolutely no true violent tendencies."

Bobbie felt as if cold water had been dashed over her. She opened her mouth to demand why this wasn't in the local case file when the retired agent abruptly stood. "If you'll excuse me a moment."

Agent Ellis pushed from his chair.

"Sit down," Snow snapped at the younger man. "You think I can't go take a piss without help?"

Ellis nodded at the older man and lowered back into his seat. When the door closed behind Snow, Ellis shook his head. "I apologize for the outburst. Mr. Snow was diagnosed with Alzheimer's last year. Sometimes he's the same sharp investigator he was thirty years ago, but others…" He shrugged. "When you called," he said to Troy, "I hoped he would be able to provide some insights from his personal notes. I had no idea Randolph Weller had advised in any capacity on this case. This is—" he glanced at the other suit in the room "—unexpected, to say the least."

"There's nothing in our files either," Troy confirmed.

Bobbie turned to Kessler. "Did you know about this?"

Kessler held her gaze for several seconds. "We need to speak privately, Detective."

"What would we possibly have to talk about, Kessler," Bobbie argued, instantly affronted, "that the rest of the room can't hear?"

Ellis was out of his seat before Bobbie's demand stopped echoing in the room. "I should check on Mr. Snow."

When he'd left the room, Kessler turned to Troy.

The lieutenant met her hard stare with lead in his own. "I'm certain you're aware, Agent Kessler, that this is my jurisdiction and my case. Detective Gentry is here at my request. Unless she asks me to leave the room, I'm not going anywhere."

Bobbie wanted to give him a high five. "He stays."

"Very well," Kessler said, a warning tone in her voice. "We know Agent LeDoux called you yesterday morning when he was supposedly calling his attorney. You tell me what he said and we'll let the issue go. You refuse and I'll inform Atlanta PD that you're all theirs. They're just itching to get their hands on anyone who was in Zacharias's house the morning he was murdered."

"What proof do you have I was in his house that morning?" Bobbie demanded. "You're aware I visited Weller on a previous trip to Atlanta. I spoke with his attorney before my visit to the prison." It was true. She simply didn't add the part about their conversation having taken place on the phone.

"LeDoux is in way over his head," Kessler

warned, rather than answer her question. "You would be well advised to stay away from him. His superior, Supervisory Special Agent Pitts, has placed Agent LeDoux on administrative leave. Nothing he says or does is official at this point."

"I haven't seen or spoken to LeDoux since that phone call." Bobbie met her relentless stare. "Anything else?"

"The same goes for Nick Shade. He's on our radar and not in a good way."

"Nick Shade has saved my life more than once," Bobbie argued. "He's taken down at least a dozen serial killers your people couldn't find."

"We know all about Shade," Kessler said. "We want him almost as much as we do Weller. In fact, we've already issued a BOLO on him as a person of interest in this ongoing investigation. We have reason to believe he's helping his father evade capture."

Bobbie laughed. Nothing could be further from the truth. "No one wants Weller back in prison more than Nick."

Kessler smiled. "We'll see. Keep in mind, Detective Gentry, we're watching you closely. One misstep and you're mine, are we clear?"

Bobbie turned to Troy. "Did that sound like a threat to you?"

"Definitely." He stood. "Agent Kessler, at this time we don't require the FBI's assistance on this case. At any point that we do, I'll contact Agent Ellis. If you have any additional questions regarding our investigation, you can take them up with the liaison officer or the chief."

Kessler held his gaze for a moment before she stood. "I'll speak with the chief."

Troy gave her a two-fingered salute. When the door closed behind her, he muttered, "Bitch." He glanced at Bobbie. "Excuse my French."

Bobbie gave her head a shake. "I was thinking the same thing." She hesitated a second. "I'm sorry you're caught in the middle of my private war. I've never met Kessler before, but she strikes me as the kind of agent who isn't going to walk away without a battle."

Troy shrugged one shoulder. "I can take care of myself, Bobbie." He settled back into his chair. "So if this Dr. Weller was involved with Treat Bonner, does that give you some idea of why he would risk coming to Savannah now?"

"Not yet, but it's a starting place."

Troy leaned forward and searched her eyes as if he worried she might hold out on him. "Is there a chance Weller killed the Sanderses?"

"The manner of their deaths is not his MO, but it's possible he had someone else do it for him."

"What about his son? Is he a killer, too?"

"No." Bobbie wished Nick could be here. Working together, they might be able to ferret out Weller far more quickly. Lieutenant Owens was right—the FBI wanted to turn him into something he wasn't. "He's a hunter. He's taken numerous serial killers out of play."

Troy nodded slowly.

"It's a lot to absorb."

"Is there something between the two of you?"

Bobbie wished she knew how to answer that one.

He held up a hand. "Sorry. I didn't mean to get personal." He frowned. "I guess I still don't get why Weller would come to Savannah. Doesn't exactly seem like the place to go when on the run from the cops and the feds."

"If he's here, and I believe he is, he has an objective. He won't stop until he accomplishes that objective."

"Which means—" Troy slumped back in his chair "—there will be more bodies."

Bobbie nodded. "There will be more bodies."

He stood. "Well, I guess we'd better get out there and figure out how your serial killer is connected to my case."

It sounded so much easier than Bobbie suspected it would be. The one thing she knew with absolute certainty was that they would need Nick to get this done.

Seventeen

The Bonner home was small with an even smaller attached garage surrounded by trees on a larger than average city lot. The neighborhood was probably considered up-and-coming since a handful of properties were under renovation. The rows of houses badly in need of maintenance reminded Bobbie of the one she rented in Montgomery. According to Troy the Bonners had lived in the house for fifty years—from the day Mr. Bonner had carried his new bride over the threshold.

Bobbie noted the wheelchair ramp on the far end of the porch as she climbed out of his Tahoe. Troy also mentioned that Mr. Bonner had suffered a spinal cord injury just before the couple's only child had been born, leaving him paralyzed from the waist down. A stroke last year left him unable to speak or to communicate in any way.

Troy was right about Lucille Bonner having had it rough.

Even so, the woman seemed to have a green thumb. Bright red and purple mums overflowed the pots stationed on the steps leading up to the porch. Autumn's fallen leaves had banked against the boxwoods that bordered it. Green, yellow and orange pumpkins were stacked on either side of the door. As Troy knocked, Bobbie stood back and allowed him to take the lead. He knew the Bonners. They would feel more comfortable with him than with a stranger. The distance would give Bobbie an opportunity to observe Lucille Bonner's reactions to Durham's questions.

When she opened the door Lucille Bonner didn't appear the slightest bit taken aback. "Troy, what a pleasant surprise." She immediately opened the door wider in invitation. "Y'all come on in. The air this morning's got a bite to it."

Troy waited for Bobbie to go in first. As she did, he said, "This is Detective Gentry from Montgomery."

Lucille's smile widened. "What you doing so far from home, Detective Gentry?" She closed the door behind them. "You thinking about moving down here?"

Bobbie propped a smile on her lips. "No, ma'am, just visiting. I'm assisting Lieutenant Durham with a case."

He leaned toward Bobbie and said, "Troy."

"Troy," she echoed with a nod.

A dog—a beagle—struggled to his feet and trotted over to inspect the new arrivals.

"Go on now, Jelly. Don't be sniffing the company." To Bobbie and Troy, Lucille said, "Please sit down." She gasped and pressed a hand to her chest. "Oh my. Forgive the mess." Lucille hurried to the sofa and gathered the scattered gossip magazines. "Thomas and I just got back from Atlanta late last night. I was too worn out to pick up the place this morning."

"How is Mr. Bonner?" Troy asked.

"Oh, he's all right," Lucille said. "They want him to get back in physical therapy. His poor old body is just wasting away. Lord knows I do all I can." She clasped her hands as if she might pray. "I'll just have to try and do more. I'm all he has, you know."

While the two discussed how Troy's parents were getting along, Bobbie took a seat on the sofa. The dog, Jelly, made several circles around his bed before deciding to plop back down. The home had that closed-up smell as if the windows were never opened and the blinds were always drawn tight. Nothing particularly bad, just a little musty. The decor and furnishings were slightly faded, a couple of decades old but still serviceable. Other than the pile of magazines, the living room was tidy. Framed photos of their son, Treat, sat here and there. Several more hung on the walls. The final photos, obviously taken just prior to his disappearance, showed a young man with a big, furry dog.

"That was our boy," Lucille said, following Bobbie's gaze. She picked up a framed photo and sat down in one of the two matching, well-worn recliners. "He was such a handsome young man. And that's Shep." She laughed. "Treat said the big old furry animal looked more like a sheep than a dog."

"Anytime I saw Treat, I saw Shep." Troy settled on the sofa next to Bobbie. "If you don't mind, Mrs. Bonner, we wanted to talk to you about Treat."

When Lucille set the photo aside and looked up, her eyes were bright with emotion. "I could talk all day about my boy. He was my angel for the short while we had him. What would you like to know?"

"Looking back," Troy said, "is there anything you recall that should have been investigated more thoroughly?"

While Lucille spoke frankly about Detective Mike Rhodes's incompetence, Bobbie studied her. She was an attractive woman. At sixty-eight she appeared fit. She dressed well and her shoulder-length hair was freshly colored a light brown. No telltale gray roots. The touch of pink on her cheeks suggested she still liked to wear makeup. Her nails were recently manicured and accented with a soft shade of pink, as well.

The lull in the conversation gave Bobbie an opening. "Just before his disappearance, did anyone make threats against Treat or your family?"

Lucille blinked rapidly for a second or two as if needing to keep the tears at bay or to hide her surprise at the question. "Why so many questions after all these years? Have you finally found him?"

"I'm sorry," Troy rushed to clarify. "We haven't, but there has been a major development in the case of the missing children."

Though a number of children had gone missing in the past thirty or so years, he didn't have to explain which children he meant. Lucille's expression instantly closed. "Oh? What do you mean, a development?"

Bobbie held back more of her own questions and waited for Troy to explain. She reminded herself that this was not her case, not her jurisdiction. She was here solely at his invitation. He could rescind that invite at any time if she stepped on his toes. Though she doubted he planned to do so.

"I realize you've been out of town. No one called you?" he asked.

Lucille shook her head. "Why would anyone call me? Please, Troy, just tell me what's happened?"

"Dr. Sanders and his wife were murdered."

For several endless seconds Lucille didn't move. Bobbie counted each moment. Shock and something like horror peeked past the older woman's casual demeanor. "What on earth? Was it a robbery?"

Troy shook his head. "No, ma'am. You know those statues he made to help folks remember the children who went missing?"

She nodded, the movement jerky.

"I guess whoever murdered the Sanderses wanted to reveal a dark secret they'd been keeping. They pushed over some of the statues and damaged others enough for us to find the bones hidden inside. The coroner has already identified three sets of the remains. Braden Cotton, Heath Wilson and Alice Cortland. They're reasonably sure the fourth set belongs to my sister, Brianne."

Lucille's hands went to her mouth. "Sweet Jesus." The words were muffled. The tears she'd been holding back rolled down her cheeks.

When the silence dragged on with her soft sobs, Bobbie said, "We're in a race against time, Mrs. Bonner. The man I believe may have murdered the Sanderses is extremely dangerous. You probably remember him from when he interviewed Treat. His name is Dr. Randolph Weller."

Her breath caught and her hands fell back to her lap. "The psychiatrist who turned out to be a serial killer?"

"I'm afraid so," Bobbie confirmed.

"He's here?" She looked from Bobbie to Troy.

"Yes, ma'am." Troy gave a nod. "We believe he is. If there is anything you can tell us about the time he spent with Treat, it could be useful in helping us determine his intent."

Her fingers entwined and twisted nervously. "I wasn't allowed in the interviews." Her lips quivered. "Mike wouldn't tell me anything. He treated my boy like he was guilty from the moment that charlatan told him about her vision."

The bitter edge in her voice when she said the deceased detective's name told Bobbie that in addition to considering Rhodes incompetent, there was no love lost between her and the man in charge of the Foster girl's rape and murder case. Nor did she have any warm and fuzzy feelings for Amelia Potter.

"So you never saw or spoke to Dr. Weller?" Bobbie asked.

Lucille shook her head adamantly. "I can't believe he escaped prison." She kept her attention on Troy. "Should we be afraid?"

Though her eyes widened, Bobbie didn't hear any true fear in her voice.

"We can't be certain why he's come to Savannah," Troy said. "But we can assign a surveillance detail to your home if you'd feel better."

"I just can't believe it." Lucille pressed her fingers to her cheeks again instead of responding to his offer of a detail. "Bill is dead. Murdered."

"Were you close to Bill Sanders?" Since she didn't mention the wife, Bobbie didn't either. Troy had said the Bonners and the Sanderses attended different churches. Clearly their tax brackets were vastly different. Where was the connection between them?

Lucille blinked repeatedly. "He…he took care of Shep. Treat loved him."

"Do you have any thoughts on who might have been responsible for Treat's disappearance?" Bobbie pressed.

The woman stared at Bobbie for a long while before answering. "I've asked myself that question a thousand times over the past three decades. I wish I knew."

Bobbie opted not to pursue the answer the lady clearly didn't want to give.

"No one has tried to contact you about Weller?" Troy asked, framing the question he'd ask before slightly differently. "Or about Mr. and Mrs. Sanders's murders?"

"We…" Lucille shrugged. "We don't have a cell phone and I've never cared for watching the news. I can't even remember the last time I watched television." She gestured to the old-fashioned floor model television. "That old thing was Treat's. He loved his cartoons."

"Mrs. Bonner," Bobbie said gently, taking another approach, "we know what happened to Treat was wrong. He was falsely accused based on circumstantial evidence. It was a terrible, terrible mistake. Do you believe someone related to the Foster girl hurt him somehow?"

The older woman's expression shifted to one of surprise. "Of course not. The Fosters were devastated by what happened to their precious daughter, but they knew my boy didn't hurt her. I don't know who took him, but it was not the Fosters. They suffered the same way Thomas and I did."

The answer wasn't the one Bobbie had expected but if the woman sincerely felt that way, it was a good thing. "Do you believe Treat's disappearance had anything to do with the children who went missing scarcely three weeks later?"

Bobbie hoped Durham didn't feel she was trying to take over the interview. Maybe she was. She should back off and let him lead from here.

"I do," Lucille said to Bobbie's surprise. "It was too big a coincidence otherwise. We all thought they had been taken like those other children. You know, the ones that were murdered by that cult group over in Charleston."

"If we operate under that theory," Troy pointed out gently, "we would be assuming Dr. Sanders was part of the cult you're referring to and that he took Treat."

"No!" Lucille's face flushed with something like outrage. "Bill—Dr. Sanders would never have hurt Treat."

"But he did hurt the other children," Durham reminded her.

Lucille covered her face with her hands for a moment. Her shoulders shook with more of her soft sobs. "It had to be his wife." She wiped her eyes and lifted her gaze to Troy's. "He would never have hurt anyone. It had to be that crazy bitch."

Lucille broke down then, not even attempting to hide her weeping. While Troy moved to her side, kneeling next to her chair to comfort her, Bobbie tried to piece together the puzzle. Why would Lucille despise Sanders's wife so much that she felt completely ready to blame her for the murder of the children? Was there bad blood between the two? The human element was the most difficult aspect of a cold case. Memories faded. Those that remained were often jumbled or recalled the way the person wanted to remember the moments in question rather than the way they actually happened.

The decades that had elapsed between the abductions and the discovery of the remains made this case all the more difficult. One glaring detail was undeniable: Weller had been involved, at least on the fringes.

Lucille promised to make herself available for any other questions they might have. She also assured them that she would call if she remembered anything else potentially useful.

Outside, Bobbie asked, "Questioning Mr. Bonner isn't possible? He can't write with either hand?"

"He can't," Troy confirmed. "Before his stroke he tried to take his life a couple of times. Lucille has always been very protective of him." He opened the vehicle door. "Since he can't communicate with us, I don't see any point in upsetting his daily routine."

When she'd climbed into the SUV and fastened her seat belt and he'd settled behind the wheel, he turned to Bobbie for a long moment before he worked up the courage to ask the question she suspected was coming next.

"I noticed the scars." He touched his wrist. "Will you slug me or pull out that Glock of yours if I ask about those?"

Bobbie stared out the windshield for a time. Until a few weeks ago she wouldn't have answered a question about that part of her life except to her shrink—and she only talked to him because it was required for her to stay on the job. But she'd learned that if she ever intended to get on with her life, she had to be willing to touch the past. To acknowledge that it happened and that those years before…were the best in her life so far and that she missed them with all her heart.

"After I was released from the hospital, the only thing I wanted to do was die." The chilling memory sliced through her like a knife. "My husband and my little boy were gone. I was the one who brought home the monster who took their lives. I didn't deserve to live."

He drew in a deep breath, then released it. "I know that place."

Bobbie nodded. "You were a child. I was a grown woman who was more focused on her job than on her family."

"I'll be sure to tell myself that next time I'm drowning in a bottle of Jack."

"Unfortunately alcohol never worked for me." She was relatively confident he'd had an encounter of the eighty- or ninety-proof kind last night. Bauer had tried drowning his grief that way, too. God she missed him.

"Lucky you." He started the SUV.

The curtains in the front window of the Bonner home shifted as if someone had been peeking out. "Where to next?" Bobbie made a mental note to ask Potter if she was aware of any tension between Nancy Sanders and Lucille Bonner.

There was something about Amelia Potter that made Bobbie want to take a closer look at her background, as well. She should ask Troy but she didn't want to tip her hand about her prior knowledge of the woman.

"The parents have had some time to digest the news—I say we interview each family and see what they may have recalled—if anything."

Made sense to Bobbie. The search for more remains was ongoing. No new results from the lab. What else could they do but interview those who were involved in the case?

"I thought we'd start with Deidre and Hoyt Wilson and then move on to Shelia and Wayne Cotton before talking to Mr. Cortland. We can drop by Ms. Potter's shop on the way back to headquarters."

"Did you talk to *your* parents last night?" Bobbie noticed that he'd left them out of the lineup.

He pulled away from the curb. "I did but mostly my mother cried and my father just stared at me like he wished it was me who'd been murdered instead of my sister."

"I'm sure he doesn't feel that way." The accusation was more of Troy's guilt talking. Bobbie recognized the MO. Standard operating procedure for survivors, according to her shrink.

"Maybe."

"All the players in this case, except Bonner and Potter, still attend that same church?"

"They do. First Baptist on Bull Street."

"You're a member?" Bobbie didn't really need to know. She was curious.

Church had never been high on her priority list. She hadn't set foot inside one since before her husband and son were taken from her. Except in the line of duty. It wasn't that she blamed God for their deaths. Mostly she had blamed Him for allowing her to live. Slowly but surely she had regained the desire to keep living, or maybe to start living again. Nick had been a major part of that milestone, too.

"I used to be a member," Troy confessed. "I haven't attended since I graduated high school and left for the Marines."

"What about the Sanderses?"

Troy braked for a traffic light. "Never missed a Sunday according to their neighbors." He glanced at her, a frown marring his brow. "You think the church is related to the case."

"I'm not sure yet," she admitted. Troy was still frowning at the idea when she asked, "You said Bonner's husband was in a construction accident?"

A moment passed before he nodded. "That's right. He fell off a roof or something. Anytime I've ever heard it mentioned, it was followed by the adamant statement that it was a miracle he survived."

Bobbie did a quick mental run-through of the background info she'd read on each player. "Was it mentioned somewhere in the case file that the Cottons owned a construction business?"

Troy nodded slowly, then glanced at her again.

"Give me a minute." He tugged out his cell and made a call. "Hey, Dee, what was the name of the construction company where Mr. Bonner worked?" He listened for a half a minute. "Thanks." He ended the call and put his phone away.

"Well?" His surprised expression had a new surge of adrenaline firing in Bobbie's veins.

"Cotton Construction." He braked for another intersection. "Just another of those intersections you talked about."

"That's right."

All they needed was to find the right one.

Eighteen

11:30 a.m.

Edward Cortland awoke in a pool of sweat and piss.

He shuddered, then groaned as it hurt so very badly just to breathe. For a moment he tried to determine what had awakened him. A beeping or something. Didn't matter. Why oh why had he ignored the pain so very long? If Allison hadn't grown worried about his weight loss and then noticed how jaundiced he was, he might still be wondering what the hell was wrong with him.

He was dying. Advanced pancreatic cancer... Allison had cried so hard when the doctor explained the damning test results.

His heart hurt as he thought of his dear, sweet Allison. He should never have told her the terrible, terrible secret he had been keeping all these years. He was a selfish son of a bitch. She would still be here with him if he hadn't been so damned selfish. All of the pain and agony they had suffered was his fault.

No matter what Bill Sanders and that insane wife of his had done, Edward knew where the true guilt lay. He had killed their precious girl as certainly as he had his beautiful wife.

The sobs rocked his frail body for a few minutes, maybe several minutes. He could no longer judge the passage of time. He'd buried Allison on Thursday, today was... Saturday.

Had it only been two days?

He wished he was dead already.

A new crescendo of pain washed over him. He groaned with the agony of it. God, how was he supposed to live like this? The pain was overwhelming. His body betrayed him a little more every hour of every day.

A nurse came in each morning to feed and dress him. She would return this evening to prepare his dinner and to bathe him and put him to bed. Between her visits, he slept. He took his pills and he slept. Friends called but he was in no condition to have visitors. The nurse reminded him that soon he would require around-the-clock care.

Soon he would die. The sooner the better.

He groaned and reached for the bottle of pain pills on the bedside table. No visitors. He'd told the nurse he would accept no visitors and that he would be staying at home until he was carried out feetfirst. He'd seen his old friends at Allison's funeral. That would be the last time until they gazed upon his thin, lifeless body in his casket.

Funny, the others hadn't rushed to his home and demanded why he'd told his wife what they did all those years ago. So very odd. The pain pills made his thinking fuzzy. Maybe they had. The drugs also made him forgetful. Or perhaps Allison had not told anyone. Unlike him, she may have been strong enough to take their awful secret to her grave with her.

Edward was a coward. Always had been really. He was typically the first to come up with an idea but he preferred that others execute it.

He clutched at the bottle and dragged it toward him. He shook it. *Empty.* A frown pulled at his face. The nurse should have checked to see that he had all that he needed within reach before she left this morning.

Summoning all the strength he possessed, Edward threw back the covers and forced his failing body into an upright position. When he'd gained his balance, he stood. One staggering step at a time he made his way into the bathroom. He fumbled through the bottles on the counter. His heart beat faster and faster. Where were his pain pills?

A wave of fierce agony washed over him and he had to brace himself against the counter.

Where the hell had that stupid bitch put his pain meds?

Holding the wall, he made his way out of the bathroom and the bedroom and into the hall. The distance to the stairs appeared so very far, but he knew it was really only twelve or fifteen yards. Slowly, he made his way there. Sweat poured down his face by the time he sat down on the first step. His body had started to shake with the pain. Long ago, as a young man, he'd volunteered at a homeless shelter. He'd seen the pitiful old men who were drug addicts. The lack of nourishment and exercise had eaten away at their bodies, leaving nothing but flabby skin and brittle bone. Every step had been a mountain to climb, each breath a shallow draw. How their fragile bodies had shaken.

The memory was like looking in the mirror at what he had become in the past few weeks. Even his penis had shriveled into nothing.

One by one he scooted down the steps. When he reached the bottom, he had to sit for a brief period before he dared to stand. Slowly he hauled himself up and started toward his destination. He hit the table in the parlor, causing the large vase atop it to crash to the floor. He didn't care. The housekeeper would take care of the mess. He needed to get to the kitchen. There was a newly filled bottle of meds on the counter next to the sink and two more in the cabinet next to it. His personal physician, an old friend, had ensured Edward had whatever he needed. Since there was nothing else they could do for him, keeping him comfortable was the goal. Soon he would be totally bedridden and on a morphine drip, but he refused to be stranded that way until there was no other choice.

By the time he reached the kitchen, he was sweating profusely, his vision was failing and the ability to stand without holding on to something had deserted him. He overturned a chair on the way to the sink.

Edward froze. Ironically his vision cleared. The countertops were clean. Nothing, not a bottle or glass or anything at all sat on the gleaming white marble. Had the housekeeper been here this morning? She knew better than to touch his meds.

"Fuck."

Outrage thundered inside him. Where was his cell phone? For the love of God! Had he left it upstairs? He reached for the house phone. There was no dial tone. He hit the necessary buttons and listened again. Still no dial tone. He tossed the useless instrument across the room.

He needed his goddamned pills!

Edward tore open cabinet doors and drawers. He flung contents aside…over the counters…onto the floor…wherever, he no longer cared. No pills! Where the hell were his pills?

Maybe the nurse or the housekeeper had put them in the refrigerator. It was the only place he hadn't searched. Stupid cunts! Holding on to a chair and sliding it along with him, he made his way there. The pain screamed inside him. He moaned.

No pills in the refrigerator.

Edward dropped to his knees.

He was so tired. The pain was too much.

His body slumped to the floor and he flopped onto his back.

He stared up at the kitchen light. Each breath was a tremendous struggle. The pain was like a thousand knives cutting him up inside.

Something blocked the light.

He blinked. Tried to make out the face staring down at him.

"What happened Edward?"

He frowned, tried to say her name, but he couldn't speak. He couldn't think. Why was she here? His mind was going around and around just like the room. He must be confused.

"Don't worry, Edward. I have what you need. What you *deserve*."

He opened his mouth, whether in an attempt to speak again or for the promise of a pill that would provide blessed relief he couldn't say for sure.

Fingers prodded his mouth open wider. He thought he saw another face in the light. Were his housekeeper and his nurse here? Something poured into his mouth. His tongue laved at the objects. His pills! He tried to swallow, but there were too many. The pills kept spilling into his mouth.

Oh yes! More! Thank God! He just needed to swallow.

"There you go," a singsong voice resonated around him.

Edward tried to swallow…to close his mouth, but it was too full.

Fingers shoved the pills deeper into his throat. He gagged.

Can't breathe...

As he choked and gagged and sputtered, a face lowered next to his. "Don't worry, Edward, the others will be joining you soon."

Nineteen

Myrtlewood Drive
12:00 p.m.

Troy parked on the cobblestone drive and turned to Bobbie. "I'm really sorry about what happened back there." He shook his head. "Wondering where their boy was all these years is hard enough, but to reach this stage in your life and then discover what that bastard did to him—it's hard. Really hard. The Wilsons are usually nice people."

"I didn't take their refusal to talk with me in the room personally. I'm an outsider. This is a painful time. I completely understand."

Mr. and Mrs. Wilson had flatly refused to talk to Troy unless Bobbie waited outside on the porch. She'd spent the time researching Cotton Construction on Google. Savannah was a fairly large city but not so large that folks didn't know one another. Like most cities the residents were divided into cliques by neighborhoods and churches. The parents of the missing children as well as the Sanderses knew each other beyond the tragedy they shared. In the South the connection of church was a strong one. For now Bobbie was more interested in the connection between the Cottons and the Bonners and that long-ago accident. It might be nothing, but she had learned from Nick not to overlook the smallest detail. The Foster girl's murder and the Bonner family's connection to that horrific event as well as to Weller was significant somehow.

"Besides—" Bobbie glanced at the man behind the wheel "—I didn't really miss anything."

What she was missing was Bauer's funeral. Bobbie stared at the digital display of the time. The service had just started and she wasn't there. *Forgive me. I will make this right.*

"I'm hoping they'll change their minds when the shock wears off a little."

"Maybe," Bobbie allowed. She exiled thoughts of what was happening in Montgomery this afternoon. Here. Now. She could help stop more of the same travesty. Going back to Montgomery for the funeral hadn't been an option.

Ultimately the Wilsons had insisted they were far too upset to discuss the horror they had suffered all those years ago. They'd politely instructed Troy to speak to their attorney. He would answer any questions the police or the FBI had.

Bobbie had seen folks shut down like that before. It was a defense mechanism. If they refused to answer the questions, they could pretend for a little while that whatever was happening wasn't. If push came to shove, they would come around.

Like the Wilson home, the Cotton residence was a mansion of eight or so thousand square feet judging by the looks of it. While the Wilson home sat smack in the middle of downtown Savannah's historic district, the Cotton home stood on a large lot facing the golf course and the water well outside the hustle and bustle of downtown. If the grand estate was any indicator of how well what was now called Cotton Brothers Construction had weathered over the years, the company had done well.

"Wayne Cotton retired about five years ago," Troy explained, "but he still owns the company. His younger brother runs the day-to-day operations."

"Fair warning, Lieutenant," Bobbie said, "I'd like to know as much as possible about the time frame Bonner worked for the company."

"I've been thinking about that and you're right. The connection between the Fosters, the Bonners and this case is an overlooked lead that should have been explored thirty-two years ago." He reached for the door. "I can only hope it was and that Rhodes failed to write up a report about it."

As if he'd read Bobbie's thoughts on the matter, he added, "A lot of his legwork and interviews seem to have been left out of the case files."

"Maybe he felt what he was leaving out was more hurtful than relevant to the overall investigation."

Troy hesitated as understanding dawned in his expression. "The same way I did when I removed the interviews with my family."

"You're human, your father is human, so was Detective Rhodes. All the players were closely acquainted," she reminded him. "Back in the day it was a pretty common practice to ignore the technicalities of paperwork when it came to friends."

"Excellent point, Detective."

Bobbie climbed out of the SUV. "What about Detective Rhodes? Did he attend the same church?"

Troy met her in front of the vehicle. "You know, I think he did."

"That closeness impacted the investigation." Not in a good way. No need to say that part out loud. Troy was no fool.

As they walked toward the front entrance of the Cotton home, Bobbie realized she hadn't properly thanked Troy for having her back that morning. "I appreciate your saying what you did to Kessler."

"We're cops." He pressed the doorbell. "We have to stick together, especially with the feds."

Not to mention the two of them shared the sort of pain few understood.

"Apparently she isn't ready to let it go." Kessler had gone to Metro's chief.

"Don't worry." He gave her a wink. "I know how to handle bullies like Kessler."

Bobbie hoped he realized exactly what he was promising. Kessler wasn't the only fed they had to worry about. Pitts, LeDoux's superior, was apparently involved. She had expected that BAU would help with the search for Weller. What she hadn't expected was to be one of their persons of interest. The worst part was the way they appeared intent on railroading Nick.

The door opened and Wayne Cotton stared at them. Bobbie didn't need an introduction. The man had the same bright green eyes she'd seen in the photograph of his son. His dark hair had grayed but there was no mistaking the eyes or the chin. This was Braden Cotton's father.

"Afternoon, Mr. Cotton," Troy said. "Sergeant Lawrence should have called to let you know we were coming."

Bobbie had met most of Troy's unit. Freda Lawrence was about the same age as Bobbie. Divorced and attractive. She wore her adoration for Troy like a neon sign. Maybe the two had a thing like the chief and Owens back home.

"She did. Come in, Troy." Cotton considered Bobbie a moment. "So this is the detective who came all the way from Montgomery, Alabama, that we've been hearing about."

"Yes, sir. This is Detective Bobbie Gentry."

Bobbie extended her hand. "I appreciate your taking the time to speak with us, sir. This is a difficult time."

Cotton accepted her hand and gave it a quick, firm shake. "We appreciate any and all efforts to find justice for the children." He closed the door behind them. "Unfortunately my wife won't be able to join us." He began moving away from the door. "A migraine hit her this morning and she'll be down for the day." He shook his head. "Poor thing. She's suffered with those hideous headaches all her life."

While Cotton led the way deeper into the home and Troy chatted amiably with him about the opening dates for deer hunting season, Bobbie scrutinized the place. The decorator had used a light hand. The discreet taupe on the walls was interrupted only by the occasional understated piece of art. An elegant table with a lovely vase was expertly stationed beneath a chandelier. Fine, thick rugs graced the rich hardwood floors. The furnishings in the great room they entered were equally elegant yet that lived-in look was evident. The leather was worn comfortable. Well-washed throws and soft pillows adorned the sofa and chairs. The mansion was grand but it was undeniably a home.

When they had all settled around the conversation area, Troy kicked off the interview. "Mr. Cotton, when we last spoke I asked you to think about whether there was anything new you recalled from the days immediately before or after Braden was abducted. Have you had a chance to do that, sir?"

Bobbie watched Cotton's face as he prepared to respond. Perhaps it was his obviously close relationship with Botox or an innate ability to keep his feelings hidden, but the man gave the term *poker face* new meaning. His shirt and trousers sported crisp seams and expertly pressed creases. The dark colors accentuated his tan. She seriously doubted he'd gotten that tan on a construction site.

Cotton patted his right hand against the center of his chest as if he'd suffered a pang there. "Shelia and I discussed this last night." He sighed. "I fear that was the cause of her migraine. We simply can't remember anything that would have given the slightest hint that trouble was coming before...that night."

Troy asked, "You never noticed the Sanderses showing any particular interest in your son. You never had words with them or any sort of trouble?"

"God no. We considered Bill Sanders a friend." He turned his hands up. "Nancy was a little more difficult to relate to. She stayed to herself. Never joined any of the other wives for tea. There was a rumor she suffered from depression, but I can't say for sure. I do remember there was a time years and years ago when she didn't leave the house for months. I believe she had several miscarriages. You know they never were able to have any children." He shook his head. "The truth is, a great deal of the time around the abductions is nothing but a blur. After Braden...was gone. We had a very difficult time moving on. If not for the other children..." He shook his head again as his words drifted off.

The Cottons had a son and a daughter who were older than the son they lost. Both were married and lived in the greater Atlanta area.

"Mr. Cotton," Bobbie said, drawing his attention to her, "do you remember the accident Thomas

Bonner had when he worked for your construction company?"

Not the first line of surprise or confusion appeared on his unreasonably smooth face. "Of course. It's not often that one of the company's employees is injured, but it happens."

"Did the Bonners receive a settlement after the accident?" Bobbie pressed.

"My father was in charge at the time and he made the decision not to provide any sort of settlement," Cotton said. He shifted his attention to Troy. "What does Thomas Bonner have to do with the disappearance of the children?"

He made that leap damned fast. "Is there a connection between the two?" Bobbie said before Troy could answer.

"How could I possibly presume to know the answer to that question, Detective?" Cotton was irritated now—it resonated in his tone.

"Why did your father decide not to provide compensation for Bonner's fall?" Bobbie pressed.

Cotton adjusted his jacket. "If you must know, Thomas Bonner was drinking on the job. The rumor was that he and his wife were having problems. Whatever his personal problems, he fell off that roof because he was drunk." Cotton stared hard at Bobbie. "My father kept that part out of the report so the insurance company would pay his medical bills. I'm certain my father felt that was adequate compensation."

"Why would he do that, Mr. Cotton?" Bobbie

had him on the defensive now. "If the accident was Bonner's own fault, why do anything at all?"

"Because my father was a Christian, Detective. That's what Christians do." His irritation had shifted to outrage. He turned back to Troy. "What is this, Troy?"

The interview ended shortly after that. Cotton remembered nothing beyond what was in the original reports and Bobbie had her doubts as to whether he would be inclined to answer any more of her queries.

Troy didn't speak as they loaded back into his SUV. When he shifted into Drive and drove away from the ostentatious home, he finally said, "You know, you see people every day and you think you know them, but I'm beginning to think I don't know any of these people."

There were several things Bobbie had expected him to say when they were alone again. That she shouldn't have pushed Cotton about the Bonner incident. That her questions weren't relevant and those damned irrelevant questions had shut down the interview. The statement he'd made was not at all what she'd anticipated.

"His answers—up until the end—were oddly matter-of-fact," she said. "Thirty-two years is a long time. I guess maybe I'll feel different when I'm that far out from my own personal tragedy." Would those memories one day be nothing more than pieces of her life shelved in the "hurtful past" section? She couldn't imagine ever touching those memories and not feeling the sharp ache of loss.

Troy checked traffic before pulling out onto the street. "Maybe I'm the weird one then because I don't feel one bit different than I did thirty-two years ago when I realized I'd lost my baby sister."

"Everyone—"

"Deals with grief differently," he interjected.

"We all process pain in different ways." Bobbie thought about the exchange for another moment. "I don't understand why Cotton would get so fired up over a question about an accident that happened nearly half a century ago. One he said himself that his father took care of in a more compassionate manner than necessary."

"Do you think the accident is relevant to what happened to the children?"

"No." Bobbie checked her cell, wishing again that Nick would change his mind about working with her. "What I think is relevant is the way all their lives intersected back then. These aren't merely residents of the same city or neighbors or members of the same church or even statistics in the same tax bracket, they're *all* of the above."

Bill Sanders loved taking care of animals, but he had inherited a great deal of property and family money. The same could be said for the Durhams. Troy's father had been a cop until he retired, but he had inherited well. As Troy said, they were far closer to the Cortlands' tax bracket than Potter's.

"Except for the Bonners and Amelia Potter," he reminded her.

"Except for those two, yes." Bobbie thought about the way Nick analyzed a killer's movements. "Of all the available children in Savannah, the killer—presumably one or both of the Sanderses—selected those five children and yet there were never any demands for ransom. Have you found any indication that the Sanderses were going through any sort of financial trouble at the time?"

"None."

"Then the real question we need to ask is why those children were taken? What did those families have in common besides tax brackets, neighborhoods and church? The difference between Amelia Potter and the others may explain why her son's remains are not accounted for and Treat Bonner's disappearance is still unexplained."

Troy glanced at her. "You're thinking if we find the underlying connection between the five—no, the six—families, we'll find the motive."

"I believe so."

The sooner they found that answer, the sooner they might be able to figure out what Randolph Weller had to do with any of it beyond evaluating Treat Bonner.

Driving back into the heart of Savannah, Bobbie worked at clearing her mind of the mounting frustration. It was almost Halloween. The creepy decorations and harvest colors were everywhere. The last of autumn's leaves were scattered across the streets and sidewalks. Most of the folks in the downtown shops were dressed in some form of costume. Last year she'd hurried home from work a little early so she and James could take Jamie trick-or-treating. He'd been dressed as the Stay Puft Marshmallow man. A smile tugged at her lips. The costume had made walking a bit of a balancing act for him.

Miss you so much, baby.

Bobbie blinked away the memories and decided her current dilemma was easier to deal with. Nick should be part of this. His decision to step completely out of her life was unfair. *Deep breath.* She couldn't pretend not to understand what drove him. This was his way of protecting her not only from Weller, but from him. Didn't matter that she was a grown woman fully capable of taking care of herself. He, of all people, should know as much. The person he really didn't trust was himself. He was so damned afraid he would become his father. That fear had burrowed deep inside him and hardened like ice.

Troy pulled to the curb and parked. Bobbie pushed aside thoughts of Nick and focused on the task at hand. Someone who knew the Sanderses' ugly secret had murdered them. That someone was very likely involved somehow with the missing children. Bobbie intended to do all within her power to help Troy solve the mystery. And to help Amelia Potter learn the fate of her little boy. She'd wondered long enough. Maybe along the way Bobbie would see whatever it was that Weller wanted to show her.

He'd warned her that what was coming would take all the courage and tenacity she possessed to survive. Was that because little Noah Potter had been about the same age as Jamie? Or was the warning about some danger to Nick? Maybe to her.

Show me what you want me to see, you bastard, so we can get on with the business of taking you down.

"You coming?"

Bobbie banished the thoughts and reached for her seat belt. "Absolutely."

The Cortland home was another of Savannah's historic beauties. According to the plaque posted at the sidewalk, it was one of the first homes built in Ardsley Park. The bride-white siding and massive columns and half-round upper balcony were jaw-dropping. Bobbie had read in the case file that Edward Cortland was a banker just like his father and grandfather before him. The family had opened the first independent bank in Savannah more than a century ago.

Troy pushed the doorbell and they waited. The trickle of the bubbling fountain in the center of the front yard and the occasional buzz of a passing car were the only sounds. Glass sidelights and an arched transom turned the classic six-panel door into a welcoming masterpiece. The leaded glass twisted and tilted the image of the spiral staircase

that wound its way upward in the entry hall beyond the closed door.

When no answer came, Troy pressed the bell
again and followed up with a firm knock.

"Maybe Mr. Cortland decided to return to St.
Louis with his nephew for a while." Bobbie's instincts hummed. The memory of standing at Lawrence Zacharias's door and finding it unlocked kept
flashing in her head.

"Maybe." Troy walked over to one of the front
windows and peered in. "Shit."

He drew his weapon and rushed back to the
door. He gave the knob a twist. Locked. He charged
it a couple of times, forcing it open and rushing
inside. Bobbie was right behind him, her Glock
at the ready. He nodded for her to go left and he
went right.

Just beyond the entry hall, a table stood in the
center of the parlor, the vase that had sat atop it
had fallen and shattered on the floor. Past the parlor was a dining room. *Clear.*

Listening intently above the sound of her own
blood roaring in her ears, Bobbie moved into the
kitchen. She stopped cold.

An overturned ladder-back chair lay next to the
breakfast table in the middle of the room. Drawers
and doors stood open, their contents tossed about.
Kitchen utensils were scattered over the tile floor.
No blood.

Bobbie eased cautiously into the room. Troy appeared at a cased opening on the other side of the kitchen.

"What the hell happened here?"

"The rest of the downstairs is clear?" Bobbie asked, drawing his attention to her.

He nodded. "Still gotta check upstairs."

Troy knew the family. He'd just given the poor man the news about his missing child late yesterday. His wife had been buried mere days ago. For the first time the lieutenant allowed his emotions to show. His hands shook and his face paled.

Bobbie said, "Call it in and have a look around outside."

When his gaze snapped to hers, she added, "You're familiar with the kind of car he drives. See if it's in the garage. If not, check with the hospitals. Maybe his health took a turn for the worse. I'll check upstairs."

He gave a quick nod and reached for his phone.

Retracing her steps, Bobbie returned to the entry hall and started up the winding staircase. Troy's somber tones as he spoke to dispatch sent a chill tumbling over her skin. Did the Cortlands have something to hide? His wife had committed suicide for some reason. Why after thirty-two years had she suddenly decided she couldn't live her life any longer?

The upstairs hall and sitting room were adorned with the same lovely antiques and elegant decorating Bobbie had seen downstairs. The walls were a soft cream throughout with satin white trim. No rugs on the hardwood. Most of the chairs and sofas she'd spotted were leather. There had been no cut flowers in the broken vase downstairs. No sign of pets. Allergies?

She checked the first three bedrooms. All were clean and tidy. All were clear of foul play. When she moved into the master everything changed. The room smelled of death, a distinct sickly sweet odor of the dying. The covers were tousled and a pill bottle and water glass lay on the floor next to the antique bedside table. Like the other rooms, no framed photos sat atop the tables or the dressers. None hung on the walls either. She checked the en suite bath and the massive walk-in closet. *Clear.*

She hesitated as she prepared to exit the bedroom. A smaller door was hidden by the door leading back into the hall. Bobbie opened the door that was only a couple of inches taller than her five-eight. She felt for a switch on the wall and flipped it. An overhead light glowed to life. The room was approximately eight by ten feet. Maybe an extra closet or a nursery.

Whatever it had been, it was a shrine to Alice Cortland now. The photos Bobbie had expected to see scattered throughout the house covered every inch of wall space in this hidden room. Toys and stuffed animals were piled nearly to the ceiling in one corner. A small pink cushioned mat, like a kneeling pad one would use in the garden, lay in the center of the room. All around the mat were prayer candles.

The image of Mrs. Cortland coming into this room and praying for her child every day and night for thirty-two years sat heavily on Bobbie's chest. As horrible as her child's death had been, at least Bobbie had known. These people had lived in uncertainty for half their lives.

Had the Cortlands learned the Sanderses killed their child and the others and decided to have their revenge? Except Mrs. Cortland walked into that lake before the Sanderses were murdered. The idea that she would take her life when her husband needed her most still nagged at Bobbie. Had a man as ill as Mr. Cortland been able to carry out what Bobbie had seen at the Sanders's home? Not likely.

Another possibility nudged Bobbie's instincts. *The lake.* Mr. Cortland may have decided to go to his lake house and do exactly what his wife had done.

Bobbie rushed from the room, ran down the hall and took the stairs two at a time. Outside, official vehicles were already screeching to halts on the street. When she reached the back door she spotted Troy. He stood near a large fountain ensconced in the center of the secluded gardens nearest the house. Lush shrubs and vibrant flowers surrounded the seating area, complete with an outdoor kitchen that had been designed specifically for entertaining.

None of those material things mattered to the Cortlands now. Allison Cortland was dead and buried and Edward Cortland lay facedown in the fountain, a water lily stuck to his back.

"If this is a homicide, and it sure as hell looks that way," Troy said, his voice grim, "why would Weller do this?" He shook his head. "I can't come up with a single damned reason he would care about this case or these people much less go to the trouble to drown a dying man in his own backyard in broad daylight. Where is he going with this?"

Bobbie had to admit she was as baffled as Troy. "That's the million-dollar question."

He shook his head again. "This is fucking crazy."

Bobbie hoped the lieutenant understood that things were going to get a hell of a lot worse before this was over.

As if Fate had decided to provide immediate proof that things were going to get far worse, three suits, one being a skirt, abruptly appeared around the corner of the house. How the hell had Kessler gotten word so quickly? The scene had barely been called in. Bobbie exhaled a weary breath. Maybe while Troy was dealing with Kessler, she could call Nick.

"I need a minute," she said to Troy. He nodded his understanding and Bobbie turned to walk away.

"What's your hurry, Detective Gentry?" Kessler demanded. "Walk me through what we have here."

Bobbie wished she had slipped away a few seconds sooner. "This is Lieutenant Durham's crime scene. You're aware that I'm only here in an advisory capacity."

On cue Troy launched into an explanation of what they'd found, which was nothing beyond the body floating a few yards away.

Hands on her hips, Kessler shook her head. "This isn't Dr. Weller's work."

Troy glanced at Bobbie. Kessler noticed.

"I see you've already come to that conclusion."

Bobbie figured keeping her mouth shut was her best answer. No, this was not Weller's work, but that didn't mean he hadn't orchestrated the kill.

"I believe this is his son," Kessler announced with a confirming nod. "There's something going on in Savannah, Lieutenant," she said to Troy. "And it's somehow related to Dr. Weller's past. Quantico is sending two of their best profilers to help us out here. Whatever secrets the players in this case are keeping, Nick Shade believes they will draw his father here. I would advise you to press those involved to come clean before it's too late."

Bobbie was too stunned for several seconds to speak.

Kessler turned to Bobbie, her smug expression evidence she fully comprehended just how much her conclusion had rattled Bobbie. "When you speak to your friend again, you should tell him that I'm on to him."

The agent executed an about-face and marched away, her entourage following.

"What the hell was that all about?"

Bobbie stared after the bitch determined to drag Nick onto the wrong side of this. "I wish I knew."

If the FBI could somehow come up with enough evidence to suggest Nick had prompted his father's escape and was now playing a macabre game with him, their own mistakes would be overlooked.

Or maybe Kessler or someone higher up the food chain had some personal stake in proving guilt lay elsewhere.

Either way, Kessler's point about Weller having secrets here was far too accurate. Weller would not risk hanging around otherwise.

Maybe Weller was setting up some sort of payback for his son.

Twenty

Luke Durham waited next to Delores Waldrop's car. For as long as he had known her, Delores had parked in the same spot. She was working late tonight. The woman did that most every damned night. She had for as long as he could remember.

He'd always been able to depend on her. When he'd been in charge of the homicide unit she had been his right hand in the office. When Brianne went missing, she'd held him up. They'd both been ashamed of themselves when comfort had turned to something more. No one had ever known, but they had known. For a long while he and Delores had beat themselves up about stepping across that line, but they'd worked past it. Their friendship and professional respect for each other had weathered that ugly storm.

When that FBI agent had contacted him on Thursday evening and told him what he had to do to protect his son, Delores had been there for him once again. She'd pulled Mike Rhodes's notes on the case and given them to Luke. He'd added Bobbie Gentry's name and number just like he was told. Delores had refiled the notes without asking a single question.

Luke had wanted to go to Troy and tell him about the agent's visit, but he'd been too damned afraid to take the risk. He'd already lost his son, but he refused to take a chance with Troy's life. He'd done what he had to do and he had no regrets.

Except now people were dying.

Bill and Nancy Sanders were dead. Edward Cortland was dead… God only knew what would happen next. He'd begun to wonder if Allison's death had really been a suicide.

This horrific nightmare and all the secrets surrounding it had evolved into something even more sinister. There was no telling what would happen next.

Delores had promised to keep him up to speed on the investigation, but she'd gotten cold feet after what happened today. Luke had to make her see that she couldn't let him down now. She had to trust him.

The side door opened and Delores walked out. She was barely three yards from her car when she saw him.

"You shouldn't be coming out alone like this after dark," he warned. Luke had always given her a hard time about not taking more precautions leaving work alone this late.

"I can take care of myself." She clicked her car fob, and the lights flashed in response. She opened the driver's-side door and tossed her bag inside. "If you've come to ask for any more favors I'm afraid I'm fresh out."

Luke moved closer to her. "I swear I didn't get you into anything illegal or immoral."

One thinly arched brow lifted higher than the other. "That would be a first."

"Dee, you know that's not true." He wanted to hug her and remind her that he still cared, but that would be veering to close to that line they'd crossed all those years ago. "You have my word. What I did then and now were necessary."

"Are you going to tell me why?" She crossed her arms over her chest. "You added her name to those notes, didn't you?"

Luke nodded. "I didn't know why until Bill and Nancy's bodies were found." He closed his eyes and shook his head. "And the children." His heart squeezed. "Someone knows what really happened and vengeance is descending. Whatever's coming, I will not regret protecting Troy."

"What about protecting yourself?" Dee lifted her chin and stared at him. "We both know you made a mistake when the Bonner boy went missing."

He had, damn it. He had. "I deserve whatever happens to me. But I have to protect Troy and

Heather." What he'd put them through already was unspeakable. What he'd allowed to happen to his little girl… God Almighty. His baby girl had paid for his sin.

Delores closed her hands into fists and pressed them to her forehead as if the decision she had to make was a battle raging in her skull. Finally she looked up at him. "I'll do whatever you need me to do."

Luke couldn't help himself—he hugged her. He hugged her with all his might and prayed that he could somehow make this right.

But then, he'd been a fool before.

Twenty-One

Bobbie tossed her bag onto the bed in her room and stretched her back. She was beat. Not one person along the block where Cortland lived had seen anyone coming or going from the property. The home security system had been turned off. His private nurse, who had prepared his breakfast that morning, swore she had reset the alarm when she left around ten.

The security company confirmed the nurse's statement. They also confirmed that the Cortlands had never installed video surveillance as part of their system. Bobbie would never understand why some wealthy people assumed they were untouchable. Just living in the prosperous neighborhood he lived in put Cortland at a higher risk for a home invasion. The lack of security as well as the decision not to hire a full-time nurse after his wife's death had left him vulnerable. On the other hand, his wife had only just died. She imagined the man had still been reeling from the shock of her death as well as learning of his own impending death from terminal cancer.

Like the Sanderses, Cortland's murder had nothing to do with a home invasion. Beyond the obvious search for his pain medication, nothing in his home had been touched.

There was no question in Bobbie's mind that the three were targeted and eliminated for reasons related to the long-missing children. And somehow, those children were connected to Weller.

But what if they were wrong? What if this entire case was nothing more than a distraction to allow Weller more lead time in his disappearing act? He was a brilliant man. He would know exactly how to manipulate everyone involved to ensure all eyes were on the drama he had somehow set in motion.

No. Bobbie refused to believe all of this was nothing but smoke and mirrors. Lawrence Zacharias had wanted Amelia Potter to have a photo of Nick. Bobbie highly doubted the attorney had done this as part of a master plan to help Weller disappear. It was a warning of some sort or a clue. If Zacharias had been taking care of Weller he wouldn't be lying in a morgue in pieces. Weller would only have murdered his old friend if he was no longer of use to him.

Zacharias had screwed up and Weller had taken him out. It was the only logical explanation.

The faster they put the pieces of this puzzle together, the more quickly the dying would stop.

With Dr. Mather's help, she and Troy had recreated Cortland's murder. He'd come down the stairs in search of his medication. The full bottle the nurse had left on his bedside table had somehow been emptied—presumably by the killer. His killer had been waiting for him downstairs. About two hundred pain capsules had been shoved down his throat and then his mouth had been duct taped shut. He'd still been wearing his pajama bottoms when he was dragged to the fountain and placed facedown in the water.

Mather felt confident the autopsy would confirm Cortland had been alive at the time his face was plunged into the cold water.

Bill and Nancy Sanders, Allison and Edward Cortland, all had died from the same cause—asphyxiation. Was the killer attempting to ensure his victims died the same way the children presumably did, from a lack of oxygen? But the Cortlands were parents of one of the children.

Did that mean the parents were somehow involved in what happened to those children thirty-two years ago? Was that the real intersection that tied the players together?

If that was the case, the one part of this puzzle that didn't fit was Amelia Potter.

Ignoring the hour, Bobbie grabbed her bag and left. Downstairs, she exited the inn and crossed the street to where her Challenger waited. Her cell phone flashed a warning that it was dying. She started the engine, plugged the phone into the charger and pulled out onto the quiet street. She'd called Nick and left him a message about Cortland, but he hadn't returned her call. He hadn't returned her call about Kessler either.

If he didn't call her back tonight, she was going to hunt him down. She lowered the window and allowed the cold air to blast her face. She wanted coffee and daylight. She wanted this damned night to be over. Recently nights seemed far longer... far lonelier.

Bobbie shook her head. All this time she hadn't felt a damned thing except the agony of loss—until Nick came into her life. Now she wished she didn't feel this new kind of emptiness that came from his pushing her away.

Keep your head in the case.

River Street was quiet. No traffic. Yet finding a spot to park in front of The Gentle Palm was not happening. She parked up the block and on the opposite side of the street. She locked her car and walked quickly back toward the shop. It was dark inside but upstairs there was still a light on. Hopefully there was a doorbell or something at the entrance that would alert Potter up on the second floor. When she reached the door she found what she was looking for and pressed the buzzer.

She took a breath and considered the possibility that Cortland's murder could be related to a disgruntled employee at one of the many banks the family owned. Not likely. Cortland's murder had been extremely personal in nature. His killer wanted him to suffer before he choked to death. If the murders were about the children and revenge, then all the players were at risk.

Troy had offered to provide a surveillance detail for each family and all had turned down the offer, including his parents. Bobbie hadn't been surprised the Durhams had passed. Troy's father was a retired cop. No cop liked to be told he needed help protecting himself. In fact, she had insisted Troy call off the detail watching her and use that resource elsewhere. To her surprise he had conceded.

The one decline of a security detail that really surprised Bobbie was Amelia Potter's. She lived alone. She should have accepted protection. Maybe if Bobbie explained the threat in greater detail the woman would see reason.

A light came on in the shop and Amelia appeared beyond the glass door. She was dressed for bed in a white cotton gown and a well-loved blue knit shawl wrapping her shoulders. Bobbie wondered if she had some sort of camera to see who was at her door or if she was so foolishly trusting. Maybe even after the passage of thirty-two years, she still had little care for her own safety. Bobbie doubted she would ever feel that sort of fear again. She had fallen down on the most important job of her life—protecting her son. What else mattered? Maybe time didn't heal that particular pain and regret.

Amelia unlocked the door and pulled it open wide. "Is there any news on who murdered Mr. Cortland?"

Bobbie stepped inside. "Not yet. We're still investigating his death."

The older woman's face lined with pain. "I said a prayer for whatever family he has left."

Bobbie searched her face, looking for any sign of fear. She found none. "I wanted to drop by to make sure you understood how much danger you could be in. We have reason to believe his murder is related to the Sanderses' murders and most likely to the children."

Amelia closed the door and locked it. "Would you like some tea?"

Bobbie almost said no. "Do you have coffee?" She would kill for a cup right now.

"I have one of those single-cup coffeemakers." She indicated that Bobbie should follow her. "Not all my customers are tea drinkers."

"Lucky for me."

Amelia led the way beyond the counter and through the cased opening. The space behind the storefront provided storage for her shop as Bobbie had expected. There was a small kitchenette as well as a door marked Restroom. On the far side of the room was an exit. Besides the shelves of boxed goods, there was another small table and two chairs. A narrow staircase led to the second floor.

"Cream or sugar?" Amelia tucked a pod into the machine and closed the lid.

"No, thanks." Within seconds the scent of fresh brewed coffee wafted in the air. Bobbie's mouth watered.

"Please, sit." The older woman indicated the table and chairs.

The more comfortable Amelia Potter was, the more likely she was to be receptive to Bobbie's questions, so she pulled out one of the chairs and took a seat. Steaming mug of coffee in hand, Amelia joined her. She set the mug in front of Bobbie. "Here you go."

As soon as the taste landed on her tongue Bobbie hummed her appreciation. "That hits the spot."

"Did Randolph Weller kill him?"

Bobbie searched her face. "He's a person of interest in the investigation."

"You know him well?"

"I know enough. Randolph Weller is a monster. He's murdered dozens of people, including the nurse who helped him escape custody. He mutilated their bodies in the most depraved ways." She held the other woman's gaze, urging her to listen up. "He's extremely dangerous."

"Why is he here? Why this case?" She shook her head, worry clouding her features. "Why now, after all these years?"

"I wish I knew the answers. The only connection we've found is that he evaluated Treat Bonner after the Foster girl was murdered. Whatever his reason, it's significant enough that he's willing to risk capture. As twisted as he is, the man is brilliant. He has an objective, we simply don't see it yet. Bad for our team."

Amelia rested her elbow on the table and rubbed at her temple. "I saw his picture in the newspaper. I'm certain I've never met him."

"Thirty-two years is a long time," Bobbie suggested. Like before, Potter didn't look at Bobbie when she spoke of Weller.

"I don't know him."

Bobbie decided to go in a different direction. "You said before that you never experienced any sort of warning that Noah was in danger. Looking back, do you still feel the same way? Maybe you were busy and you ignored your instincts."

Amelia closed her eyes for a moment and then said. "I've always been so sure of my feelings…of my knowing." She shook her head. "Except that once. When it counted the most." Her gaze rested on Bobbie's. "The answer is no. I didn't feel it coming."

You couldn't have saved him.

Bobbie took a breath and said what needed to be said. "You know that I lost my son, too."

Amelia nodded. "I do. I also knew you were coming to Savannah. I didn't know your name or why, but I saw you in my dreams." She pulled the shawl closer around her. "After your visit to my shop, I went to the library and used one of their computers to learn what I could about you. I'm sorry for your loss."

"I only mention my personal experience," Bobbie went on, her voice more unsteady than she would like, "because I understand how you might ignore your own safety. I urge you to take this threat very seriously."

Amelia assessed her a moment. "The way you do?"

Bobbie decided not to take offense at her question. "I'm a trained cop. I know how to deal with him. You can't possibly comprehend what you're up against."

Amelia smoothed a hand over her shawl. "I made this while I was pregnant. I wrapped my son in it when he was an infant." She lifted her gaze to Bobbie's. "I've kept it close every night since he was born." She smiled. "And I pray, every night, that he'll come back to me."

Bobbie held her tongue. Why shatter her peace of mind by telling her that was in all probability not going to happen?

"I know it's foolish, but it makes me feel better to imagine that he's out there somewhere with a good life." Her smile returned. "With a woman who loves him and maybe a child."

Her words made Bobbie want to squirm at the need to get up and walk around the room. She shook off the discomfort and changed the subject. "Do you own a weapon?"

"No." Amelia laughed softly. "I've never really had to worry about my safety. Most people think I'm a witch or something far worse. They aren't likely to tempt fate by trying to harm me."

"You really should rethink allowing a temporary

security detail. Weller won't be put off by who or what you are."

She drew in a sharp breath and suddenly stiffened, her shoulders going back and her fingers tightening in her beloved shawl.

"Are you all right?" Bobbie lowered her coffee mug to the table and curled her fingers into a fist, resisting the impulse to reach out to the woman. Some people didn't like to be touched under any circumstances.

As if she'd said as much out loud, Amelia abruptly reached across the table and took Bobbie's hand. "You're worried about everyone else," she said, her voice urgent, "when it's you he really wants."

A few strained minutes later Bobbie left the shop and stepped into the cold night air. She drew in a big breath and let go the tension that had climbed deep into her muscles. From the moment she was briefed on the case all she wanted was to find the connection between Weller and the children. For reasons not completely clear to her yet, she suspected Amelia Potter was the key. Somehow she was far more deeply entrenched in this than merely being the parent of a victim.

Bobbie crossed the street and hurried toward her car. The music from a club somewhere nearby drifted in the night air. She hugged herself and rubbed her arms. She'd almost reached her car when she saw *him*.

Nick waited, leaning against the driver's door

as if there wasn't a BOLO out on him, as if Weller wasn't out there hoping to ruin him or worse.

She defied her initial reaction to seeing him and mustered the anger she'd felt last night. "I thought you wanted to be alone."

He pushed off her car but stopped short of moving toward her. Instead he stood stone still and waited for her to come closer.

When she stopped in front of him, he said, "I owe you an apology."

She hit the fob, unlocking the car. "Get in. In case you haven't heard, there's a BOLO for you."

He rounded the hood and climbed into the passenger seat while she slid behind the wheel. For half a minute they sat in silence.

When he remained quiet, she said, "Kessler, that FBI agent from Atlanta, is certain these murders are your way of drawing your father here for some sort of showdown. She's setting you up for a murder rap."

"I'm aware."

The words, spoken as if he'd just told her the weather forecast or the time of day, infuriated her. "You mentioned an apology."

"I shouldn't have left the way I did."

She kept her gaze trained forward though she felt his burning into her profile. "That's right, you shouldn't have."

"I don't want you to be hurt anymore, Bobbie. You've been through enough."

"I'm a big girl, Nick. I'm a trained officer of the

law and I've worked as a homicide detective for seven years." She drew in a big breath. "In case you've forgotten, I survived the Storyteller and I survived Steven Devine. Your protection isn't what I need."

If that wasn't clear enough for him, then he wasn't half as smart as she'd thought.

Another long stretch of silence elapsed.

"*I* am not what you need."

"We've had this discussion." She was not going to argue with him. "Thank you for the apology. I guess I'll see you around."

She started the engine and waited for him to get out.

"We should work together." The words were spoken with heavy reluctance. "This once," he added quickly. "As much as I want to focus solely on finding Weller, the children deserve justice. I'm beginning to think finding one will give me the other."

Bobbie turned to him. "And after that?"

He held her gaze, his resolute. "There is no after that."

"All right." Hurt speared her. "How do you want to do this? It's not like you can waltz into the police headquarters and sit in on any briefings."

"You focus on the investigation and we'll analyze what you learn whenever we can. I'll be close."

"Fine."

"Good."

With one last fleeting look, he got out and disappeared into the night.

Twenty-Two

Troy sat outside the house where he'd grown up. The house that had been a happy home for the first six years of his life. Birthdays, Christmases, Thanksgivings. The whole Durham crew, including extended family and close friends, would gather to celebrate. The split-level ranch was the perfect kid-friendly space. There was a pool and woods in the back. Just the kind of place to raise kids.

Except Troy's mistake had shattered that dream. He had torn his mother and father apart. He remembered how they'd slept in separate rooms after Brianne went missing. His mother slept in his sister's bed every night. His parents no longer kissed each other goodbye or shared those secret looks they thought he hadn't noticed. They rarely touched each other at all. Their lives had stopped the day he failed to protect his sister.

"Way to go." He'd screwed up his whole family in one moment of stupidity.

Take care of your sister, Troy. Mommy's counting on you.

That was the last time his mother looked at him with pride in her eyes.

Why the hell couldn't it have been him?

Exhaling all the air in his lungs, he got out of the car. Nothing annoyed him more than the feel of oxygen-rich air filling his lungs once more. He had no fucking idea why his worthless heart kept beating.

His parents were still up. The downstairs lights were on. He'd called hours ago and given them the news. His father would likely have preferred to hear it from anyone else, but that was too bad. No matter how much they hated him, they were still his parents and he would do what he could to protect and help them for as long as he was breathing. Didn't matter if they wanted him to or not.

When he'd first come home after years away, it had torn him up to see how old they looked. He'd spent so much time anywhere but at home, he hadn't been prepared for the consequences of time. His father's heart attack had forced Troy to see that he was no longer the strong, capable man who had busted kneecaps as a cop for better than forty years. He was old and worn-out and weary from loss.

But it was the hurt in his mother's eyes that damaged him the most. She always dredged up a smile for Troy. Always prepared a good dinner for his weekly visit. She talked endlessly about what she and her book club friends were reading. She never talked about Brianne. Never. Troy knew his sister's room was exactly like it had been the last time she'd slept in it, though he hadn't been inside it in twenty-five years. The last time he'd dared to go in there, his father had come unglued and told him never to touch his sister's things again.

At the door, he raised his hand to knock but it suddenly opened. His father, clad in the same brown housecoat he'd owned for as long as Troy could remember, turned and shuffled away, leaving the door open. Troy stepped inside, closed and locked the door. The smell of fresh brewed coffee drew him to the kitchen. His mother poured a cup and placed it on the table. His father dropped heavily into the chair at the head of the table. He reached for the cup of coffee, his hand shaking as he lifted it toward his mouth.

How could so much be the same and yet everything had changed?

They were like strangers stuck with the same last name, in the same town with the same friends and neighbors, stuck in this tragic twilight zone.

"You want coffee?" his mother asked. "I doubt any of us is going to get any sleep."

"No coffee for me, ma'am."

"Have a seat." She gifted him with a dim smile as she took her own seat.

"No, thanks. I just came by to make sure you're

all right." Troy stood just inside the kitchen door. On Sundays when he came over for dinner they used the dining room. He felt like an outsider in this kitchen. This was the place where he and Brianne had eaten oatmeal every morning. They'd made macaroni art and cookies at Christmas. He no longer belonged in here or even in this house.

"Already told you we don't need a security detail," his father snapped.

Troy shifted his attention to him. "I'm not here about the security detail."

His mother's face paled.

"You've attended the same church with the Cortlands, Wilsons and Cottons your whole lives. You were friends. Brianne and I played with their kids. We all knew the Sanderses. We took that old hound dog to him when she got sick." Troy summoned his courage. "Why Brianne? Why the others? Of all the children in Savannah, why did he take them?"

No one spoke or even looked at him—it was as if someone had suddenly pushed Pause on the movie of their lives. Anger overrode his good sense.

"I remember the hushed meetings between the two of you," he said to his father, accusation thick in his tone, "and the other fathers. Something was wrong and it started when the Foster girl was murdered."

Outrage flashed on his father's face. "You don't know anything!"

Troy stepped closer to where he sat. "You might

not have been in charge of the investigation, but you were aware that Randolph Weller was called to evaluate the Bonner boy. You had to know and yet not one word about it was in the file. Why is that? Why are so many of Detective Rhodes's reports missing?" He hitched his thumb at his chest. "I'm astonished at all that's missing from the case file. Every time I interview someone, I learn something else that should have been documented. How did that happen?" He braced his hands on the table and leaned closer to his father. "Why did *you* allow it to happen?"

His mother abruptly stood and walked out the back door. The screen door slammed against its frame, the sound like a slap in his face. He straightened and forced himself to take a breath.

"Is that what you came here to do?" his father snarled. "Upset your mother? Haven't you hurt her enough?"

His father was right.

Troy backed up a step. "Whatever you think of me, whatever happened all those years ago, if you want to protect her, then you'd better listen up. This bastard Weller is here for revenge or some sort of twisted game." He turned his hands up. "I can't even begin to see how any of this ties to him or what his goal is, but it's real. It's happening. Something's even more wrong than we know with what happened all those years ago and now the people who were a part of it are dying. If you know something that can help me, for God's sake tell me."

"Go do your job," his father blustered. "You're wasting your time here."

Troy nodded. He'd been wasting his time hoping for his parents' forgiveness for years. Hell, he didn't know why he expected them to forgive him when he couldn't forgive himself.

Twenty-Three

Hoyt Wilson felt ashamed.

He had done a number of things in his life that he regretted and he had tried to make up for those. He had endeavored especially hard to atone for one sin in particular. That vile deed had cost him dearly. The very idea that Wayne Cotton had called to demand that they meet at the church, of all places, was unconscionable.

This was God's house. How could they even talk about such evil within these holy walls?

Hoyt shook his head. "Charlie Grogan told me the police are investigating the possibility that someone Edward fired murdered him. The FBI agent who came all the way from Atlanta says that serial killer they're looking for had nothing to do with Edward's murder. And then she mentioned his son. I'm completely confused."

Wayne whirled on him. "Are you senile? Have

you finally lost the final remnants of any good sense you ever possessed? Our high and mighty Mayor Grogan has no idea what the FBI is doing. He knows what they want him to know. The damned chief of police isn't even sure."

Anger stirred in Hoyt's belly. He tried hard to be a patient man. Never to say anything unkind about anyone, but Wayne Cotton was sorely testing his limits. "I came here this morning like you asked, but I'm not going to stand here and put up with your attitude."

"Someone knows what we did," Wayne snarled. "Don't you see? It's no longer our ugly little secret. Edward is dead because he was the one who provided the place for disposing the body. Maybe that's why Allison walked into that lake. Maybe she wanted them to drag the water so they'd find his damned bones."

Hoyt shook his head. "How would Allison know? We agreed never to tell anyone, not even our wives."

"Edward was dying." Wayne exhaled a heavy sigh. "He told me he confessed to Allison and that's why she killed herself. Fucking old fool."

"He didn't tell me that."

"Of course he didn't," Wayne mocked. "He knows you don't like to discuss those things."

Fury simmered inside Hoyt. For thirty-two years he had hated Wayne Cotton. He'd pretended nothing had changed. Acted as if they were still pals for all to see. "We should never have listened to you."

Wayne laughed long and hard. Hoyt's fingers curled into fists to prevent reaching out and strangling the son of a bitch. Maybe Edward had told his wife, but no one else had ever known. Not Bill Sanders. Not even Luke Durham had been certain they were the ones who took that boy. He'd suspected but he hadn't known for sure.

"It's a little late to whine about that now," Wayne said. "Besides, Edward was the one who came up with the plan."

Hoyt shook his head. "No, no. It was *your* idea."

Wayne glared at him. "Are you calling me a liar?"

Hoyt ignored his demand. He did not want to talk about this anymore. He preferred not to think about it at all, but there was no help for it now. "It's Lucille Bonner. She figured out what we did and she took our babies." Agony swelled in him like a massive black tidal wave. His little boy would not have suffered this awful end if not for their actions. That one snap decision had cost them all far more than they would have ever dreamed.

"We all thought she was the one." Wayne fired back. He laughed then. "She was fucking crazy and that Potter bitch, hell she was even crazier. You were afraid to even pass her on the street."

"I wasn't the only one who was afraid." They'd all been afraid of Amelia Potter looking into their eyes and seeing what they'd done.

"Obviously she wasn't the one we should've been worried about," Wayne snapped.

"*Obviously* we didn't understand how deep the betrayal went," Hoyt snapped right back. "Bill and Nancy are dead. Our children—" hurt howled inside him "—were in that fucking cemetery all these years. Bill, at the very least, had to be involved."

Sanders had played the part of good friend all these years. He'd spearheaded the search for the children when they went missing. How could he do such a thing? Dear God, Hoyt wished he didn't know these things…wished he could go back in time and undo all the ugliness.

Wayne threw up his hands. "Maybe they were all in it together." He paced back and forth in the small meeting room. "Bill may have helped Lucille plan and execute every step. I'll bet he was fucking that crazy old bitch. Her husband sure as hell hadn't been giving it to her."

"You should be ashamed," Hoyt growled. "Her husband was injured working for your father. If she hadn't been rushing to the hospital she wouldn't have had that accident and that boy of hers wouldn't have been born brain damaged. Your family should have helped the Bonners, instead your father fired the man before he was released from the hospital."

Wayne stepped in toe-to-toe with him. "Don't pretend to be better than me. You're just as guilty as I am. Each of us took our turn beating him."

"He wasn't supposed to die!" Hoyt shook with the anger and the self-loathing charging through his chest.

"But he did," Wayne snarled. "Somehow that bitch figured out what we'd done and she got even, didn't she? Apparently, our old friend Bill helped her."

Tears burned Hoyt's eyes. She had taken their babies and they couldn't tell a soul they suspected her. They'd watched her every move but they'd had no proof. They'd threatened her. Hoyt closed his eyes. So many horrible, horrible words. She'd just smiled and said she had no idea what they meant.

So they'd kept their mouths shut and never told a soul.

"You were the one," Hoyt accused, his voice wobbling. "Don't you dare try to pin it on Edward. If you—"

Wayne scoffed. "You're pathetic."

"I won't talk about this anymore." Hoyt held up his hands and backed away. "I can't do it."

Wayne pointed a finger at him. "We have to ride this out and keep our mouths shut just like we have all these years."

God have mercy on them. Now Hoyt understood what this impromptu meeting was about. "You're worried I'm going to tell." He shook his head. "It's too late to come clean now. My boy is dead." Renewed rage sparked inside him. "They're all dead and nothing we do now is going to make a difference."

"Make sure you remember that when the police knock on your door," Wayne warned. "Edward is dead and so is his wife. There's a strong possibility we'll end up the same way, but I will not have my family's name ruined by a mistake we made thirty-two years ago."

Except it hadn't been a mistake. Hoyt walked out of the room and then the church without looking back. No. What they did to that poor mentally challenged boy had not been a mistake.

It was premeditated, cold-blooded murder.

Twenty-Four

Troy slid into the booth and braced his forearms on the table. "I appreciate your agreeing to have breakfast with me."

Bobbie relaxed into the vinyl leather seat. She was beat. Too many nights without a decent amount of sleep...*too many murders*. "We both needed a break." She summoned a smile. "According to one of the brochures at the inn, this is home to the best breakfast in the city."

A faint smile tugged at his lips. "It's in the top five for sure."

Edward Cortland's friends and neighbors had reiterated that he was depressed and grieving the recent loss of his wife but none had any idea if there was anything new going on in his life. Cortland had kept to himself since the funeral. Not the first neighbor had seen any strangers near his home. A forensic tech had discovered his cell phone in the house. No calls or text messages to unknown recipients showed up. Of course his phone records—cell, home and business—might tell a different story, but obtaining those records took time.

Without any real leads as to where the danger was coming from, it was difficult to know how to warn the public. Ellis, the local FBI field agent was happy to assist in the investigation no matter that Kessler appeared disinterested. That bitch had an agenda—making Nick the same sort of monster his father was.

Bobbie could not allow that to happen. Nick had reluctantly agreed to work with her. For that she was grateful. Their chances of beating Weller were far better if they worked together.

Troy surveyed the diner before meeting Bobbie's gaze once more. "I'm worried about my parents."

And why wouldn't he be? Parents of one of the missing children were dead. The murder of the Sanderses and the revelation of the children's remains weren't likely a mere coincidence. Troy had a right to be concerned about the safety of his parents.

"They still refuse a security detail?" The Cottons and the Wilsons remained adamant that security was not necessary. If his personal security systems could have saved him, Cortland wouldn't be at the morgue this morning being dissected. For such intelligent, well-educated people, their decisions were about as logical as trying to sell matches in hell—unless they had secrets of their own.

"I'm not really surprised by that part," Troy admitted. "There's something else." He looked away for a moment before coming clean. "One or both are hiding something."

The waitress arrived and Bobbie paused until she had deposited the stoneware mugs on the table and poured the steaming coffee. When she was gone, Bobbie said, "I understand this is very personal, but I'll need a little more detail."

Troy stared out the plate-glass window, watching the traffic for a time. "My old man was a lieutenant at the time, like me. Violent crimes." He shook his head. "The department should never have allowed him to be a part of the investigation."

Even in a city the size of the Savannah, the police department was a family. Sometimes the rules were ignored when it came to one of their own. "I didn't see any reports completed or signed off on by your father." Bobbie had been aware Troy's father was a retired cop, but she hadn't known he'd been involved with the case of the missing children. "I assumed he stepped aside and allowed Rhodes to take charge."

Troy made a sound that could in no way be mistaken for a laugh. "He and his captain grew up together. The chief at the time wanted all his best cops on the case. They weren't about to ask him to stand aside."

"You believe his involvement compromised the investigation somehow?"

"I honestly don't know. There was something

going on back then." He peered into his coffee mug. "It was more than the pain and fear and grief—at least with my father. He was on the edge all the time. He was never home. My mother cried every waking hour."

Bobbie propped her forearms on the table, matching his stance, and leaned closer. "You could be describing my life the first eight months of this year. Your parents had a right to feel all those emotions and more." She closed her eyes and shook her head. "Losing a child hurts like nothing else in this world. Nothing makes the pain go away."

Troy scrubbed a hand over his jaw. "Maybe I'm using this as some way to excuse what I did. Hell, I don't know anymore."

Bobbie knew. This man had punished himself for three decades. She reached out, placed her hand on his. He lifted his gaze to hers. "You were a child yourself. It was a terrifying time for you. Besides the guilt you felt, you were experiencing uncertainty. Your parents were in a shaky place that made your whole world feel off balance and out of control. It was way too much for a six-year-old to handle."

He turned his hand palm up and closed his fingers around hers. "Thank you."

"Balancing the pain and guilt isn't an easy task. Keeping it inside only makes it worse." God, she sounded like her shrink. She shook her head. "Granted, giving that advice is a hell of a lot easier than incorporating it into your life. I haven't been fighting this battle nearly as long as you, but it takes a toll."

"Tell me about Weller," he urged. "Not the part I can read in the FBI reports or on Google. Tell me about *him*."

It was far easier to track a killer when you knew what made him or her tick. "He's brilliant." She thought of the one time they had met—the way he looked at her. "He's envious of his son—of the idea that he doesn't crave the kill. The truly startling part about him is that I think he actually loves Nick. I think it unsettles him as much as it surprises anyone who notices."

"Why is he here?" Troy's fingers instinctively tightened on Bobbie's. As if he'd belatedly realized, he drew his hand away. "Is there a chance he was involved with the Sanders murders?"

Fair question. They had touched on it before. "The FBI's reports will tell you that he claimed something about his victims inspired him. Made him want to deconstruct them and that's probably accurate for the most part. But the nurse who helped him escape, she was chopped up the same way and I doubt his motive had anything to do with artistic inspiration. He had an objective and she was a way to accomplish it. I think the Sanderses are like the nurse. They were somehow necessary to what he hopes to accomplish in Savannah. As for whether or not he killed them, I don't believe he did. As much as he wants to accomplish his endgame here, his self-preservation instincts are far too strong to play so fast and loose."

Bobbie hesitated before sharing the scenario she'd been toying with.

"What're you thinking?" He searched her eyes, his showing the kind of desperation she knew far too well.

"It's possible he formed some conclusion about who took the children since he evaluated Treat Bonner. He's known certain things about the case all these years and now he plans to expose those long-buried secrets. Whatever his objective it's related to Nick. There's something about this case he wants him to see. Some wrong or hidden aspect that no one has found. Maybe he wants to show that he can be the hero if he chooses." Bobbie shook her head. "I'm doubtful about that last part."

Troy weighed her words for a moment. "If Weller is doling out some twisted form of his own justice, my parents' names could be on his short list. How can I protect them if they won't tell me the truth?"

"Put a surveillance detail on them without their permission." The chief had done it to her more than once.

"He'd spot it in a New York minute."

"Would it help to divide and conquer?" Bobbie hated the idea of suggesting he attempt to get his parents alone, one at a time, and question them. His mother was likely the weaker link. She might talk if the father wasn't around.

"What do you have in mind?"

· "I could interview your mother." She shrugged. "It can't hurt to go at this from a different direction."

"I would really appreciate it."

Their food arrived. The scent alone had Bobbie's appetite revving up. As they ate, she contemplated the possibility of Durham's father being involved even if his actions proved nothing more than his looking the other way. As ugly as it was, it was a distinct possibility based on how sloppy Detective Rhodes's work appeared to have been. At this point Bobbie had decided it was less about disorganization and more about protecting someone.

When she had scarfed down the last scrap of eggs and pancakes she could handle, she pushed her plate aside and thought about the most logical options. "Do you ever recall your parents socializing with any of the other parents, including the Fosters?"

"I remember the occasional church picnic or social with all but Ms. Potter and Mrs. Bonner. They didn't attend the church where we went. All the fathers served in one leadership position or another at the church."

The waitress paused at their table and refilled their cups.

When she'd moved on, Bobbie said, "Your father and the guys never went fishing or hunting? Bowling?"

Troy cracked a real smile. "They weren't friends like that, at least my family didn't fit into that social circle. My father's real friends were cops."

"The families were the wealthy and the powerful. Is it possible any or all of them were suffering from financial woes?" She hesitated and then forged on. "Were insurance payouts collected on the children?"

For a moment he looked taken aback then he shook his head. "There's nothing in the case files about insurance payouts. I imagine if there were any they were hardly substantial."

She wasn't so sure how he would take her suggestion but it was the only logical option. "We need to be talking to your father's cop friends. Those who worked with him at the time will know if steps were overlooked or purposely left out of the reports." Getting them to say as much was a whole other issue.

Troy picked up his cup and then seemed to decide he didn't have the stomach for another sip. "That could start a war."

"What do you mean?"

"Half the cops in Metro are second or third generation. They'll see through what we're doing right out of the gate and shut it down."

"Let me try speaking to your mother," Bobbie offered. "We'll see where things go from there."

Troy agreed to set it up. As they exited the quaint building, Bobbie hesitated at the passenger door. "Have you interviewed everyone who was on the force at the time the children were abducted?"

"Twice. The story is always the same. Rhodes did everything he could do. His partner, Freddie Chapin, did everything he could do."

Before Bobbie could ask, he added, "Chapin was shot and killed in the line of duty seven years after the abductions."

Well, damn. "Maybe there really is nothing to know other than the sheer desperation of parents scrambling to find their children. It's an unimaginable place to be."

He exhaled a heavy breath. "You're right. I'm sorry. I guess this case is bringing back a lot of bad memories for you, too."

Bobbie hitched the strap of her bag a little higher on her shoulder and confessed, "It's not my favorite kind of case, but murder is never easy."

"Thanks for coming all this way and—" he shrugged "—for staying. You could easily have turned right back around and walked away."

Not as long as Weller was out there. *And Nick.* "It's what we do."

"A good cop doesn't stop until the job is done," he offered.

Except it was never really done. There was always another depraved killer out there like Randolph Weller or Steven Devine...or Gaylon Perry.

And another victim.

Willow Road
1:00 p.m.

Heather Durham opened the door after the second knock. Surprise lit her eyes. "Bobbie." She glanced over Bobbie's shoulder and didn't see Troy and her surprise turned to fear. "Has something happened?"

"No. Nothing new," Bobbie assured her. "I just had a few minutes and I wanted to ask you a couple of questions if you have a moment."

Bobbie had watched the house for the past hour. Finally about three minutes ago Troy's father had pulled out of the driveway and headed toward town. There was no way to guess how long he would be gone, so getting straight to the point was imperative.

"Well, certainly." Heather opened the door and stepped aside. "Would you like something to drink? Tea or coffee?"

"Coffee would be great." Bobbie shivered. "I haven't been able to get warm all morning." She wished she'd brought thicker socks and a heavier coat.

"Let's go to the kitchen. I have some homemade pumpkin pie if you're interested." She laughed softly. "It's Troy's favorite."

"Sounds great." Bobbie couldn't remember the last time she'd had pumpkin pie.

"Please sit down." Heather gestured to the round table in the center of the large kitchen.

Bobbie pulled out a chair and took a seat. She waited until the coffee and pie were served and Heather had joined her at the table. "I know the events surrounding your daughter's disappearance are painful, but it's important that we know as many accurate details as possible. A case like this is particularly difficult with so much time under the bridge. Folks with good memories who are willing to talk are priceless."

Heather picked at her pie with her fork. "What would you like to know?

"Having a child missing is unimaginable heart-break and incredible stress," Bobbie began. "That level of intense emotion generally leads to high tension."

"It was the most painful time in my life." Heather set her fork aside. "I wouldn't wish that kind of pain on my worst enemy."

"Being involved with the investigation must have been immensely difficult for Mr. Durham."

She nodded. "More than you can imagine." Her breath caught and she put a hand to her chest. "I'm sorry. Of course you know exactly how that feels."

Bobbie gave a sad nod. "That's the reason I wanted to speak with you personally. I do under-stand how you feel."

A moment of knowing silence passed between them.

"Ask whatever you need to ask," Heather of-fered.

"Was there anything you felt Mr. Durham and the others investigating the case should have done differently?"

Heather shook her head. "I'm certain everyone on the case did all within their power to find the children. Luke would never have let our child or anyone else's down."

"But there was tension between the two of you."

She looked away a moment, then said, "The tension Troy noticed during that awful time had nothing to do with the case."

Bobbie waited—there was more?

"Luke was having an affair with Delores Waldrop."

Definitely not the answer Bobbie had expected to hear. "I'm sorry. I know that must have made life even more difficult."

She cradled her cup of coffee. "Honestly, if he'd been able to find Brianne and bring her home, I wouldn't have cared how many affairs he had. In fairness to them, Delores had just lost her husband after an extended illness. She was in a bad place. With the long hours she and Luke were spending together, it was a miracle it didn't happen sooner. She came to me later and apologized."

"You accepted her apology?" Bobbie wasn't so sure she could have been so forgiving.

"Not the first time." A sad smile touched her lips. "But she just kept coming back. She offered to resign from her job. Luke did the same. Maybe I'm a fool, but I really do believe they were sincerely miserable that they had allowed it to happen. In the end, I had to let it go. I love my husband. Delores is a good friend to both of us."

"Luke is a lucky man." Bobbie shifted directions. "What about the other parents? Did you notice any unexpected behavior or tensions among them? Or with the Sanderses?"

Heather considered her question. "Since Troy asked, I've gone over and over those first few days and weeks after Brianne and the others vanished. There was something going on between Luke and the other fathers. It was as if the others, Hoyt, Wayne and Edward were on one side and Luke was on the other. I chalked it up to his being involved with the investigation. I'm sure there were moments when he made them feel as if they were suspects. In truth, their relationships never recovered."

"What about Bill Sanders?"

"Bill." She inhaled a breath as if simply saying his name was painful. "He kept trying to play peacemaker. He threw himself into the part of advocate. He focused on rallying the community to help with the search and then the healing."

She looked away but not before Bobbie saw the battle she fought to hold the tears back.

"I can't believe he did this." The tears won the battle.

Half an hour later Bobbie still felt stunned as she drove away. Heather had asked her not to tell Troy about the affair. Bobbie agreed. The affair was irrelevant.

Some secrets should stay secret.

Twenty-Five

Heather Durham's comment about the fathers having some sort of issue after the children went missing had stuck with Bobbie. Since both Wayne Cotton and Hoyt Wilson had repeated nearly word for word the same responses to Troy's questions when they were interviewed about Cortland's murder, Bobbie decided they should be interviewed again. Only this time without advance notification.

Troy had agreed without hesitation.

He pressed the doorbell of the Wilson home a second time.

Another minute passed before the locks turned and the door opened. Deidre Wilson stood in the doorway. "Troy." Unable to conceal her surprise, she looked from him to Bobbie. "Has something else happened?"

Deidre Wilson was a petite woman. Her short, curly locks were the same red her little boy had sported in the case file photo. The natural-looking color reminded Bobbie of the old commercial her mother used to repeat after having her dark hair highlighted. *Only her hairdresser knows for sure.* Dressed as if she'd spent the day at Neiman Marcus shopping for the latest fashions, Deidre's jade skirt and matching silk blouse complemented her pale complexion and fiery hair.

"No, ma'am, nothing else has happened. Detective Gentry and I have a few more questions for you and Mr. Wilson. Is he home?"

"Actually," she said, "he's not. He's over at Wayne's—Wayne Cotton's. I think they're playing a round of golf. Can I have him call you?"

"That won't be necessary, Mrs. Wilson," Bobbie spoke up. "I'm sure you can clarify the few issues we have with your previous statement. May we come in?"

"Issues?" Deidre frowned. "What issues?"

"We'll only take a moment of your time, ma'am," Troy pressed.

Deidre looked from one to the other. "All right," she conceded. "Come on in."

When they had taken seats in the parlor and the lady of the house had offered the expected refreshments, Troy allowed Bobbie to take the lead.

"Mrs. Wilson, you and your husband stated that you hadn't spoken with Mr. or Mrs. Cortland recently. When you attended Mrs. Cortland's funeral, it was the first time you'd seen Mr. Cortland in several weeks. Is that correct?"

Deidre seemed to assess the question. "Yes. We're so busy, you know. I'm involved in so much charity work. I started an advocacy center for the mothers of missing children twenty years ago. So often there are no proper support services for those left behind. After I lost my little boy, it was very important to me to help others cope with the same sort of nightmare."

"The work you do is above and beyond," Troy commented. "It's a great service to the community."

Deidre smiled, her face flush with pride. "It's not nearly as important as what the police do," she offered. "Finding justice for the children who are taken and…and oftentimes harmed, is far more vital. Are you any closer to determining why Bill would have done such an awful thing?" Her voice quivered on the last.

"We don't believe he worked alone," Troy admitted, "but we still have a long way to go sorting out what happened."

Deidre put a hand to her chest. "When I first learned that my Heath was dead—I mean, I should have known after all these years, but I always hoped." She drew in a deep breath. "When you told us what really happened, I fell apart. I couldn't believe anyone I knew would do such a horrible, horrible thing. Once I pulled myself together, I realized that, at this point, all that mattered was justice. What else is left?"

Bobbie watched the determination and something like hatred harden in the other woman's eyes. "I'm certain your department will do all within their power to solve this puzzle and find justice for the children."

Deidre blinked away the emotions and squared her shoulders. "Do you think Hoyt and I are in danger from that serial killer? What's his name? Randolph Weller? Is he really running around Savannah killing people?" She put her hand to her chest again. "I've been hearing all these awful things on the news."

The media had latched on to the Weller story and turned it into a true Halloween boogieman horror story. In truth, they weren't far off the mark. So far Bobbie had managed to duck the reporters whenever they descended on Troy. The last thing they needed was the media dragging her life story into the circus they were quickly creating.

"I'm concerned about that, too," Troy said.

Bobbie resisted the urge to give him the thumbs-up. The man had just found the perfect opportunity to push the idea of a security detail.

"Oh my." Deidre looked from him to Bobbie and back. "Should I be concerned that he's coming for us next?"

"At this time all I can say is that I would urge you to reconsider the security detail I offered."

Deidre hesitated, then sighed. "I think you're right. We do need a security detail. Thank you, Troy. You're a good man. The world needs more like you."

Outside, as they loaded into Troy's SUV, Bobbie shot him a grin. "Good job."

He grinned back at her, the first genuine one she'd seen since they met. "Let's see if we get so lucky next time."

As they left, Deidre Wilson waved from the front door. For a woman who was frightened for her safety, she hadn't been in any hurry to close the door and lock it behind her. Instead, she remained on the porch, watching until they had driven away.

Myrtlewood Drive
4:50 p.m.

Shelia Cotton didn't appear the slightest bit surprised at their visit. Bobbie suspected Deidre Wilson had given her a call. After all, what were friends for?

A couple of years younger than Deidre, Shelia was a fashionable dresser. Her elegant slacks were navy and her cashmere sweater was the same dark blue. Shelia was tall with brown eyes and dark hair that she wore draped around her shoulders. The lush mane lacked even the slightest hint of gray. She carried herself like a dancer. Unlike Deidre who helped her husband with his grocery store chain, Shelia had been a stay-at-home mother to their two older children.

"Wayne will be sorry he missed you," Shelia said to Troy. "He's off discussing a new mall project with his architectural team."

Troy nodded. "I would have thought he'd be on the golf course on a Sunday afternoon."

Shelia waved off the idea. "Please, he never golfs when it's this cold."

"Deidre Wilson," Bobbie spoke up, "mentioned that the two of you spoke with Allison Cortland shortly before her death." It was a lie but Shelia didn't know that at the moment. Bobbie decided not to look at Troy just in case shock had descended on his face.

Shelia appeared taken aback for a moment. "Well," she made a breathy sound, "we've had tea together every week for forty years. Of course we spoke to her. We had tea on the Friday before... before her death on Tuesday."

"Did she appear particularly upset about anything?" Bobbie asked now that the lid was off the box.

"Of course she was upset." Shelia appeared more than a little peeved. "She'd only just found out a week or week and a half beforehand that her husband was dying." She glanced at Troy. "I'm certain you can imagine how devastating that news was."

"I surely can," Bobbie assured her. "I should have framed my question more clearly. Was she upset about anything other than the news about her husband? Deidre seemed to think she was struggling with something else."

That "deer caught in the headlights" look took hold of Shelia for a moment. "No." She shook her head, banishing the expression. "Allison didn't mention being upset about anything other than Edward. Not to me anyway."

Bobbie asked, "Were you surprised that she would take her life when her husband needed her most?" Next to her, Troy shifted in his seat.

Shelia stared at Bobbie for a long moment, then something in her demeanor changed. Gone was any sign of uncertainty or discomfort. "Allison was a good wife to Edward. She did what she thought she needed to do. Edward had the means to take care of himself."

Troy asked, "Has your husband mentioned anyone who might have wanted to hurt Mr. Cortland?"

"Edward made his share of enemies," Shelia said. "But you'd be better served speaking to Wayne about that."

"What about your husband?" Bobbie ventured. "Does he have any enemies?"

Shelia stared at her for another of those long moments. "I suppose everyone has a few."

Before Bobbie could ask anything else, Shelia said, "Should Wayne and I be worried about this awful serial killer we saw on the news? Will he try to hurt us next?"

While Troy assured her that the department was doing everything possible to stop the person or persons responsible for the murders, Bobbie watched the lady. She wasn't afraid or concerned. The idea that her question about Weller was so similar to Deidre's niggled at Bobbie.

These two women knew things they had no intention of sharing. She could feel it.

The good news was that Troy persuaded Shelia Cotton to accept a security detail, as well.

Maybe they should go at the husbands the same way, one by one and separately from their wives.

Sometimes the pieces of a puzzle had to be pulled apart before they could be properly put together.

Twenty-Six

Bobbie climbed the final set of stairs to her room. Wayne Cotton and Hoyt Wilson had stuck by their stories. Neither made the first misstep in repeating their claims. Both maintained that they had never received ransom demands or threatening contact of any sort after the abduction of their children. Both also insisted they'd had little or no life insurance on their children.

No matter how many ways she asked the same questions, the answers were consistently the same. Some would say such flawless consistency was a good indicator the two were telling the truth. Bobbie wasn't so sure. Sounded more like well-rehearsed responses to her. And why not? Cortland, Wilson and Cotton had been telling the same story for thirty-two years. Durham, on the other hand, had stayed oddly quiet. He'd given his statement in the beginning and, according to Troy, had refused to speak of the case again.

What had those men done to incur the wrath of someone—presumably Bill Sanders—ruthless enough to snatch and murder their small children? Heather Durham had noted a taking of sides, so to speak, among the men involved.

Maybe there was some tie between the Sanderses and the Foster family. Or the Bonners. But what would that have to do with the children whose remains were found in those statues? If not for money or sexual perversion, what motive would anyone have for taking those children?

The only good news she had learned today was that Troy's mother and father weren't likely involved beyond being the parents of one of the missing. Any noted tension had been about the affair and the strain put on Luke's relationship with the other fathers during the course of the investigation. She'd thought Troy would break down into tears when she recounted the conversation she'd had with his mother—leaving out the details of the affair. Instead of breaking down, Troy had hugged her for the longest time. This case was a tough one for him, but she didn't blame him for wanting to stay on top of it.

As she reached the landing on the third floor, Bobbie stalled. Amelia Potter stood in front of her door. Clutched to her chest was a paper shopping bag, the kind with handles that boutiques and higher end department stores used.

"Hey." Bobbie walked toward her—the closer she came, the more fear she recognized in the other woman's eyes. "Has something happened since we spoke this afternoon?"

She and Troy had stopped by The Gentle Palm and briefly questioned Amelia. Like the others, she was unable to provide any additional useful information. Unlike the others, Bobbie believed she was telling the truth for the most part. She still felt Amelia was leaving something out. Maybe it was nothing significant, but it was there.

"I need to speak with you privately." Laughter coming from a room down the hall snapped her gaze in that direction.

Definitely jumpy. "Of course. I hope you didn't wait too long. You could have called."

Amelia shrugged. "I don't like to talk on phones."

Bobbie dug for the key in her shoulder bag. "They can be a pain." She unlocked the door, stepped into the room and then turned on the light. "I'm sorry I don't have tea to offer you. I could call room service."

Amelia looked around as she entered the room. Bobbie wondered if the idea of ghosts concerned a woman supposedly gifted in seeing things others didn't.

"I'm fine, thank you." She glanced at the duffel bag on the floor at the end of the bed. "I brought you some things." She thrust the bag she carried at Bobbie. "I thought you might need them."

Bobbie accepted the bag. Inside were two sweaters, a fur-lined jacket and a pair of faded jeans. Thick, warm socks and even a couple of pairs of underwear and a nightshirt. Bobbie wasn't sure what to say. "Thank you. This was very kind of you."

"I rewashed them just to be sure they were fresh and clean." She shrugged. "We're about the same size. I thought these could tide you over until you're back home again."

Bobbie had intended to pick up a few things but she hadn't found the time. She'd ended up washing her panties in the shower last night. She checked the size of the jeans. Should fit. She remembered the first time she went to The Gentle Palm thinking that she needed to pick up some necessities, but she was fairly confident she hadn't mentioned as much to Amelia.

"One question." Bobbie placed the borrowed clothes on the bed, along with the bag. "How did you know I needed extra clothes?"

"Both times I saw you, you were wearing that same sweater."

Well, there was a logical answer that had nothing to do with woo-woo. "Maybe I just like this sweater."

"When you were in my shop the first time," Potter said, "I sensed you were concerned about picking up a few things."

Maybe that something else she'd been holding back wouldn't be contained any longer. Bobbie indicated the chair next to the desk before dropping onto the foot of the bed. "Have a seat." She was too damned tired to stand and finish this conversation. "Is there something else you've sensed? Is that why you're here?"

Amelia smiled but she didn't sit. Instead she pulled her sweater tighter around her. Like the shawl, it was crocheted. Bobbie imagined she'd made it herself. The one sewing project Bobbie had tried in high school when all her friends were making cute short shorts and skimpy tops had turned out badly. She hadn't attempted anything along those lines since.

"I told you that I knew you were coming before you came to my shop."

Bobbie nodded. "You did."

"I didn't tell you everything." Amelia sank into the chair next to the desk.

"I'm listening," Bobbie prompted.

"I keep having this same dream over and over. We—you and I—are in the woods." Her voice grew soft and distant. "We're running. The danger is right behind us. So very close."

"Can you see what or who it is?" Bobbie didn't really believe in fortune-telling or seeing into the future. But what she strongly believed in was some people's ability to sense things others could not. Not really a psychic ability but a heightened awareness of the world around them.

Amelia shook her head. "I only know it's close and that we're in grave danger."

"Are there any other details you can share?"

Her gaze lifted to Bobbie's. "The water. We're in the water together and we're struggling." She shook her head and looked away. "Struggling so desperately. I can see the blood. It leaks into the water and turns it a bright red."

The next second turned into five, then ten before Amelia spoke again, her attention once more settling on Bobbie. "I think one of us is going to die."

10:30 p.m.

Bobbie hurried along the alley, following the same route Nick had taken the night before last. Before leaving the inn she'd sent him a text letting him know she was headed to his place. If this was the way he wanted their interaction, then so be it. She couldn't make him see what she wanted him to see. She could only hope time would.

The moon seemed so close tonight. Her feet slowed as she peered up at it. Almost full. Tomorrow would bring a rare harvest moon for trick or treating. *Halloween.* Last year she and James had taken Jamie from door to door in their neighborhood. They'd pulled him around in the red wagon Newt had bought him for his birthday the year before.

A smile tugged at her lips as the memory came flooding back.

"That's a big wagon for such a little baby," Bobbie teased her partner.

Newt shrugged. "The boy'll grow into it. Wait and see."

And he had. Jamie had grown into the cutest, sweetest toddler. He had pulled that wagon around the backyard just like Newt said he would.

I'm so sorry I let you down, baby.

Bobbie brushed at her eyes with the back of her hand. She wished she'd brought her good running shoes. Four or five miles would definitely burn off some of this pent-up frustration. She walked faster, needing the brisk pace and cold night air to release the tension. She appreciated the clothes Amelia Potter had brought to her. For now she would reserve judgment on the other. Bobbie had never been one to believe in all that woo-woo stuff. Ghosts and psychics had been more Newt's thing. He'd had a healthy respect for those who professed to dabble in the supernatural.

As she reached the same stoop where Nick had hidden before, he stepped into her path.

She rolled her eyes. "I know the way."

His dark eyes assessed her as if he needed to ensure she was in one piece. "I was in the neighborhood."

Bobbie kept walking.

"What have you learned in the past twenty-four hours, Detective?"

So this was how it was going to be. Business. Straight to the point. Bobbie kept her attention forward and her step quick. "I'm sure you already know the cause and manner of Edward Cortland's death."

"I do."

"We've reinterviewed the other players in the case, the Wilsons, Cottons and Durhams. Nothing's changed about their statements. In fact, the statements are so eerily similar they feel rehearsed."

That was it. It was as if the parents of the children in the case had gotten together and prepared responses to any potential questions that might be thrown at them. The one time their responses had faltered was when Deidre Wilson said her husband was playing golf with Wayne Cotton. She hadn't expected the visit or the question so she'd stumbled.

"None have legal or financial problems," Nick said as they reached the alley next to his building. "Then or now."

"There were no ransom payoffs or substantial insurance payouts after the abductions as far as we can tell," she added as they climbed the stairs.

They didn't discuss the case further until they were in Nick's room. Bobbie walked straight to the case map. He'd added more photos and reports. The sheer number of details he knew about all the players amazed her.

"Who's your source in the department?" She turned to him, knowing full well he wouldn't tell her.

He hesitated for a moment, then said, "He isn't

a cop, but he's been in the department longer than most of them, including your lieutenant."

Will wonders never cease? "Thank you."

"Trust isn't the issue between us, Bobbie."

"So you're admitting that there is something between us?"

He gestured to the case map. "You came to discuss the case."

Rather than start another argument, she decided to consider his statements as progress. Focusing on the case, she looked from photo to photo. "None of this really ties together. The Fosters are connected to the Bonners through tragedy but neither is really connected to the others—beyond the fact that the Fosters were wealthy and attended the same church as the Cortlands, Wilsons, Cottons and Durhams."

Nick moved up beside her. He tapped the photo of Christina Foster. "Her murder was the beginning of the tragedies that would befall this group. She was the first domino to fall." He moved on to the photo of Treat Bonner. "He was falsely accused and then disappeared, the second domino."

"Days later the children disappeared," Bobbie picked up from there. "Four of the five were taken from the fall festival. The Potter boy was the only exception. He was taken from his bed. He was the last domino to fall."

Nick gestured to the photos of the parents. "The real answer we need to find is what do these people have in common? All except Potter and the Bonners have money and power. Why was her child added to the mix? What did she possess that put her in the same category as the others? Or was it something she had done?"

"Her statement about seeing Treat Bonner with Christina Foster triggered multiple reactions."

"Weller was called to evaluate him." Nick pointed to Weller's photo.

"He found Bonner incapable of masterminding or executing that level of violence." Bobbie studied the photos of Bonner and Foster. "Have you ever known Weller to choose victims related to a case where he was called in for an evaluation?"

"No."

"You think the Sanderses were murdered only to reveal who took the children all those years ago?"

"I do. It was both a revelation and a warning."

Bobbie surveyed the faces of the parents. "I think they were all—except maybe Potter and the Durhams—involved in what happened somehow. Something one or all did. Something Weller knew about or was somehow involved in." Bobbie turned to him. "Did you and your family ever come to Savannah when you were growing up? Did Weller have friends or connections in the city?"

"Not that I remember." As he spoke he moved the photos of the children around on the wall. He placed Christina Foster's photo first, and methodically surrounded it with the other children's, then he tapped Christina's. "As we've already established, she was the trigger."

Bobbie gathered the photos of the parents and

repeated the process, placing Amelia Potter in the center with the parents of the other missing children in a circle around her. "Her child doesn't fit with the others. He wasn't taken from the same setting as the others." She looked to Nick, her pulse rate kicking up. "He was chosen as payback for her statement to the police about the Bonner boy."

"That's why he was taken from his home," Nick agreed. "He wasn't part of the original plan."

"That's why his remains haven't been found." Bobbie put her hand to her mouth, disbelief stealing her breath. "What if he isn't dead? What if he was a replacement for the son Lucille Bonner lost?"

Nick stared at the photos for a bit before turning to Bobbie. "We may be looking at two different cases. Noah Potter was lumped in with the other children only because he went missing on the same night and in the same manner."

"If Lucille Bonner took him," Bobbie began, "where is he now?"

"I believe you and your lieutenant have a new lead to follow up on tomorrow morning."

There was something in his tone...jealousy? "I believe you're right. This is a solid theory."

"Find a connection between Lucille Bonner and Bill Sanders." Nick tapped the veterinarian's photo. "The other children may have been nothing but a distraction to prevent anyone from figuring out what she'd done."

Bobbie considered that one of the children was

a Cotton. "And maybe a little payback for what happened to her husband."

Nick nodded. "Adding the other three children, whose families had no direct ties to her, helped avoid drawing suspicion to herself. She wouldn't have minded taking something so precious from them. They were rich, powerful, likely sided with the Fosters when her son was accused. They had everything and she was left with nothing."

Bobbie turned to him. "Would the circumstances of this case have drawn Weller somehow? Intrigued him?"

Nick considered her question for a time. "As I said before, Potter would have intrigued him. I see nothing about the others that would draw his attention. His victims were typically those who, for whatever reason, couldn't or wouldn't take care of themselves much less contribute to society. None of the people involved in this case fit his preferred criteria, which indicates there's a different motive. The nurse, his longtime attorney, the driver and the courier were executed for no other reason than they were in the way of an objective. He made no attempt to turn them into art by painting the scene of their deaths."

"We've never talked about why he kills." When Nick's gaze lit on hers once more, she went on, "I know he claims his victims inspired him, but what made him need to kill to capture that inspiration? What perverse hole in his soul did all those murders fill?"

Every killer, even serial killers as heinous as Weller, had motives. They had histories and reasons they became what they became. Not that any reason was an excuse to commit murder, but it gave a glimpse into the killer's soul.

"You're looking for his profile, is that it? You didn't like the one the feds created?"

"I haven't been privy to the profile the FBI created for Weller." She studied his face, looking for any hint of what he was thinking. "I'm certain you created his profile long ago." Nick was as good as any profiler at the FBI's illustrious BAU. He didn't like to talk about Weller so they had never delved into the subject of how he became a notorious serial killer. She'd done some research on him, but she wanted to know what Nick thought... what he *felt*.

"He was born in Chicago to parents who were hand-to-mouth factory workers. They had nothing. They lived in a small apartment over a butcher shop."

"Were they loving parents?"

He stared at her as if the question hadn't occurred to him, but she knew that wasn't true even before he answered. "According to my source they were, yes. They spent money they didn't have to spare feeding beggars, even going so far as to allow hungry strangers to spend the night in their apartment rather than freeze on the street."

Bobbie shuddered as her mind conjured images of slabs of meat in display cases. She'd been in a couple of butcher shops. There was a smell she suspected couldn't be washed away even with bleach. The smell of freshly cut, chilled meat and cold blood had no doubt been a part of Weller's everyday life.

"Was there ever any trouble with the beggars they took in?"

"Only once. Mr. Thompson, the owner of the butcher shop, warned Weller's father that he could no longer bring in strangers off the street, even for a meal."

"Sounds like the Thompsons were looking out for him." Bobbie felt no sympathy for whatever Weller had suffered.

"Most days when Weller came home from school, his parents were still at work," Nick went on, "so he hung out in the butcher shop. The man and his wife had no children of their own so they enjoyed having him around. The butcher, Mr. Thompson, took Weller with him when he made his weekly trips to the packinghouses where Weller routinely played on the killing floors. Sometimes he was even allowed to use the large meat cleavers to help cut the hogs."

"Jesus." What kind of person allowed a child to play where animals were being slaughtered much less allowed them to participate?

"It wasn't as strange as you think," he countered. "At the time grade school children were taken on tours of the stockyards and packinghouses. Watching the hog slaughter was a major event in Chicago during the better part of the twentieth century."

Bobbie attempted to see beyond the matter-of-fact tone and expression he maintained. "How do you know all this? Did he tell you stories about his childhood?" They had talked about Nick's childhood but he hadn't mentioned stories about Weller's childhood.

"No, he never spoke of his early life. I interviewed Mrs. Thompson ten years ago, when she was ninety-seven. She still remembered him. She'd never made the connection between the child she enjoyed as if he were her own and the serial killer in the news."

Before Bobbie could ask, he said, "I didn't tell her. I saw no reason." He shrugged. "She died three years later on her one hundredth birthday."

"What about your grandparents? Were they still alive when you were a child?"

"My mother was a foster child. She never knew her real parents and she despised her foster parents, so I never knew them. Weller's parents died in a suspicious fire at the factory where they worked when he was twelve."

"Who took him in after that?"

"The Thompsons. He lived with them until he went off to college. According to Mrs. Thompson, he never showed the slightest emotion about their deaths. He came home from school, Mr. Thompson informed him what had occurred and he asked what was for supper. He sat stoically at the funeral. Never shedding a single tear."

"She never noticed anything odd about him?"

Nick considered her question a moment as if he had grown weary of the subject. "When Weller was sixteen, her husband found him in the bathroom at the packinghouse masturbating after helping on the killing floor. She said things were never the same between them after that. She cried when she confessed that from that point until he left for college her husband beat him often."

Was that childhood enough to turn Weller into the monster he became? Bobbie couldn't say, but she did see one conspicuous fact. "So neither of his parents was a killer?"

"Not as far as anyone knew."

Bobbie folded her arms across her chest. "So you looked into it?"

"I did."

"So much for DNA making monsters." Rather than give him the opportunity to debate the statement, she surveyed the case map and announced, "We make a good team."

He tensed at her words, but she wasn't taking them back. It was true. When she refused to look away from him, he reluctantly met her gaze. "Talking about Weller's childhood doesn't change anything. This is only temporary, Bobbie. When this is over, I'll be gone."

She shook her head. "You just can't admit that you feel something for me."

"You've mistaken basic human compassion for something it's not. I lost the capacity to feel anything more profound long ago."

He started to look away but she stopped him with a hand on the center of his chest. He flinched at her touch. "As long as your heart is still beating—" the strong pounding beneath her palm confirmed her belief "—there is no limit on what you can feel."

He pulled her hand free of his chest but didn't immediately let go. "Not the way you think."

When she would have argued, he released her. "I should walk you back."

Bobbie let it go for now, but the debate was far from over.

Twenty-Seven

Over the years Randolph Weller often thought of Savannah. Quite a lovely place if one had a taste for the dankness of the river and the constant influx of rude tourists. Speakeasies, historic architecture and hauntings had never been on his bucket list. No, he'd never anticipated visiting Savannah again.

He'd expected the dead to stay buried along with the secrets this oldest city in Georgia harbored just for him. A smile eased across his lips when he considered that his friends at the *F...B...I...*were no doubt scratching their heads and wondering why he would risk coming here. There was an entire task force dedicated to the theory that perhaps the events in Savannah were nothing more than a ploy to distract them while he slipped out of the country and far, far away.

Actually, leaving had been the plan, but this city

had not been a part of it. Regrettably, he'd had to take a detour. He drew in a deep breath, savored the stench of death. The man in the other room was very near that much-feared threshold. No need to bother with him. The woman, however, was quite another matter. She had disrupted Randolph's carefully laid plans. Apparently she had forgotten that he'd already given her an enormous gift. He shook his head. Where was the gratitude? No one appreciated the sacrifices of others these days. What a disgrace.

Until recently Randolph had chosen not to take the life of anyone who really mattered. He had prided himself on selecting those who were a waste of DNA and those who lived their lives for nothing more than to drain society. Really, his efforts to make the world a more beautiful and peaceful place had never been appreciated.

Be that as it may, he wasn't here to wax poetic about the atrocities the common man did every day of his tragic existence. He was here to attend to a mistake he himself had made so many, many years ago.

He glanced at the grandfather clock that stood next to the front door. It was late. He'd waited long enough. With a quick flick of his hand, he overturned the ceramic lamp on the marble topped table next to his chair. The crash shattered the silence. The rustling of covers sounded and then the pad of bare feet on the cold hardwood floor.

The overhead light switched on and she stood

in the doorway, squinting at its brightness. The yellow flannel gown she wore covered her from neck to toes. Her hair was a mousy brown cloud of tangles. When her eyes had focused behind the glasses, her breath caught.

"Good evening, Lucille." He gestured to the sofa. "Please, join me. We have some catching up to do."

She hesitated as if weighing her options. Should she run screaming back into her room and attempt to call for help? Since there were no exterior doors on that end of the house and he'd severed the old-fashioned landline that supplied phone service to her home, there was no help there. To reach the front door or the kitchen door, she would need to move past him. Her options were sorely limited.

"Please," he repeated. "Let's not make this more unpleasant than it needs to be."

She took a step in his direction and then another and another until she reached the sofa. Finally she settled onto the worn cushions.

"Now. Was that so difficult?"

She clasped her hands in her lap. "Why are you here?" Her voice was rusty with sleep and fear.

Randolph laughed. "Why, Lucille, aren't you the one who called my attorney and told him it was imperative you speak with me about the *children*?"

She blinked like an owl. "I didn't know what to do. Cortland told his wife what he'd done. She came to me and asked if I took her child."

"And what did you say, Lucille?"

"I... I told her to leave, that I had nothing to say to her."

Randolph nodded knowingly. "But that wasn't the end of it, was it, Lucille?"

She fiddled with the fabric of her nightgown. "She wouldn't believe me. She just kept on and on until I told her everything."

"A very foolish mistake."

She flung her arms in exasperation. "What choice did I have? She just wouldn't shut up. The next day she walked into that lake and never came back out. I thought everything would be okay after that."

"Ah, but it wasn't."

She shook her head. "It only got worse."

"Tsk. Tsk. I'm afraid you've brought this fate upon yourself, Lucille. I gave you an opportunity all those years ago and you took advantage of my benevolence."

"I... I wanted to show them." She trembled with the fear mounting in her aged body. "They had everything and they took what was mine—the only thing in this world that mattered to me. I just wanted them to feel what they'd made me feel. You told me that was a natural reaction to what I suffered."

"Indeed," he allowed. "When they took your son, you had every right to want revenge. To want to make them suffer that same loss. Your mistake was in having second thoughts. You let me down, Lucille. You should have drowned those children yourself and left their little bodies floating in the Savannah River for all the world to see."

She dropped her head again. "I was afraid. They were so young and innocent. Practically babies. As much as I wanted to hurt their parents, I couldn't kill those babies."

"So you went to your lover."

Her head shot up. "Bill made me happy. We made each other happy. We were both so miserable."

How truly wretched. "Misery does love company."

"He wanted to help me."

"But his wife intervened while the two of you were in her home—in her *bed*—fucking."

Lucille looked away. "She took them into the woods to the stream that runs behind their property and drowned them, one by one."

He sighed. "I'm certain you understand that now I must do something to finish this before it gets further out of control."

"We had a deal," she accused, drawing up a little courage. "I gave you what you wanted." Her lips quivered with the fear no doubt coursing through her veins. "Don't forget that part."

His patience was at an end. "Where is he?"

She shook her head. "I won't tell you. He's suffered enough. He isn't the sweet boy I lost, but he's mine."

"Very well. I'm certain you know I will find him." Randolph should have been far from here

already, but this business had cropped up and he'd
had no choice but to attend to it personally.

"Please," she beseeched. "He needs me. My husband needs me."

Enough. Randolph stood. "Come to me, Lucille."

Without moving off the sofa, she peered up at
him. The plea for mercy in her eyes a waste of his
time as well as her own. "I'll take him and go away.
Please don't do this."

"He should have died all those years ago like
the others. It's time he did."

"No," she cried.

He reached for her, she tried to scramble away
but she was not nearly fast enough. A few quick
slams of her head into the table's sleek marble top
and she stilled. He entwined his fingers in her hair
and dragged her through the living room to the
kitchen. He opened the side door and pulled her
down the two steps to the small, attached garage.
There was no car parked inside, but there were
numerous boxes of junk. Randolph had already
cleared a spot and placed the necessary items he
would need there.

"Dear, dear Lucille, you thought you were so
smart." He stretched her out in the middle of the
cramped space. "I'm afraid I have neither the time
nor the proper setting to prepare a true work of art,
but I'll do the best I can."

He picked up the ax. "Did you really believe I
wouldn't come back to take care of this person-

ally?" He watched her for a moment, enjoying her desperation as her head moved from side to side in an attempt to regain control of her faculties. "If only you'd kept your mouth shut, none of this would have been necessary."

Randolph raised the ax and brought it down on the knee, shattering the patella, sliding through ligaments and cartilage and separating the femur and tibia. Blood spurted and Lucille tried to scream, the sound a feeble howl.

Randolph closed his eyes for a moment and enjoyed the pulsing pleasure of her fear. There was no fear purer than that which came with the knowledge that death was imminent.

He raised the ax a second time.

Twenty-Eight

A US marshal and a GBI agent; Ellis, the FBI agent from the local field office; Special Agent Angela Price from BAU; and the Chatham County sheriff as well as half a dozen members of Metro circled the table in the main conference room. Bobbie had chosen a chair at the back of the room near the door. Troy had stood his ground about her inclusion in the meeting. His chief had backed him up. Troy had boldly asked her to sit next to him with the others but she had declined. A seat close to the nearest exit was a far better position in her opinion.

Savannah's Chief of Police Jim Cafaro glanced repeatedly at Bobbie during the briefing from the federal agents at the table. She had anticipated her name would come up and the feds hadn't disappointed her. Price was the profiler who had come from Quantico to work with Montgomery PD when the Storyteller returned. But she wasn't the only one painted with the broad brushstrokes of their suspicions. While Bobbie's motives weren't to be trusted, Nick was portrayed as a criminal.

Troy spent far too much time countering their remarks with examples of how Bobbie had proven invaluable to the investigation so far. She didn't actually agree with him but she appreciated his backing her up.

According to the report Ellis read from, the feds hadn't found any connection between Weller and the missing children either.

So why are you here, you bastard?

Better question, why the hell hadn't Weller contacted her again? She'd come to Savannah as he'd obviously wanted. What did he want from her now? If Weller had made contact with Nick, he hadn't mentioned it.

Sleep had eluded her last night after the meeting with Nick.

It would be so much easier to be angry with him if she didn't so thoroughly understand his position. Whether he admitted it or not, he was afraid. His father had convinced him that he, too, would one day feel the urge to kill. Nick had taken great care to never put himself in a position where he might have to take a life. His decision to come to Montgomery to help her had put him in exactly that position where it was either kill or be killed for both of them. Afterward he had retreated back to the shadows and was determined to stay there. Bobbie worried that as soon as Weller was stopped, Nick would disappear completely.

The possibility that she might never see him again was not one she was willing to accept.

Bobbie's phone vibrated and she reached into the pocket of her borrowed coat to check the screen. *LeDoux.*

Since the folks around the table were deep in debate as to whether or not Weller was even in Savannah, Bobbie was able to slip unnoticed from the room. Delores waved at her as she hurried through the lobby. Bobbie gave her a wave back. She couldn't help thinking about the affair. So many secrets.

Outside the cool air reminded her that the year was slipping away. Thanksgiving and Christmas would be here before she knew it. Cold settled in the center of her chest at the realization that this would be her first significant holiday season without James and Jamie…without Newt. And Bauer. A year of terrible firsts.

The thought made her feel so very alone.

But you have Nick…for now.

LeDoux waited near her Challenger. She checked the street and hurried across it.

He glanced around. "We should sit in the car while we talk."

Bobbie unlocked her car and slid behind the steering wheel. LeDoux settled into the passenger seat. He looked as if he had been wearing the same clothes since they ran into each other three days ago in Zacharias's house. Like her, he also looked as if he hadn't slept much since that early morning run-in either.

Had it only been three days? It felt like weeks.

"Shade won't respond to my calls."

"Maybe he doesn't trust you." She was still on the fence as to whether or not she trusted LeDoux. Telling him that she and Nick were working together again was more than she was prepared to share.

When the silence dragged on, she glanced at the purportedly fallen agent. He stared straight ahead.

He said, "It's Rodney Pitts, my superior. I think he uses Kessler to do his dirty work, but he's the one."

Bobbie stared at him until he met her gaze. "What do you mean? Pitts hasn't been here. His name hasn't even been mentioned. And Kessler went back to Atlanta. She doesn't believe Weller is involved."

LeDoux shook his head. "First, don't believe anything she tells you. She's the one who kept Weller happy with basically whatever he wanted, except his freedom, of course. Second, it's Pitts who runs the show. You haven't heard his name or seen his face because he keeps plenty of degrees of separation between himself and the dirty work. He's too smart to set himself up to go down. If anyone goes down, it'll be Kessler."

"Do you have any proof of this?" If either agent was involved, there had to be one hell of a motive.

"You'll just have to trust me on that one."

Bobbie laughed. "Like I'm going to trust you without some sort of proof. The last time I trusted you, I was almost dragged into your troubles by your friends in the suits."

"I like how you got a heads-up." He turned to her then. "You couldn't have done me the same courtesy?"

"Why would Kessler or Pitts have facilitated Weller's escape and then pretend to want him captured? Without proof, all you have is an unfounded allegation."

"I didn't say either of them facilitated his escape. To the contrary, Kessler—under Pitts's direction—did whatever necessary to keep him comfortable and cooperative *in* prison. Now he's out there. If he's found, he'll likely reveal how the two facilitated his needs. Not such a good stepping-stone for their careers. I don't think they want Weller found, I think they want him dead."

"I have no problem with that ending." The sooner Weller was erased from this planet, the better for all mankind.

"They won't stop with Weller," LeDoux argued. "They'll want to take out anyone he might have told or who might have figured out what they've done. Like Shade." He met her gaze once more. "And the two of us."

Suddenly his theory made way too much sense. "Not that I'm saying I agree with your theory," Bobbie warned, "but what do you need me to do?"

Why else would he want to see her? He wanted something and since he wasn't involved in the investigation, he likely needed someone inside.

"Watch your back. Urge this cop, Durham, to keep the feds out of the loop. And tell Shade to stay clear of the whole damned shooting match."

"I can do that."

Silence settled between them for a moment.

"I really need you to trust me, Bobbie."

She told him the truth. "I'm not sure I can do that."

"When we were in that place...with Perry..."

Bobbie closed her eyes against the memories of Gaylon Perry aka the Storyteller.

"I would have done anything to save you," he went on, "because I understood that what he did to you was my fault."

She turned to him, saw the stark devastation on his face. "You were desperate to catch a serial killer."

"I used you to lure him in. I knew he'd be drawn to you. I put my need to solve the case ahead of your safety...of your family's safety."

Her eyes burned but she would not cry in front of him. She would not.

"We have to find Weller," he reiterated, "before Kessler gets to him. She's still here. She isn't going anywhere until she finds him and kills him. Pitts will make sure she gets the job done or goes down."

A burst of anger knocked the softer emotions

to the back of Bobbie's mind. "Why would Pitts or Kessler provide Weller with anything he could use against them? What you're suggesting doesn't make sense."

"Pitts used him to make a name for himself. His ability to gain Weller's cooperation has set his career on track and gotten him a fucking book deal. Kessler had her own career goals. Weller did things for her, too"

"Things?" Bobbie cleared her throat. "What the hell does that mean, LeDoux?"

Her cell vibrated again. Troy.

Where are you?

"That's all I can tell you for now," LeDoux said.

"I have to go." She reached for the door.

He touched her arm. "Don't trust anything you hear coming from the Bureau, Bobbie. Pitts is spinning this to his own benefit."

"Don't worry." His admission about using her echoed in her ears. "I don't trust anyone associated with the FBI."

Bobbie walked away without looking back. As she reached the front entrance to the headquarters building, Troy exited.

"I had a call." She shrugged. "I needed some privacy."

He acknowledged her excuse with a nod. "We're going to interview Lucille Bonner again. Agent Ellis provided documentation that Bonner met with Weller two times after he evaluated her son."

"Why would she lie about meeting with Weller?" Bobbie matched his stride as they headed for his car.

"Beats the hell out of me."

Anderson Street
11:10 a.m.

"Her car is in the driveway," Bobbie pointed out. Troy had knocked several times and still there was no answer.

He drew his weapon. "I'll have a look around back. Keep knocking."

Bobbie reached around and rested her right hand on the butt of her Glock while she pounded a couple more times on the door.

The beagle that belonged to Bonner hadn't moved from the front of the garage. Bobbie had never owned a beagle but most dogs barked when someone knocked on their master's door. This one—what was his name?—appeared content to lie with his nose pointed toward the garage.

Jelly. That was it. "Hey, Jelly." Bobbie walked toward him. "Where's your mama?"

The dog looked at her without moving his head. As she drew closer he growled and showed his teeth.

Damn. He'd seemed friendly enough on their first visit. "Is your food in the garage? Did Mama forget to feed you this morning?"

Moving nothing but his eyes, the dog watched

as Bobbie eased closer to the set of handles in the center of the garage doors. The doors were the carriage style that opened outward rather than rising overhead.

As her hand landed on the iron handle Jelly growled another warning. "It's all right, boy. Let's see what we've got here."

Bobbie released the latch and swung the doors outward. Jelly shot to his feet and bounded inside. Her weapon leveled and ready for any threat, the morning sun poured over Bobbie's shoulders and filled the interior of the small one-car space as the coppery scent of coagulated blood rushed into her lungs.

Lucille Bonner lay on a white sheet that had been spread on the stained concrete. Her body had been hacked into the eleven pieces used in Weller's MO. The pieces had been rearranged in the same bizarre, broken mannequin manner as all his victims. On an expanse of the dingy wall at the rear of the garage a painting of Lucille in her current state had been drawn for all to see.

"Holy shit." Troy moved up beside Bobbie.

"This," she said, her heart pounding, "is Weller's work."

While Troy rounded up the dog who had already tracked through the blood, Bobbie stepped carefully around the mangled body. She studied the poor woman who had died such a horrifically violent death.

"What the hell did you do, Lucille?"

The forensic unit arrived within minutes. Uniforms were instructed to canvass the neighbors. Agent Ellis showed up, his cell phone attached to his ear. Bobbie imagined he was on the phone with Kessler letting her know she had been wrong about Weller not being in Savannah. An ambulance had come and taken Mr. Bonner to the hospital for evaluation. He appeared unharmed and oblivious to the violence that had happened in his home.

Bobbie took a couple of photos with her cell and sent them to Nick, then she left the scene to the forensic folks. On the back porch, she found Troy.

"They find anything inside?"

Troy shook his head. "I was about to check the basement."

"Basement?" Bobbie hadn't noticed a basement entrance in the house.

He gestured to the double doors at the back of the house that sat at a forty-five degree angle to the ground and seemed to open carriage-style. Back home they called it a root cellar. Chains and a lock lay on the grass next to the doors.

"Mind if I join you?" She thought of the old hole in the ground that Devine had used to hold the women hostage only days ago. Maybe that was where Lucille Bonner had kept her secrets, too.

Troy hitched his head in an affirmative. "Underground exploration is always better with company."

Bobbie followed him to the end of the house. Lots of older homes back in Montgomery had root cellars or old-style basements. Some had dirt walls and floors. Others had stone or brick but most were just plain old dirt.

The doors opened outward, the same as the garage doors had. With his flashlight in one hand and his weapon in the other, Troy slowly descended the narrow steps. Bobbie kept a reasonable distance in case they ran into trouble. The dark hole smelled like the one where she'd found the women Devine had kidnapped. Dank and musty, a little like urine and feces.

The beam of the flashlight reflected against something metal. Troy traced the beam over the object. Twin bed. The metal kind with rusty, metal springs and a thin, dingy mattress. As they moved closer she could see that one leg had been broken free of the bed and lay on the packed dirt floor. The metal leg was shinier than the rest of the bed.

Where a chain rubbed against it.

"She kept someone chained down here," Troy said, his voice soft with disbelief.

"I was thinking the same thing." Her heart thundering, Bobbie slowly surveyed the space. The bed with its broken leg. A table with a kerosene-type lamp and a book, *Gulliver's Travels*. There was an old-timey pot with a lid that had served as a toilet for whoever had been chained in this hole. Drawings made with crayons hung on the rock walls.

"Do you think she kept her son hidden down here all this time?" Bobbie spotted a stuffed dog, the kind a small child would love. "Or maybe the Potter boy?" She'd shared her thoughts with Troy about the possibility that Bonner had taken a replacement for her son.

"Great minds think alike."

"If that's the case, where is he?"

"If Weller killed his mother, maybe he took the boy." Troy grunted. "Boy? He wouldn't be a boy now. He'd be a forty-eight-year-old man—or thirty-five if her guest was Noah Potter."

Bobbie stared at the broken chains. A very strong man who was likely not happy that he'd been locked away in a basement for the past thirty-two years.

Had he heard his mother's cries as Weller hacked her into pieces?

Where the hell was he now?

Twenty-Nine

The chief of police had designated the case the highest priority, so the autopsy on Edward Cortland's body had already been completed. Lucille Bonner's would begin first thing in the morning. Unless the lab came back with some unexpected drug in the systems of the vics, there wouldn't be anything new, which was why Bobbie was surprised when Weston called and wanted to see Troy.

As he drove, Bobbie considered what she'd seen at the Bonner home. A BOLO had been issued for Treat Bonner in the event he was the prisoner from the Bonner basement. The FBI had taken a photo of him as well as the one of Noah Potter from thirty-two years ago to have age progressions done. It would take some time before the FBI's findings filtered down to the local police, but when the photos arrived, they would be circulated on social and media outlets. Had whatever happened to Treat

Bonner all those years ago made him uncontrollable? Did his mother fear him? What kind of mother kept her son chained in the basement, particularly after he was cleared in the Foster case? Was Treat the one who murdered Cortland and the Sanderses?

Bobbie couldn't imagine what might have been done to Noah Potter if he was the one who'd been held in that basement all those years.

As soon as they arrived at the coroner's, they were escorted into Weston's office.

"You have something new for us?" Troy asked, a hopeful note in his weary voice.

Weston opened the file on his desk. Bobbie found herself leaning forward in anticipation.

"You asked us to work with the lab to find something that might tell us whether the fourth set of remains belonged to the Potter boy or to…your sister."

Seated next to her, Troy's posture changed, stiffened. His fingers curled around his chair arms. Bobbie felt for him.

"We believe," Weston went on, "the children's clothes were removed to ensure the concrete mixture adhered to their skin. Since human hair can survive for centuries if properly preserved, we had hoped to find usable strands in the concrete. Unfortunately, it appears the moisture in the mixture sped up the decomposition process of the keratin."

"Then you have nothing new." The hope Bobbie had heard in Troy's voice had flatlined—his disappointment was painful to hear.

"I believe," Weston began, "we've found enough to call the identity of the final set of remains discovered at the pet cemetery. A few tiny threads of nylon fabric were encased in the concrete tomb with the fourth child."

Bobbie spoke up, "I thought there were no traces of clothing found." He'd just said they believed the children's clothes were removed before they were entombed.

"We thought so, too, but in the area where the child's head would have been there were tiny bits of fabric. My colleague, Dr. Mather, believes this is from a product that would have been composed of cotton and nylon. The cotton, of course, decomposed but the nylon remained." Weston looked from Bobbie to Troy. "The nylon bits are pink. According to the statements made by the parents when the children went missing the only child wearing anything pink when she disappeared was—"

"Brianne," Troy said. "She wore a pink ribbon in her hair."

"I have to say it's not conclusive," Weston allowed. "We'll still pursue a DNA comparison, but with this new find and the size of the bones, it's my opinion the remains are Brianne's."

Troy stood and reached across the desk to shake the man's hand. "Thank you, Dr. Weston. I'll let my folks know."

Bobbie, too, thanked the coroner as they left his office. Troy didn't speak until they were outside on the sidewalk. He looked around the street as if searching for something. Bobbie understood. He needed something to kick or someone to scream at. Some way to rid himself of the mounting grief no doubt burgeoning inside him.

Bobbie reached out to him, put her hand on his arm. "I'm so sorry. At least now your family can have some sense of closure."

He pulled Bobbie into his arms so fast she lost her breath. Though he never made a sound, she felt the shuddering sobs rocking his body. She allowed him to hold her for as long as he needed. Bobbie closed her eyes and remembered the day she had been told her son was dead. She had survived three weeks of hell—the kind of hell no other victim of the Storyteller had survived—for one reason: to get back to her little boy. Only he was dead, too.

Sometimes no amount of preparation for the worst and no amount of time was enough.

Willow Road
5:52 p.m.

Bobbie followed Troy's lead as his mother ushered them inside the house where he'd grown up. Mrs. Durham eyed Bobbie speculatively as if she regretted what she'd shared on her last visit. The woman needn't worry. Bobbie would never expose her secret.

Troy's father muted the evening news as they entered the living room. "Y'all figured out who killed Cortland yet? I just heard about Lucille Bonner."

Troy waited for Bobbie and his mother to settle before he took the end of the sofa nearest his father. "We have a number of leads."

"Which means you don't have jack shit." The older man turned his attention back to the silent screen.

"We do have an update from the coroner's office," Bobbie spoke up, mostly because she wanted to shake Luke Durham. When was he going to stop punishing his son for his own mistake?

Durham stared first at Bobbie then at Troy.

"Dr. Weston found a few trace fibers encased in the concrete with the fourth set of remains." Troy glanced at his mother. "The fibers were pink. We believe—"

Heather Durham burst into tears, her sobs loud in the room.

Bobbie reached across the sofa and took her hand. The other woman held tightly to Bobbie.

"We believe," Troy repeated, "the remains are Brianne's."

"What about the Potter boy?" his father asked. He tried to look unfazed but Bobbie noticed the tremor in his hands before he tightened his fingers on the arms of his chair.

Troy shook his head. "We haven't found his remains yet. I'm sure you've heard about what we found in the basement of the Bonner home."

His father looked away. "I heard something

about it. That woman went a little crazier than she already was when she lost her son. God only knows what she'd been doing."

"When can we make final arrangements for our little girl?" Heather struggled to regain her composure.

"I'll talk to the chief," Troy offered. "I don't see any reason why any of the remains should have to be held any longer. There's nothing else they can offer us in the way of information. Dr. Weston can keep what he needs for the DNA."

Heather nodded and dabbed at her red eyes.

"I wanted to talk to you again," Troy began, "about a security detail. Or you could come stay with me for a while."

His father focused his attention back on the television screen. "We're fine right here. I can protect my family."

Bobbie felt the tension in the room escalate.

"You didn't protect Brianne," Troy said, anger simmering in his voice.

Heather started to cry again. Luke shot a scalding look at his son. "That was your job. You're the one who let her down."

Troy stood. "You're right. I did let my little sister down, but I was a child. You were her father. You're the one who should have known whatever the hell was going on with Lucille Bonner and her son. You should have known Bill Sanders was not who he appeared to be. You—" he pointed a finger at his father "—let us *all* down."

Bobbie stood and touched his arm. "We should go."

"That's right." Luke got out of his chair. "You should go. You think you can come in here and upset your mother and then accuse me of not protecting my family." He shook his head. "Get out. We don't need anything from you."

Heather ran from the room, her sobs echoing through the house.

"Mr. Durham," Bobbie urged, "Troy wants to protect you and his mother. Randolph Weller is extremely dangerous. Whatever he's here to do, he won't stop until he accomplishes his goal. If you're keeping anything about what happened—"

"Don't come into my home," he shouted, "and accuse me, Detective."

"Sir," Bobbie put a hand against Troy's chest to prevent him from interfering, "I'm not accusing you of anything. I'm trying to make you see that you and Mrs. Durham could be in grave danger because someone else may believe you know something about what happened all those years ago. Whatever you're keeping to yourself could seem irrelevant to you, but it may not seem that way to Weller."

Durham threw up his hands. "I have nothing else to say." He turned to Troy. "Go. I need to comfort your mother."

Troy hesitated but then he relented. Bobbie followed him to the front door. He paused again but changed his mind. It wasn't until they were in his SUV and had driven away that he spoke again.

"For the life of me I can't understand why he would cover for Bill Sanders or anyone else involved in this."

Bobbie had to admit the man's reactions were off. Way off—even for a man still harboring guilt for an affair all those years ago. There had to be more than what his wife knew.

"Unless he knows something he only now recognizes would have made a difference."

Troy shook his head. "I just hope it doesn't get him killed."

Thirty

Nick watched as Amelia Potter locked the door to her shop and reversed the sign from open to closed. The woman stood for a moment and peered out into the darkness as if she felt someone watching her. He couldn't get an accurate read on her. Her past was uncluttered and unremarkable beyond a few issues in high school before she dropped out.

She was born in Boston but moved with her family to Atlanta when she was only six. Her high school record showed drug issues and the suggestion of emotional problems. He found no police records or any other kind of history—good or bad—between age sixteen and eighteen. Then, a few months after her eighteenth birthday, she showed up in Savannah, got a driver's license and cleaned houses for the wealthy. Less than two years later her child was born. There was no record of a marriage or divorce before or since. On her son's birth certificate the father was listed as Nathan Crowder. Crowder, deceased, had been a local handyman.

Shortly before becoming a mother, Potter opened The Gentle Palm. The people he had interviewed under the guise of writing a book on Potter claimed she was kind and helpful. During her early years in Savannah she had become close friends with a Camille Balfour who likely funded her business endeavor. Balfour had refused to speak with Nick.

Had Potter's son been taken as punishment for her statement about seeing Treat Bonner with the Foster girl? Since she moved to Savannah from Atlanta, was it possible she had known Weller? There was something about her that felt vaguely familiar. Had she been a patient of Weller's? He'd found no record but that didn't mean her parents hadn't taken her to the prestigious psychiatrist.

Had she sensed his evil way back then? Was that what had sent her fleeing to Savannah?

Perhaps when Weller came here to evaluate Bonner, he found her again. Had he murdered her son, allowing everyone to believe he simply disappeared along with the others? There was nothing in Weller's past kills that suggested he ever worked in a team—not until the Steven Devine murders. It wasn't impossible that Nick as well as the FBI had not discovered all of Weller's murders.

The urgency that stirred in his blood warned

that he was onto something. The need to talk to Bobbie was nearly overwhelming.

He pulled his cell from his back pocket and opened to a photo of her. As hard as he'd tried not to, he had grown too close to Bobbie. She had been right about his feeling more than he wanted to admit. Finding and stopping the Storyteller had been his goal when he first saw Bobbie. The only way to find him had been to watch and wait for him to come back for the one victim who got away. Bobbie was that lone survivor. Nick had watched her for months, learning all he could about her. He'd broken into her house and watched the home videos of her and the family the Storyteller had murdered. He'd memorized every part of her, the way she laughed—before her life was devastated—the way she smiled up at her husband…the way she kissed him.

Nick had wanted her to look at him that way, for her to kiss him and want him. Not once in his adult life had he wanted anything the way he wanted Bobbie. But he could not have the kind of life she and her husband had shared. *This* was his life. Living in the shadows, tracking the most heinous killers.

A few hours ago he had watched from a safe distance as she and the Savannah detective exited the coroner's office. He had hugged Bobbie and Nick had felt the kind of pain he never imagined he would feel again…not since he lost his mother.

No matter what he felt, he could not give Bobbie what she deserved. A man like Durham could. He could love her.

Nick could only bring more tragedy to her door.

He had spent his life avoiding taking a life at all costs. Whatever else he was, he never wanted to be like Weller. Protecting Bobbie had forced him to take a life. The fact that he had savored that moment confirmed his worst fears. He was destined to be like the monster Weller was. Killing was in his DNA, no matter what Bobbie wanted to believe. Every ounce of restraint and focus he could muster would be required to stay on track. Hunting down the depraved killers no one else could find and seeing that the local authorities captured them had to be his singular objective.

He would not drag her into that life or expect her to wait for him while he was gone for months at a time. She deserved better.

In time she would forget him.

Nick pushed those thoughts away for now. He had a job to do.

The photos from the Bonner crime scene Bobbie had sent him clearly showed Weller's work. No question. Was Weller tying up loose ends? Had he used Lucille Bonner somehow in the travesty that happened here thirty-two years ago?

Weller was close. Nick could feel him. The bastard was keeping a low profile. Other than Bonner, someone else appeared to be doing his dirty work.

But who? Better yet, why?

It was possible someone else not connected to

Weller was involved and responsible for Cortland's murder as well as those of Bill and Nancy Sanders, but it seemed impossible to separate the murders. The victims were far too closely associated.

Nick started to fade back into the darkness but the jingle of the bell over the shop door across the street stopped him.

Amelia Potter stepped onto the sidewalk, the glow of the streetlamp like a halo over her. A white cotton gown flapped against her legs in the cold breeze. She pulled her blue shawl more tightly around her and stared directly at Nick.

He should have moved, but he did not.

"Who are you?"

Her words traveled across the night wind and brushed across his senses. He didn't answer. He knew if he didn't she would speak again, and he wanted to hear her voice a second time.

Her hand went to her chest as if her heart were pounding in fear or anticipation. "What do you want from me?"

The wind picked up a wisp of her hair and slid it across her face before dropping it back to her trembling shoulder. She was afraid.

Nick withdrew, stepping into the darkness and away from her too-seeing eyes.

She'd asked who he was but she knew.

He was the son of a monster.

His phone vibrated with a text from Bobbie. She was ready to meet.

But he wasn't.

He couldn't talk to her tonight. He couldn't have her near or smell her skin.

Instead, he returned to the alley near her room and waited. When she appeared, he stayed out of sight and followed her to his building. When she'd given up on finding him, he followed her back to the inn.

In time she would forget him.

Thirty-One

Happy Pets Cemetery
11:30 p.m.

Wayne Cotton stared toward the street. Where the hell was Hoyt? He'd demanded this meeting. His text had said it was urgent that they meet tonight.

After those divide-and-conquer interviews with their wives, both Wayne and Hoyt understood that Troy Durham and that detective from Montgomery were watching them. They couldn't possibly have any evidence but they were suspicious.

What better place to meet than this cemetery? The police had finished here already. The crime scene tape had been removed. Wayne glanced toward the clinic and the house where the people he had considered friends had lived. He hoped Bill and Nancy Sanders were burning in hell.

No matter that thirty-two years had passed, Wayne still felt the pain of losing his youngest son. His mistake had cost his child's life.

He would never forgive himself.

He shuddered as he thought of the way Edward had died. Who the hell would have done such a thing? If Hoyt wasn't worried that one of them was next, he damned well should be. Which was exactly why Wayne had brought his gun with him. He checked the weapon tucked into his waistband at the small of his back. He was nobody's fool.

He gazed across the cemetery to what remained of the broken statues. How had the children ended up here? Had Bill helped Lucille kill those babies because he was fucking her?

What the hell? No matter that Bill had no children of his own, surely to God the man hadn't traded the lives of those innocent children for pussy.

"Piece of shit."

Wayne closed his eyes and shook his head. He had no right to judge anyone. If he and the others had left that Bonner retard alone, none of this would have ever happened. God knew he'd made his share of mistakes over the years. His wife had always overlooked his indiscretions. But Shelia could never know what he and the others had done. None of the wives would have forgiven them…

Though he had forgiven Shelia for her affair with that fucking Irish gigolo. *Whore.* But then, she'd only fucked him, she hadn't killed him.

He closed his eyes and cursed himself. His wife might never have strayed at all if he hadn't been so busy bedding all those other women. He was the whore.

Lucille Bonner was his biggest mistake. He'd screwed her every Tuesday afternoon for months back when her husband worked. How else was he supposed to occupy his time before he went off to college? The first thing the crazy bitch had told his daddy when her husband had his accident was that her baby was Wayne's. His daddy had paid her plenty to keep her mouth shut about that part, but she'd rubbed it in to Wayne every chance she got. He'd lived in fear that one day she would tell the world that her retarded kid was his child. So, yes, he'd taken the first chance that came along to be rid of the bastard.

He cleared his head of the ugly memories. That had been the beginning. Lucille figured out what they had done and she'd gotten her revenge.

A shadow fell over him and Wayne turned, expecting to see Hoyt.

What the hell? Wayne opened his mouth to demand an explanation. He saw the wood coming a split second before it slammed into the side of his head. He stumbled back, staggered around in an attempt to regain his balance. He could not. The world kept spinning. He tried to blink. Couldn't. He dropped to his knees. In front of him a small tombstone read "Spot. You will be missed."

Another burst of pain exploded in his head and the world went black.

Thirty-Two

"Two blows to the head," Dr. Weston said as he pointed to Wayne Cotton's battered and swollen head. "One to the area of the temporal bone, which certainly could have ruptured the meningeal artery. But the one that stopped him cold was the injury here." He pointed to the back of the victim's head. "In the area of the occipital bone." Weston looked up at Bobbie. "The driver—the wood as it's known in golfing terms—is the murder weapon. Despite being called a wood, the head of this particular driver is titanium. I play occasionally, when I have the time."

The golf club handle stood upright, the head of the club inside the victim's mouth. Bobbie swallowed. Damn.

"Once he was down," Weston went on, "the killer turned him onto his back and shoved the head of the club as deeply into the victim's mouth as possible. *If* he was still breathing at that point, he would have quickly asphyxiated. Of course, when the autopsy is complete we'll know if there were any underlying injuries that may have contributed to death."

"Thank you, Doctor." Troy gave the man a nod and then ushered Bobbie out of hearing range. "We've got Bonner all chopped up and Cortland and Cotton asphyxiated, one on his pain pills, the other with his golf club. Would Weller do this?" He gestured to the sickening scene behind him. "Just when I think I've figured out a motive for these murders, something else happens that turns the whole situation in a different direction."

They had talked about the theory that Bonner took the other children as a cover for taking the Potter boy to replace the son she lost. The only way that scenario worked was if Bill and Nancy Sanders had been in on it with her. Or maybe it was the other way around. Bonner may have known what Bill and Nancy were up to with the children and she seized the opportunity to replace her son.

But why would any of that matter to Weller?

Had Edward Cortland and Wayne Cotton figured out what the Sanderses did all those years ago and decided to have their revenge? If that was the case, then who killed the two of them? Bonner might have killed Cortland but she sure as hell didn't kill Cotton considering she was already dead.

"He could have, yes," Bobbie said, answering Troy's question. "Or he could have had someone else do it. But nothing we've found in this case tells us why. There just isn't a logical motive for him to risk capture to do all this."

"Goddamn it!" Troy scanned the cemetery.

Forensic techs were combing the area. The Cadillac Cotton had driven to the scene was being processed and prepared for transport to the lab. Uniforms were canvassing the neighborhood. So far no one had seen or heard a damned thing. A man walking his dog at dawn had spotted Wayne Cotton's body and called 911.

"This is out of control." Troy shook his head. "Five people are dead and the only one we can reasonably say Weller is responsible for is Lucille Bonner. The others are a goddamned mystery."

"Six if we count Mrs. Cortland," Bobbie reminded him. "I think it's safe to say her decision to take her life was related to this."

"Fuck." He scrubbed a hand over his jaw. "I'm sorry."

Bobbie smiled sadly. Troy Durham was a truly nice man. "If there is ever a time to say *fuck*, this is it."

"How the hell are we supposed to find our killer when it feels like we have two different murderers with two different agendas?" He shook his head. "Neither one leaves a speck of evidence."

Too many crime dramas had taught perps how *not* to give themselves away. If this was the work of one of Weller's colleagues, he would be well versed in covering his tracks. The truth was, in

Bobbie's opinion, these murders felt far too personal to be random kills made by someone with no vested interest.

Troy set his hands on his hips. "Let's start treating these murders as two separate cases. Bonner is clearly Weller's kill. The feds can deal with finding him. But the others, they're about the children. We might make some headway on that one if the Wilsons or my damned father would start talking. He's hiding something. It's damned time someone told the truth."

"They're afraid."

Troy looked around. "They damned well ought to be."

Delivering the news to Shelia Cotton had been difficult for Troy. He'd known these people his whole life. Thankfully, her oldest son lived in Charleston and was able to come over right away. In her grief, she hadn't been able to answer many questions. She had no idea where her husband's cell phone was. They hadn't found it at the scene and it wasn't at his home. She had gone to bed early and had no idea he'd left the house until she woke up and found his side of the bed cold and empty.

"We should give the others something to think about," Bobbie suggested, holding up her phone. She'd taken photos of both Edward Cortland's body and Wayne Cotton's.

Troy nodded. "If that doesn't shake loose the truth, nothing will."

West Duffy Street
11:45 a.m.

The first time they had come to the Wilson home, Troy had told her the house had functioned as a church for the first hundred years after it was erected. Hoyt Wilson's father had bought and renovated the abandoned church as a wedding present for his only son. Evidently living on sacred ground hadn't prevented the Wilsons from becoming caught up in the travesty that occurred thirty-two years ago.

Hoyt Wilson opened the door after Troy had rung the bell three times. "What do you want now? Can you think of nothing to do but bother us when we're grieving the loss of yet another dear friend?"

"Sir, we feel you and your wife are in imminent danger," Troy explained. "It would be in your best interest to take some time to answer a few of our questions."

"I've had enough of your questions. I'm calling my attorney," Wilson threatened.

Bobbie noticed that Wilson kept the door close to his body. It wasn't much of a leap to conclude he was hiding something.

"Perhaps we could speak to your wife," Bobbie suggested.

As if she'd been standing behind her husband, Deidre Wilson elbowed her way between him and the door. "What's going on here?"

Beyond her trendy four-inch high heels, Bobbie spotted a suitcase. "Are the two of you planning a trip?"

Troy spotted the suitcase then. "Mr. and Mrs. Wilson, you're both currently persons of interest in a multiple homicide investigation. I'll need you to stick close to home until further notice."

Rather than argue, the Wilsons simply closed the door in their faces.

While Bobbie sent Nick a few more details on Cotton's murder, Troy instructed the cop assigned to the Wilsons' surveillance not to let them out of his sight.

He took a call on his cell as he strode toward her. The changing expression on his face had her bracing for more bad news.

When he reached the SUV, Troy said, "That was my father. He's ready to talk."

Willow Road
1:00 p.m.

Bobbie stopped Troy with a hand on his arm before he climbed out of the SUV. "There's one thing I've been meaning to tell you."

He hesitated, impatience emanating from him like heat rising from the asphalt at the height of summer.

"Since Bonner was obviously murdered by Weller, Agent Kessler will likely show up again." Bobbie shook her head. "Don't trust her. I think maybe she has her own agenda." The idea that the deception went all the way to Quantico had her seriously worried for Nick's safety.

Troy stared at her for one endless moment. "Is that what your friend Nick Shade told you?"

Bobbie instinctively drew away from him. "You still have someone watching me?"

"Only because I'm worried about you."

Frustration and anger stirred—mainly because she hadn't spotted the tail—but she held it back. "He didn't tell me." She had to protect Nick as well as LeDoux. "*Kessler* did."

"How's that?"

As much as Troy wanted to hear what his father had to say, he waited to hear Bobbie out.

"She insists Nick is a killer and he's not."

"The two of you are...*close*?"

Bobbie wished the answer was yes. She wished she could find comfort in a simple, uncomplicated relationship with a man like Troy Durham— a good, kind man like James had been. But she wanted Nick. "I know him. He isn't responsible for any of this."

Troy nodded. "Okay. I don't know Kessler and I don't know Nick, but I trust you, Bobbie."

"Thank you."

As they approached the front door of the home where he had grown up, she wondered if the answers he was about to learn would give him any comfort. All the words in the world hadn't comforted her eight months ago. She'd found the justice her son, her husband and all the other victims deserved but even in that there had been no real comfort. They were still gone.

Luke Durham opened the door before his son knocked. If his face was any indication of what was coming, Bobbie hoped Troy had braced himself.

Luke led the way to the living room where Heather waited.

"He won't tell me what's going on." Tears spilled down her cheeks.

Troy looked to his father. "I guess we're about to find out."

Bobbie would have preferred he comfort his mother by sitting beside her. Since he didn't, she did. Heather grabbed Bobbie's hand and held it in a death grip. "Please tell me what's happening."

Before Bobbie could say a word, Luke spoke. "When Christina Foster's body was found, everyone went a little crazy." He exhaled a big breath. "We all knew her. Knew her family. Went to church with them. We were close." He nodded sadly. "Whatever the cost, we were determined to find the truth. When the Potter woman came forward and claimed to have seen Treat Bonner with Christina we…we became judge and jury." He fell silent for a moment.

"I think you're leaving out the part about executioner," Troy growled the words.

Next to Bobbie, Heather made a keening sound. Troy couldn't know this—he was fishing. Bobbie would have done the same thing.

Luke shook his head. "I had nothing to do with

that. When Wayne brought up making the boy talk by whatever means necessary, I shut it down immediately."

"But your words didn't stop them." Troy charged up to his father. "They killed that poor boy, didn't they?" When his father didn't answer, he demanded, "Didn't they?"

"I don't know." Luke held up his hands stop-sign fashion. "But my gut said they did. We spent days searching for him. I did everything in my power to get one of them to tell me the truth. They wouldn't talk. Not a word. Then the FBI let us know that Christina's killer was a serial killer they'd been tracking for months. He confessed to killing her. He knew details he couldn't possibly have known unless he killed her. And eventually DNA confirmed as much. The bastard died in prison."

"But it was too late for Treat Bonner, wasn't it?" Troy growled.

His father nodded. "I confronted Wayne and the others again, and they still wouldn't break."

"Tell me why they were never officially investigated." Troy shook with the fury in his voice. "Tell me how they got away with what they'd done." His father dropped his head and his mother fell against Bobbie, dissolving into sobs. "Tell me, goddamn it!"

"I pushed and pushed to get the truth, but no one would break. Then one night, Cortland had a few too many and he kept saying it wasn't supposed to happen. They only meant to teach him a lesson. When I tried to get some answers from him, he shut down. We were at the fall festival. I told him to sober up and we would figure it out the next morning."

Bobbie's heart stopped in her chest. That was the night the children went missing.

Both men lapsed into silence. Troy stared at his father, the reality of what happened next devastating him all over again.

"I knew Lucille took them." The older man started to cry. "I knew it. We tore her house apart. I personally interrogated her to the point that my captain had to pull me off her. But there was no evidence. None. There was nothing I could do. I had no idea Bill Sanders had helped her. Our little girl and the others were…just gone. We turned this goddamned town upside down."

Bobbie held Heather close.

The two men stood in the middle of the room saying nothing for half a minute.

"All these years you allowed me to believe what happened to her was my fault."

"What could I do?" the older man demanded. "There was no proof. No witnesses. Nothing. For the record, I never blamed you. Your mother never blamed you. You blamed yourself no matter how often we told you it wasn't your fault." He moved closer to his son. "Don't you remember all those times I sat on the side of your bed and told you what happened wasn't your fault?"

"Shut up." Troy backed away. "Just shut up and let me think."

"Mr. Durham," Bobbie said quietly, "where might they have disposed of the Bonner boy's body?" If the authorities could find the boy's remains, she and Troy might be able to connect his murder to his killer. Troy was wasting time and resources looking for Bonner if he was dead.

"Or could he have survived?" Troy demanded. "We found chains and a cot in her basement. Could she have been hiding him all this time?"

His father shook his head. "God forgive me but I don't know."

"God might forgive you," Troy warned, "but I never will."

"Anything you can tell us might help," Bobbie said, hoping to keep the exchange on constructive ground.

"Wayne was always the ringleader," Luke said. "Everybody else sort of followed his lead. There was this old well on the home place where he grew up. Once, when we were kids, he threw a cat in there. It made the rest of us sick but he just laughed. He wanted a dog but his mother wouldn't let him have one because of her cat. Wayne bragged that he always threw stuff that got in his way into that old well."

"Do not leave this house," Troy warned. "A surveillance detail will be right outside watching."

He walked out.

"We'll get this figured out," Bobbie promised.

"Just don't let him get himself killed," Luke pleaded.

"I'll do my best," Bobbie promised.

The trouble was she'd never been very good at keeping that particular promise.

Thirty-Three

Bonaventure Cemetery
4:00 p.m.

Nick strolled through the headstones in the historic cemetery. LeDoux had asked for a meeting. Since he still didn't trust him completely, this was as good a place to meet as any—where only the dead would overhear their conversation.

After parking his car on a street nearby, Nick had found a back way into the cemetery. He would go out that same way to ensure no one followed him when he left this place.

From the moment she arrived, he'd been far too distracted by Bobbie. Maybe if he'd had his eyes on the Bonner woman, he would have caught Weller. The bed and the chains in the cellar proved she had been keeping someone locked up. Had that someone escaped or had she freed him so he could help her contain this situation? Nick had deduced that Bonner had been involved in taking the children as revenge for her son's death. The only logical answer for the chains in the cellar was that she had kept the Potter boy, which would explain why his remains were not found. If her son had still been alive, there would have been no reason to keep him hidden since he had been cleared of Christina Foster's murder.

At this point with the Sanderses, Cortlands and Wayne Cotton dead, it was fairly easy to surmise they were all tangled in this web of deceit and revenge. The most logical scenario was that the Cortlands, Cottons and likely the Wilsons had exacted vengeance on behalf of the Fosters all those years ago. Only they'd made a mistake. Then Bonner with the help of the Sanderses had retaliated. End of story…except now someone seemed determined to see that justice was served on all involved.

There was only one player who appeared to be on the outside looking in.

Amelia Potter.

Nick doubted she could handle this alone. She was apparently the reason—or part of the reason— he and Bobbie had been summoned here. Weller had something to reveal. Perhaps he and Potter were making it happen.

Nick thought of the way she had looked at him… had spoken to him. Something about her had drawn him and yet repelled him at the same time.

Had she been Weller's lover?

Fury ignited in his veins as the full impact of the epiphany hit him. She was the one to watch. The others were nothing but pawns. Amelia Potter was the connection to Weller. She was the reason he was here.

The sound of a car engine cut through the silence and drew Nick's attention to the road that circled through the cemetery. He stayed in the trees until he confirmed it was LeDoux, and then he waited a minute or two more to confirm no one else showed up before he moved.

Using the cover of the trees he moved close enough to analyze the other man's body language.

When he was satisfied LeDoux was alone, Nick stepped into view.

"Shit." LeDoux drew back and glanced around. "You scared the hell out of me. Where's your ride?"

Nick ignored his question. "What do you want?"

"Supervisory Special Agent Janet Kessler," LeDoux said. "She's the one who helped facilitate Weller's reach all these years. But she had help. Rodney Pitts, my superior at BAU-2, is the power behind her. He's the one who wants you taken down."

Nick had determined that someone higher up at Quantico was the source of his trouble, but the motive was unclear as of yet. "How can you be certain?"

LeDoux glanced around nervously. "I still have my resources. I've already warned Bobbie not to trust her or Pitts. At this point she shouldn't trust anyone from the Bureau because they're all basing their efforts on what Pitts tells them."

Nick studied the other man. He hadn't shaved

in a couple of days and his clothes looked as if he'd been wearing them since he left Montgomery. "There is one thing in this life I don't have to do, LeDoux, and that's trust you."

"Whatever you think of me," LeDoux said, his own anger taking root now, "if you want to protect Bobbie, keep an eye on Kessler. Pitts isn't likely to get his hands dirty."

"I'm going to need something more than your word on that. What could Kessler or Pitts possibly hope to gain by helping Weller?"

"The position she now holds for one," LeDoux snarled. "Vernon Manley was a friend of mine. He was slotted to take over the Atlanta field office. He confided in me some of his misgivings about Kessler. The next thing I knew, he was dead and she had been awarded the promotion that would have been his. I couldn't figure it out at first, but I kept tabs on her and her interactions with Weller. But it wasn't until he escaped that I realized it was bigger than Kessler."

Nick appreciated the share, but Kessler was no concern of his unless she got between him and Weller. "I appreciate the information. Now, I have a request."

"What's that?"

Nick could ask Jessup, but he needed to see if LeDoux could still be counted on. "Amelia Potter. See what you can find on her. She's involved in this somehow."

"I can do that," LeDoux confirmed. "I might

be on admin leave right now but I still have a few good connections willing to help me out."

When LeDoux got into his car and drove away, Nick waited until he could no longer hear the engine in the distance and then he disappeared into the woods. He'd put LeDoux on Amelia Potter on purpose.

Nick needed information on Potter but more important he needed his attention focused exactly where Weller's would be.

On Bobbie.

Thirty-Four

The old Cotton family estate included nearly forty acres that abutted the marshy banks of Grove River. The grand home, along with its guest cottage and horse barns, was falling into ruins now. Centuries-old live oaks heavy with moss stood like sentinels around the once magnificent estate. The scent of camellias added a sweetness to the pungent smell of the marsh.

Once it had been deemed safe to do so, a diver was lowered into the old well. Bobbie had peered down into the seemingly bottomless pit. The rock walls were covered in moss. The wooden house around the well was on the verge of caving. A crew from Cotton's own construction company had come to shore up the shaky structure to ensure it didn't fall in with the diver down below.

Bobbie had sent a text to Nick about the well possibly being a dump site. He'd replied with a promise to have his FBI resource look into Cotton's background more deeply.

With so many of the players out of the way now, it was clear the killer was in his final phase of cleanup. Only Amelia Potter, the Durhams and the Wilsons remained. Bobbie had called Amelia to check on her. She glanced at Troy. He stood a few feet away from the well house speaking to someone on his cell. She could only hope he was talking to his father. No matter that what his father had done by holding back those details was wrong, and potentially criminal, Troy shouldn't have left things the way he had. She was all too aware of how quickly life could change. In the past ten months she had gone over her final conversation with her husband a million times. It had been Christmas Eve, her first day off in weeks. They'd made love and discussed having another child. He'd pampered her all day, cooking for her and waiting on her like she was a queen. She'd played with Jamie and relaxed. Newt and his wife had stopped by and dropped off a gift for Jamie. He'd brought one for Bobbie, too.

She would never forget the final moments with each of them. Newt hugging her and saying he would see her on Monday. James telling her to relax while he made cookies for Santa. Jamie snuggled in her lap.

Run, Jamie! Run for help like Mommy showed you!

Those were the last words she ever got to say to her little boy.

Troy tucked his phone away and Bobbie walked over to where he stood. "Call your father."

Troy looked startled and then he glared at her. "I can't do it. He should have done more. He might have been able to prevent the murders of those kids. Instead he left this to fester for all these years."

He looked away. She put her hand on his arm. It didn't matter that a forensic team and a dozen cops were swarming all around them. She and Troy were stuck on this island of pain. There was no way to escape it.

"He made a mistake."

"After my little sister went missing, that house became like a tomb. I didn't have a family anymore. That's one hell of a mistake."

Bobbie nodded. "Yeah. Okay. It's done. No taking it back. But if your father or your mother is the next victim this killer takes, will you want to look back and say you did all you could do? It's easy to point to what the right thing was or wasn't when you're looking back, but what about now? In the moment?"

"Lieutenant!"

Troy turned away from her. "Yeah." He headed over to the man who'd called out to him.

"We got bones. Human bones."

It took far too many minutes for the bones to be brought up out of the well. Dr. Weston was standing by to make whatever determinations he could at the scene. It took some more time for the coroner to pick through the remains and see what he had, placing the pieces like putting together a puzzle. By the time he'd stopped he had most of a fully grown adult's skeleton reassembled.

He finally looked up at Troy from the trace sheet. "I can tell you this was an adult male. I can't tell you how old he was or how long ago he died just yet, but I can tell you that he suffered multiple broken bones including the brain case being shattered—whether from his attacker or from the fall into the well."

Bobbie closed her eyes. At least now they knew what had become of Lucille Bonner's son.

Hull Street
10:15 p.m.

Bobbie stood in front of the window staring out at the night. She'd showered and still she felt dirty. She scrubbed at her hair some more with the towel to dry it. Using the hair dryer would have been far faster but she hadn't been able to bear the sound. She needed the quiet.

Why had Weller brought her here? At this point it wasn't clear whether he had committed any of the murders beyond Lucille Bonner's. So why play this game? Why lure her and Nick to this place where the past had collided with the present in such an ugly manner?

Tears burned her eyes. To watch Troy Durham's fractured life fall completely apart? Or to see the long-term effects of losing a child to the horror of murder? Or maybe to be around when he finally ensured that his son was destroyed or killed?

For a number of weeks now, Bobbie had thought she was stronger, moving forward. She'd felt that she had finally begun to pick up the pieces of her life. Then she'd met Amelia Potter, a woman just as lost and broken as she was. Amelia had tried to put the devastation behind her and to move on with her life even if it would never be exactly right.

Sleepwalking.

That's what Amelia had done all these years, the others, too, Bobbie suspected.

None of them had been living, and now those who were guilty were paying for their sins.

Is that what you're doing, Bobbie?

The knock on her door kept her from having to answer that painful question. She tossed the towel aside and ran her fingers through her hair. She thought about dragging her jeans back on but the nightshirt Amelia had given her would just have to suffice. She did grab her .22 before reaching the door.

She checked the peephole.

Nick.

She couldn't get her fingers to work quickly enough. When the lock finally released, she wrenched the door open. "You're taking a serious risk coming here."

There was so much more she wanted to say to him but those words were the most urgent.

His gaze touched hers then traveled down her

body before rising once more to settle on hers. Her pulse pounded harder. When she couldn't take it anymore, she said, "You should come inside."

Nick stepped across the threshold and Bobbie closed the door and locked it.

"LeDoux found a retired psychologist who says Amelia Potter spent some time in a psych ward when she first came to Savannah. Apparently she ran away from home carrying a heavy dependency on drugs. During detox she showed some violent tendencies. The psychologist ordered further evaluation but she was moved to a private facility, so he doesn't know who evaluated her. That may be Weller's connection to her and this case."

Bobbie scrambled to keep her surprise to herself. "Amelia Potter isn't a killer."

He stared at her a moment, the hunger in his eyes undeniable. Bobbie's heart pounded a little faster.

"I agree. She isn't a killer. But Weller may have some sort of obsession with her. I've recently become aware how strong an obsession with someone can be."

Bobbie took a deep breath, mostly to ensure her voice was steady when she spoke. "Maybe, like you said, he's enthralled by her ability to see things others can't." The memory of Amelia's pained words about not being able to see what was about to happen to her own son tore at Bobbie.

Nick moved a step closer. "She's a unique woman."

Bobbie nodded. "And beautiful."

Another step disappeared between them. "Very beautiful."

She managed another nod. "Yes."

"I've fought so hard to put you out of my mind."

The confession startled her and at the same time made her want to reach out to him. She resisted. This was his move.

"But I can't. I need to touch you."

"What's stopping you?"

He reached out, traced her cheek with the tips of his fingers. She could have sworn he trembled. When his hands slid down and over her body she was the one trembling. His fingers fisted in her nightshirt and pulled it up and over her head. He stared at her naked body and then he reached out and touched her, tracing each scar the Storyteller had left behind.

Bobbie couldn't take it anymore. She tore at the buttons of his shirt. He helped her release the last one and then he shouldered it off. His boots and jeans went next.

She took his hand and drew him to the bed with her. No matter what happened tomorrow she wanted this night with this man.

Thirty-Five

Amelia paced the floors. Going to bed wasn't an option. She'd fallen asleep in her chair and that dream had awakened her.

How was she supposed to sleep when the sound of her little boy crying wouldn't stop echoing in her ears?

In the dream she'd been searching for him. The woods were damp and thick. She'd stumbled so many times that even now, wide awake, her legs felt bruised and her skin felt scratched. It had been so real.

She'd found sweet little Noah in the woods. He'd been crying so hard. She'd reached for him but suddenly he was gone. No, no, she was gone. She was no longer in the woods. She was by the river. The woods had been thick; the gloom had cloaked her in near darkness.

Bobbie had been there. She had urged Amelia forward. *Run! Run!*

Amelia shuddered.

She was exhausted. Maybe a nice cup of tea and then she could try sleeping again.

Maybe tomorrow would bring peace.

She had lied to Bobbie Gentry. She'd told her she didn't know Randolph Weller but she did. He had evaluated her at that fancy private hospital where Camille had sent her. He'd been fascinated by Amelia's gift. She hadn't seen him again until after the Foster child was murdered. He'd stood across the street from her shop and watched her, only for a short while, but long enough to make her very uncomfortable.

When she'd first seen the man watching her last night, she'd thought for a moment it was him. Then he'd stepped from the shadows. She shivered and pushed the memory away.

The fact that Weller had evaluated her all those years ago could not be relevant to these murders. But why would Randolph Weller be involved in any of this? There was something here he wanted and somehow Bobbie Gentry was part of it.

Amelia shook off thoughts of Weller. When the dead refused to stay buried, it was because there was some truth they wanted others to see. There were secrets, Amelia knew. She'd felt the secrets buzzing around the other parents like a swarm of black flies. Had they finally found peace in death?

Would she die without knowing what happened to her son?

Where are you, Noah?

As much as she wanted her son to be alive and well somewhere far away from the pain of this place, the not knowing was taking a heavy toll on her soul.

Maybe Camille Balfour's prediction had been right. Maybe the end was coming for Amelia.

She hugged the shawl she had swaddled Noah in tightly around her.

"Give me strength, Noah," she whispered. "Mommy is so tired of the pain."

Thirty-Six

"For God's sake, Deidre, get in the car." Hoyt Wilson shook his head.

His wife finally scooted into the passenger seat. "You know that police officer is going to follow us."

"Let him follow us." Hoyt rammed the vehicle into Drive. "Until they lock me up, I still have a business to run and I'm not leaving you here alone."

"Don't talk like that," she whined. "You know how it makes me worry."

His dear, dear wife. She had loved and depended on him all these years. Not once had she suspected their son's death was his fault. He could not allow her to be hurt by this. This was his wrong, not hers.

"I don't understand what couldn't wait a few more hours," she complained. "Nothing good ever happens at this hour."

Hoyt grunted an agreement.

The security guard at the downtown store had called. There was something wrong in the office. The light was on and desk drawers were all open yet the door was locked, which prevented the guard from getting inside. He'd made a round at nine-thirty when the last of the store's personnel had gone home and all had been as it should be. He'd found the same at his midnight rounds, but a few minutes ago he'd discovered an entirely different situation. He'd wanted to alert the police but Hoyt preferred to look into the matter personally first. This wouldn't be the first time a thief had hidden in the store and then come out after closing expecting to rob the place. After that one incident Hoyt had hired a security guard to watch each of his supermarkets at night. Apparently the would-be thief had assumed the guard would take a nap, but Hoyt made sure the guards he hired understood sleeping on the job was not acceptable.

Deidre fumbled with her seat belt as they rolled onto the street. As she'd predicted, the police cruiser pulled out right behind them. Troy Durham had explained that the officer was for their protection. Rubbish! The boy just wanted to prove he could do what his daddy wouldn't thirty-two years ago.

Maybe they should have been charged and jailed all those years ago. Maybe he should be in jail right now. Hoyt's shoulders slumped as he drove through the darkness. He belonged in jail—he wouldn't pretend otherwise. He was the only one left now of the original three who had hurt Lucille's boy. Hurt. Ha! They had killed him. He had been lying on the ground and his chest hadn't been going up and down. Like Edward, Hoyt hadn't been about to get close enough to check his pulse. Watching him lie there, the reality of what they'd done had hit Hoyt. He'd wanted to call the police. He'd wanted to call for an ambulance but Wayne had ordered them both to go.

Just go! I'll take care of this, you fucking cowards.

Hoyt had walked away first. Edward had done so right behind him. They'd left Wayne to do whatever was necessary to finish it...to clean up.

The whole mess was that bastard's idea anyway. Wayne had always been the badass. He'd screwed around on his wife every chance he got until she paid him back in spades. He'd gone crazy when he found out. Hoyt was pretty sure he'd killed that man, too. Hell, he was the one who pushed them to take action against the Bonner boy. Thirty-two years had given Hoyt plenty of time to think and to form a far clearer perspective. Wayne had always wanted the Bonner boy out of the way. Hoyt knew he'd whored around with Lucille and maybe the boy was his. The two had certainly shared the same dark hair and green eyes. It wasn't long after Lucille got pregnant that the Bonner man fell off that roof. Hoyt wouldn't doubt that the two men had gotten into a fight and Wayne pushed him.

If so, it was one thing Wayne had never bragged about. Maybe it was karma that the poor kid was born with brain damage. No matter how Wayne pretended, Hoyt and Edward knew what he'd done. Knew that mentally handicapped boy was most likely his.

Money covered all manner of evil.

Except with God. All the money in the world couldn't protect any of them, not even Lucille Bonner, from what they had done.

He imagined they would have plenty of time in hell to ponder their sins.

Oscar Ortiz, the security guard on duty, met them at the front entrance of the store. The officer got out of his cruiser and headed that way, too.

Hoyt summoned his patience. "There's an issue in the office. As soon as we've checked on the problem we'll be right back out."

Officer Reynolds, according to his name tag, gestured to the door. "I should come in with you."

Hoyt lost his patience then. He held up a hand. "I can't stop you from following us around or sitting outside our home or business, but if you want to come inside, get a warrant. Now let us do what we came here to do."

"I'll make sure they're safe while they're inside," Oscar assured the officer.

Hoyt took Deidre by the arm and hurried inside. Oscar locked the door behind them. Officer Reynolds's expression showed he didn't like it, but keeping the door locked after closing was standard operating procedure. Before they walked away Hoyt saw the officer pull out his cell phone. Hoyt didn't care who he called. This was his store and by God as long as he was still breathing, he had an obligation to oversee it properly. All the other stores had managers but not this one. This was the original family store. Hoyt's father had managed it until the day he turned it over to Hoyt. He expected the same from his son.

The office was a modern glass-enclosed space at the back of the store. The first thing Hoyt had done when he took over the management was to remodel the old office. He'd done the same in all the stores. He wanted his employees and his customers to know that they mattered to him. Complete transparency.

If only he'd been able to be as transparent in his personal life.

"I'll be right out here, Mr. Wilson," Oscar said, "if you need anything."

"Thank you, Oscar." Hoyt searched his key ring. Where was his key? He checked his coat pockets. What the devil?

"Here." Deidre thrust a key at him. "Use mine."

Frustrated, Hoyt took the key and unlocked the door. Blood roaring in his ears, he passed Deidre's key back to her and ushered her inside before closing the door. Out of habit his faithful wife locked the door behind them. Security personnel didn't have access to this office. That wasn't the case in the other stores, but Hoyt didn't want anyone else touching his files or going through his desk. Employees and customers alike were welcome to look but no touching. It wasn't that he really had anything to hide. Frankly, the one mistake he'd made all those years ago was the only time in his life he'd ever crossed the line—legal or otherwise. He hoped that would make some difference when judgment day came.

It won't bring your little boy back. Or any of the others.

The pain in his chest that never truly went away deepened.

"Good heavens," Deidre murmured. "What happened here?"

Hoyt shook off the haunting memories. He surveyed the mess. Drawers had been pulled open. Files had been scattered across the floor. There was nothing here for anyone to find. No hidden confession about the Bonner boy. No secrets at all. He took a deep breath, tried to slow his heart. He'd been upset when he left the store last night. Maybe he'd failed to lock the door and someone had hidden in here after closing. Hoyt turned and looked at the place on the wall next to the door where he kept his spare keys.

The bottom fell out of his stomach. The spare key to the office was missing. The door could not be opened from the outside or the inside without a key. So he had left it unlocked and whoever had hidden in here had used the spare key to lock out the security guard and then to relock the door when he was ready to leave.

But for what purpose? There was no money left in here at night. Then again, like most business-men, he had his share of disgruntled ex-employees.

"I think someone's trying to tell you something, Hoyt."

"I don't know what this is about," he argued. "Let's get this mess cleaned up." These were his files. He didn't want just anyone going through them. He knelt down and started to pick up the mess.

When Deidre didn't answer him or join him, he turned to see the reason.

His wife waved to him from outside the door. He stood and moved toward her, tried to open the door but it was locked. He frowned. What was she doing?

Deidre pointed to something behind him. Hoyt turned around and saw Shelia Cotton standing out-side the glass on the other side of the office. What on earth was Shelia doing here? She was dressed all in black.

Uncertainty prickled on his skin. "Dear God." Hoyt reached for his cell phone.

It was missing. He'd lost it yesterday and hadn't been able to find it anywhere at the house or here at the store.

"Where the hell is Oscar?" Hoyt rushed to the desk and picked up the phone. No dial tone.

What on earth was going on here? He turned back to his wife. "Deidre!"

She only stared at him. He looked around beyond the glass walls that were now his prison. Where was Shelia? Then he spotted her legs. She stood on a ladder, her upper body out of sight.

This was insane! He surveyed the store beyond the office. It was dark save for the minimal lights left on for security purposes. Where in God's name was Oscar? A sound overhead stopped him. His gaze shifted upward, roved over the suspended ceiling until he saw the source of the noise. A single acoustic tile had been moved aside.

"What the hell?"

The scent of gasoline hit his nostrils before the sound of it splashing on the floor pierced his senses. It splattered on his clothes, poured across the tiled floor.

Hoyt dove for the desk. From the corner of his eyes he saw the wad of fire fall from the ceiling and then there was a whoosh.

He frantically surveyed the glass walls. Deidre and Shelia had disappeared... Where was Oscar?

Screaming echoed in his ears...*his* screams.

Thirty-Seven

Abercorn Street
10:30 a.m.

When a call from Troy awakened her at three-thirty this morning, Nick had been gone. The bed had felt as cold as ice. Bobbie's heart had hurt as she'd gotten up and hurriedly dressed. No matter how he lied to himself, Bobbie had felt the intensity in his lovemaking. He was as attached to her as she was to him. The knowledge was both a blessing and a curse.

Focus, Bobbie. This case was quickly spiraling toward some sort of climactic ending. Officer Lance Reynolds had called Troy to let him know the Wilsons had gone to the downtown store. Half an hour later the injured security guard had crawled to the front entrance and waved frantically for help.

Bobbie walked around the broken glass that had once been the walls of the store's office. The fire had been fairly easy to contain once the fire department arrived. Every door and window in the store had been opened to try and clear the smoke. There were no witnesses. The owners of the bakery across the street had seen the police cruiser arrive at the same time they'd gotten to the shop to begin baking. Then they'd heard the fire trucks. No one had seen anyone else come or go from the store. So far no other witnesses had come forward.

Hoyt Wilson had died of smoke inhalation before anyone was even aware the fire had started. Deidre Wilson had been found unconscious at the door to the smoke-filled office. She stated that Hoyt had forced her out of the office, locking the door. Then someone had struck her from behind, knocking her out. The paramedics had transported her to the hospital. A uniform had ridden with her.

The smoke detectors as well as the phone in the office had been disconnected. Oscar Ortiz, the security guard, likely had a concussion from the blow to the head he had received. Before being transported to the ER he had given a statement, as well. Considering both the wife and the guard had survived when Hoyt Wilson hadn't, Troy had pushed him hard. He hadn't seen his attacker. No one had broken into the store after it closed. He believed the perp had been hiding in the office when the store closed. Security did not have access to the office.

As if all that wasn't questionable enough, someone had turned off the cameras in the store. No video surveillance had been running since early the day before. Only two people had access to the security equipment room—Hoyt Wilson and his wife, Deidre.

Only three players had not been touched by whoever had decided to reveal these long buried secrets.

The Durhams and *Amelia Potter.*

The only one Zacharias had attempted to warn or to contact was Amelia Potter. If Zacharias intended to warn her about Weller, why send the photo of Nick? The photo was the aspect that made Bobbie believe there was more to Amelia's relationship with Weller than they knew. Yet every instinct resisted the idea that Amelia Potter could be part of these murders.

But Bobbie had been wrong before. It sickened her to think of Steven Devine.

Troy came up beside her. "The three men who took the Bonner boy, if my father can be believed," he added with a heavy dose of sarcasm, "are dead. The Sanderses are dead. I just checked in with the officer keeping watch at my folks' house and at Potter's shop. You think our killer will target one of them next?"

Bobbie noticed that he had started referring to the killer as "the killer" rather than Weller. As certain as she was that Weller was involved, Troy was right to widen the net. The case had grown so murky at this point it was difficult to tell if they had one killer or two much less the identities of either one.

"I don't know about Potter." She met Troy's

weary gaze. "Your father wasn't involved in what happened to the Bonner boy, but he did look the other way to some degree. If Weller is our killer, he won't leave your father out unless he doesn't know about his involvement, which is unlikely." Weller always had the dirty details. Every step he took would be carefully calculated.

"Weller is not a young man," Troy pointed out as he surveyed the overturned ladder. "*If* he's involved, he isn't alone."

"This case would have to be extremely personal for him to take these kinds of risks." That was a certainty if nothing else was.

Maybe Amelia Potter was that important to Weller. Maybe they had formed some sort of bond when she was in that private clinic. The woman Bobbie knew could never be described as violent in a million years. The only one of those who had been murdered who'd been described as having violent tendencies was Wayne Cotton. Yet the others were clearly involved.

There were no answers, only questions.

Supervisory Special Agent Kessler had returned to Savannah late yesterday apparently. Bonner's murder had brought her back as Bobbie suspected it would. She was here now, along with Agent Ellis; the two had shown up just in time to see the charred body of Hoyt Wilson stuffed into an extra-large body bag and then carried away on a gurney. The GBI agent who'd arrived two hours ago was in deep conversation with the Fire Marshal.

As if Kessler had felt Bobbie's scrutiny, she marched over and directed her attention to Troy. "This isn't Weller's work."

"I'm certain you didn't crash my crime scene to tell me what I already know," Troy tossed back.

"The task force is on high alert, Lieutenant," Kessler added. "He's been here—that much is clear. Your people should remain vigilant." She pivoted and strode away. Ellis followed her like an obedient servant.

"You think they'll ever find him?"

Bobbie shrugged. "I hope so."

"By the way, I went back to see my folks last night."

"I'm glad." That was the best news she'd heard all morning.

"We have a long way to go, but at least we're headed in the right direction."

Bobbie's cell vibrated in her back pocket. She pulled it free and checked the screen. She didn't recognize the number. "Excuse me." She moved away from the fray so she could hear the caller and have some privacy. "Gentry."

"Bobbie, it's Amelia."

Her voice was raw with emotion and no small amount of exhaustion.

"Are you all right?" Troy had said he'd checked in with her security detail.

"I need to see you."

A new thread of tension trickled through Bobbie. "Is something wrong?"

"I had a dream last night. I could see Noah in the woods crying for me."

Bobbie's heart ached for the woman. "I know this is very difficult. Lieutenant Durham has assured me that he won't stop searching for Noah." The child's remains should have been with the others...unless he was still alive.

"I don't think he's dead, Bobbie. I think he's somehow part of this."

Bobbie thought of the chains in Bonner's basement. The possibility that the woman had taken Noah to replace her son had come up more than once.

"If he's alive," Bobbie assured the older woman, "we will find him."

"I feel him pulling at me," Amelia urged. "It started when I woke up. He needs me. I need to go to the place I saw in my dreams."

"Wait." Bobbie couldn't have her taking off. "Stay right where you are. As soon as I can get away, I'll come to you and we'll go wherever you want." That would give Bobbie the chance to question Amelia about Weller again.

There was a long hesitation before Amelia finally spoke. "All right. I'll wait for you."

"Whatever you do," Bobbie pressed, "don't go anywhere without me."

Amelia promised to stay put. Bobbie put her phone away and went in search of Troy.

Maybe in a few hours she could get away.

She hoped if Noah Potter was alive that he

wasn't a part of this. If he was the one Bonner had kept chained like an animal in her basement, then he could very well be involved with these murders. Bobbie wasn't sure Amelia Potter could bear to discover that her sweet child had been turned into a monster.

Thirty-Eight

Troy scanned the murder board he, Bobbie and his team had created in the main conference room. They had six dead in five days, seven if Ms. Cortland was counted. No matter that there was no indication she had been a victim of homicide, her death was the first in this tragic chain of events.

He picked up the photo of Allison Cortland and placed it on the board next to her husband's. "How the hell did you people keep this secret all these years?"

He'd asked his father if the wives knew what their husbands had done. His father had always been under the impression they didn't know. Maybe that was why Allison had gone swimming alone in the frigid water. Maybe her husband finally told her the truth. A sort of deathbed confession. After being diagnosed with terminal cancer,

Cortland had advised his attorney to get his affairs in order.

Obviously someone else had learned this ugly secret.

Five children had gone missing. Four were confirmed dead and now, thirty-two years later, four of their parents were dead, too—three of them murdered.

Actually six children had gone missing. Treat Bonner might have been a teenager but his disability made him a child, as well.

If Bobbie's conclusion was correct, and Troy believed it was, Lucille Bonner was the only one Weller had personally killed. That set her apart from the others. The question was why.

Troy had teams going through the victims' houses and workplaces. An agent from the GBI was lending a hand. Friends and family were being interviewed again. Agent Ellis was pushing the DNA analysis on the hair and skin samples they'd found in Bonner's cellar. At this point Troy was leaning toward the scenario that the prisoner Lucille had kept was the Potter boy, but he wasn't about to rule out anything. The one thing he had learned he could count on in all this was to be ready for another surprise around the next corner.

Shelia Cotton and Deidre Wilson had been as forthcoming as could be expected under the circumstances. Like Bobbie, Troy felt something was off with the two women, but he couldn't quite put his finger on what. He had them under surveillance, as much for their personal safety as for keeping an eye on their activities.

His cell sounded and he snatched it from his pocket. Weston flashed on the screen. Troy hoped this was the good kind of surprise. "You have something new for me?"

"I do but I don't think you're going to like it."

Troy swore under his breath.

"The remains you pulled up from the well on the Cotton place are not Treat Bonner."

Troy groaned and collapsed onto the corner of the conference table. "What'd you find?"

"First off, based on the cranial suture lines, I feel confident these remains belong to a male victim closer to thirty than twenty. During his life he suffered a number of fractured ribs and several boxer's fractures of the second and third metacarpal bones of both hands, all of which had healed prior to his death. Based on his medical records, Treat Bonner had no such fractures. Finally, in looking at the teeth, this victim's wisdom teeth were fully erupted. Bonner's dental records showed only two of his had as of his exam three months before his disappearance. I'm afraid what you have, Lieutenant, is another victim to add to your growing list."

Just what he needed. Troy thanked the doctor and tossed his phone onto his desk. He scanned the case board again. "What the hell?"

Maybe Lucille Bonner had been keeping her son in that old cellar. But why would she keep him in hiding once he was cleared of murder? Didn't add up.

Something his father said about Cotton elbowed its way into Troy's thoughts. He grabbed his phone and called his father.

"Is everything okay?" Luke Durham asked rather than saying hello.

"*Okay* might be an overstatement, but so far no more bodies. You said Wayne Cotton once threw a cat down that well."

"That's right. I hate to speak ill of the dead but he was a bully. A smart-ass and a bully."

"Is it possible he had murdered someone before...when he was younger maybe?"

"I take it the remains you found in the well weren't the Bonner boy's."

"Doc Weston says it was likely a man closer to thirty. Maybe a scrapper. Got into fights a lot and had the boxer's fractures to prove it."

"Holy hell," his father muttered.

Troy straightened. "What?"

"Not long after their son was born it was rumored Shelia had an affair with this drifter. They called him Irish. He claimed to be from Ireland, had the accent and everything. He was always getting into fights, mostly with some man whose wife he'd...well, you know. I even hauled him in once and warned him to watch his p's and q's or move on."

"You remember his name?"

"Murphy. Jack Murphy, I think."

"Thanks. Call if you think of anything else."

Troy ended the call and frowned. If it wasn't Treat that Lucille kept in the cellar, where the hell had Cotton and the others dumped his body? If Treat was alive, where was he now? Had Weller taken Treat when he murdered Lucille? Why hadn't Weller killed her husband? Way too many questions and not nearly enough answers. Troy ran his hands through his hair. He needed coffee. This shitty day had started way too early.

A knock on the conference room door drew his attention there. Sergeant Phillip Goodwin, records section. Troy hoped he would be able to shed some light on who might have added Bobbie's name to the case file.

"Hey, Lieutenant." Phillip poked his head in the open doorway. "I did as you asked and talked to my people to see if anyone who wasn't listed on the sign-out sheet had been in the records section in the past week."

Was it possible he was finally going to get a lead? "What'd you find out?"

"According to Tate Fulton, the case file on the children was only pulled once before you asked for it on Friday. It was around eight Thursday night. Ordinarily Fulton would have been long gone by that hour but he'd been out sick all week and was way behind so he stayed late. The file was pulled that night but he doesn't know what time it was returned. Evidently before you called him to come in Friday morning."

His patience gone, Troy barked, "Who?"

"Delores Waldrop."

Shock, anger and a host of other emotions descended on Troy. "Thanks, Phillip, I appreciate your looking into that for me."

The sergeant gave him a nod and went on his way.

Before Troy could grasp the idea of what the sergeant had told him, another knock sounded. He looked up, assuming Phillip had forgotten something.

Delores beamed a smile at him. "The pizza is here. Since the task force will be filtering in and out at different times, we set the food and drink up in the lounge. Would you like me to bring you a plate?"

Troy held his anger and disappointment in check. "Can we talk for a minute first?"

"Sure." Delores stepped into the room and closed the door behind her.

There was no way to sugarcoat this. He hoped like hell Phillip was wrong. "You went to the records section on Thursday night and pulled the case file on the children."

The defeat and shame that emerged on her face warned him the records sergeant had been right. "Why?" Troy asked, not waiting for her to find a way to deny the charge.

"I did it to help you."

Outrage pushed him to his feet. "You falsified a document in a murder case to help me?"

She flinched at his raised voice. "Yes."

"Who asked or paid you—or whatever the hell—to do this?"

"I can't say."

Shock rocked through Troy. "You can't say?"

He had known this lady his whole life. She was one of the few people who understood how he felt. She had worked for Metro since she was nineteen years old. She and his parents were close friends.

Delores shook her head. "I can't say."

"Did Randolph Weller pay you to do this?"

The horror that claimed her expression then was answer enough. She quickly recovered and looked him straight in the eye. "If that's what you think, I'll give you my resignation right now."

His first thought was to accept her resignation and to send her home. Or better yet, to fire her. But then she might end up another face on that goddamned case board if, as Bobbie suspected, Weller was cleaning up the loose ends related to some secret he wanted to keep.

"Just tell me who told you to do this, Delores, and we'll figure out where to go from there."

She shook her head. "Fire me, arrest me, whatever you want to do, but I'm not answering that question."

He wanted to shake her but he suspected that wouldn't change a damned thing. She was protecting someone and it damned sure wasn't Weller. The answer slammed him in the gut. "My father... he told you to do it."

Once again her face gave him the answer without her having to say a word.

Troy reached for his cell. Hadn't Luke Durham done enough to damage this case? This time he wasn't getting away with his bullshit.

"Don't." Delores held out a hand. "You two are finally talking again. Don't ruin that."

Troy barked a laugh. "Am I just supposed to pretend he didn't do this?"

"Kessler, that FBI agent, she told him to do it. She said it was imperative if he wanted you protected."

Bobbie's warning that he shouldn't trust Kessler echoed in his ears. "You're certain about that?"

She nodded. "Your father was worried sick. He did what she told him because she claimed it was the only way to get you through what was coming."

"If Kessler wanted Bobbie here…" A cold fear tightened in Troy's throat. "Then whatever she has planned includes Bobbie."

That same icy fear cluttered Delores's face. "Oh my God. I hadn't thought of that."

"Have you heard from her?" Troy was already reaching for his cell. "She was going to talk to Amelia Potter." How long had she been gone? An hour maybe?

Delores shook her head. "I haven't heard from her. I thought she was still at the scene."

Troy held his breath as he waited for the call to connect. Bobbie's phone went directly to voice mail. To Delores he said, "See if you can get Amelia Potter on the phone."

Delores nodded and rushed from his office.

He called Lacon Hillman next. Hillman was the officer assigned to Potter's surveillance today. As soon as the officer answered, Troy asked, "Do you have eyes on Potter?"

According to Hillman she hadn't left her shop all day.

"I want you to go inside and confirm Potter's there. Call me back when you've spoken to her." Troy ended the call. He stood and headed for the door. Maybe Delores had gotten Potter on the phone. He didn't like this.

"Troy!"

He stepped into the corridor to find Delores rushing toward him. His pulse thumped harder. "Were you able to reach her?"

"Potter didn't answer." Delores paused for a breath. "You have a visitor." She moistened her lips, her eyes wide with uncertainty. "He insisted on waiting in your office. Under the circumstances, I agreed."

Was she purposely being ambiguous? "Who is it?"

"That man the FBI is looking for. Not the serial killer, the other one. Nick Shade."

"Do not tell anyone he's here," Troy warned, before hurrying past her. As he reached the door to his office, he slowed and composed himself, then stepped inside and closed the door. "Mr. Shade, what can I do for you?"

Shade met his gaze. "I'm looking for Detective Gentry."

Troy considered his options. The FBI was looking for this man. Kessler wanted this guy bad and he was standing in Troy's office, from all appearances, unarmed.

"If she isn't with you," Shade said before Troy decided what he wanted to do, "she could be with *him*. In case you don't fully comprehend the situation, as soon as Weller accomplishes what he came here to do, he will kill her."

"So he's still here?" Troy asked without answering the other man's question. Kessler had said she suspected he was gone but Bobbie believed otherwise.

"Yes." Shade glanced at the cell phone Troy still held in his hand. "Think carefully before you make your next move, Lieutenant. Her life depends on what *we* do."

"She's with Amelia Potter." Troy rubbed his thumb over the screen of his cell phone. The instinct to call for backup screamed at him. "Is there something you need?" He shrugged. Saw no point in beating around the bush. "The FBI is looking for you. Any cop on the premises could be calling you in right now."

"She's not answering her phone." Shade seemed to completely ignore Troy's warning. "Something's wrong. We can continue to debate my current standing with the FBI or we can find her."

Troy's cell vibrated, he flinched. *Hillman*. He hit Accept. "Yeah." The news was not what he'd wanted to hear. "How the hell did that happen?" As Hillman babbled about how he couldn't believe Potter had given him the slip since no one had gone in or out of the shop in the past hour, Troy tried to remember exactly what time Bobbie left. "Keep looking, I'll be right there." He ended the call. "Amelia Potter isn't at her shop or in her apartment. Bobbie isn't there either."

Shade headed for the door.

"Where the hell are you going?" Troy demanded.

"To find her. You coming with me?"

Thirty-Nine

"**H**e was here." Amelia Potter moved toward the river. "It was dark and he was afraid." She turned to Bobbie. "He was crying."

Bobbie surveyed the murky water. If Noah Potter ran from the Sanders home and ended up here that night... Jesus. His little bones were likely at the bottom of that river. "It's possible he may have escaped." It was a hell of a long shot but Bobbie hated to deflate the woman's hopes entirely.

Amelia moved closer to her, the sharp wind flapping her sweater around her jean-clad legs. "I know I sound crazy." She turned and stared out over the water. "It's been thirty-two years. If he was alive, why wouldn't he have come home? Why wouldn't he have tried to find me?"

"We know Mrs. Bonner kept someone in that cellar," Bobbie allowed. "It's possible she could have kept Noah since her son was gone." She refused to share the other possibilities that went along with that theory.

Amelia looked toward the cemetery. "My heart won't let me believe he was here all this time." Her lips trembled. "I've dreamed so often of where he could be. Far away on another continent or maybe as close as Tennessee. I imagined what he might be." She smiled. "A schoolteacher or a doctor. Maybe a scientist. He's handsome of course. And smart." Emotion filled her eyes. "Then I wake up." She sighed. "I've come to this very spot so many times over the years. I didn't even know why. I just felt the need. I had no idea the other children were so close." Her gaze settled on Bobbie's. "How can I have been right here so many times and not have known?"

"I wish I had an answer for you." Bobbie rubbed her hand over her back pocket as if by sheer force of will she could recharge her phone. The damned thing had died on the drive over here. Her charger was back in the room.

Amelia had called her from a shop two streets over from her own. She'd said she needed to get away from the officer watching her. Bobbie recognized the MO. She'd pulled that same move plenty of times.

"Amelia—" Bobbie moved toward her "—it'll be dark soon. Lieutenant Durham will be worried about us. It's not safe for us to be out here alone." Bobbie had her weapon but she was no fool. Being overconfident could get you killed fast in a situation like this one.

The older woman grabbed Bobbie by the shoulders. "Please, just tell me the truth. Please."

Bobbie instincts started to hum. "I'm not sure what you mean. Why would I tell you anything else?"

Amelia pulled her close and hugged her hard. "He told me you could tell me everything."

When Bobbie would have pulled free of her hold, the other woman reached down and grabbed her weapon. Bobbie tried too late to snatch it back. Amelia threw the Glock into the water.

"What the hell are you doing?"

"Dr. Weller called me," she said, her voice frantic. "He told me that you know what happened to my son. He said you could take me to him."

Shit. "Amelia—" Bobbie reached for the other woman "—I need you to listen very carefully. I found out about your time in that clinic. Was Weller one of the doctors who evaluated you?"

For a moment Amelia simply stared at her, then she nodded. "It was a terrible time in my life. I made mistakes. Camille helped me get the treatment I needed. Dr. Weller helped me, too. He came to see me three times. He was always so kind. Then, after the Foster girl was murdered, he visited me again. He was so proud of how well I'd done for myself and my child. I couldn't believe what I read in the paper about him. I never saw what he really was. How could I not know?" Her chest shook with her sobs. "How could I not see any of the evil so close to me…to my baby?"

"He fooled his own son," Bobbie urged. "Please believe me when I say he's a monster. He will kill us both. You have to tell me exactly what he told you to do."

Amelia shrugged. "He just told me you could tell me the truth."

Bobbie tried a different tactic. "I'll tell you everything I know. I swear. First you have to tell me exactly what he said. Every word."

Amelia blinked once, twice. Her grief had overridden her good sense. "He said I should bring you to the place in my dreams. I've dreamed of this place so many times. I knew that meant something. He said I should disarm you if I could so you wouldn't try to arrest me. Please." She searched Bobbie's face. "Please tell me what happened to my son."

"Weller lied to you. I don't know what happened to your little boy. He's using you."

Potter drew away. "He said he was leaving but that he wanted to give me this one thing. The truth about my son through you."

Bobbie turned all the way around, searching the gloom beyond the trees and headstones. He had to be watching. There were so many places for him to hide.

"We have to get out of here." Bobbie grabbed her by the arm.

Amelia pulled away. "No. He said you would tell me the truth."

"He lied, damn it. This is a setup." Bobbie grasped her arm once more and started toward the car. "We have to get out of here."

Amelia dug in her heels. "No."

Bobbie understood it was her grief making her irrational. Finding the remains of the other children had opened that painful place again. She wasn't thinking straight. "Randolph Weller is a master manipulator," Bobbie warned. "He has murdered dozens of people. Please, Amelia, think. Why would I lie to you?"

"Why, indeed?"

Bobbie spun around.

Weller.

Fuck.

Bobbie pulled Amelia behind her. "You really are risking everything, Weller."

He turned his hands up, then pulled his jacket lapels open and showed that he was unarmed. "I have complete faith in you, Bobbie. You would never allow yourself to be tailed by our fine boys in blue. You are far too good for that. So I know we're alone."

"Do not hurt this woman," Bobbie warned, her anger building with each breath she took. "You've done enough damage here."

"Quite the contrary," he argued, "I didn't have to do anything. You see, Edward Cortland's confession to his wife set all this nasty business in motion."

"His wife is dead."

"A minor detail," Weller offered. "Before taking that final swim, she shared the ugly truth she had learned from her husband and from Lucille Bonner with her closest friends. Apparently, after watching dear Allison lowered into the cold, cold ground, the ladies decided to do something about what their husbands had done."

"You expect me to believe Deidre Wilson and Shelia Cotton are responsible for all these murders?" The idea that he could be telling the truth was not lost on Bobbie. Numerous small details suddenly fell into place.

"They did, indeed. They took care of the Sanderses first. Then they gave their husbands what they deserved, one by one. Their plan was rather ingenious."

As Weller talked, Bobbie slowly ushered Amelia backward. The one thing he liked almost as much as killing was listening to the sound of his own voice.

"Why did you kill Lucille Bonner? Hadn't she suffered enough when her son was torn away from her?"

Weller sighed. "The entire ordeal has been quite tedious, but Pandora's box was opened and there was no turning back. When Lucille called Lawrence, he, of course, loyally passed along the message." Weller shook his head. "His death was so unfortunate. I depended upon him for quite a number of things. Sadly, he had grown a conscience in his old age."

The picture was beginning to clear for Bobbie. "You knew Bonner took those children."

"The poor thing came to me, desperate for counseling. I was one of the last people who did anything nice for her son. She had no one else to talk to. I only allowed her to regain her confidence. I encouraged her to tell me what she wanted to do to the people who had hurt her and her son. She was desperate to make them feel the way she had felt. To torture their children the way they'd tortured her sweet, mentally deficient boy. Who knew she'd follow through?"

"You're a sick piece of shit, Weller."

"Do you want to hear the rest of the story or not?" he snapped. "I have my doubts about the good lieutenant's ability to sort out all the details."

Bobbie smiled at the idea that she'd gotten under his skin. "So tell it already."

"Lucille found herself incapable of overcoming one simple stumbling block—those infernal second thoughts about killing the children. After all, her son had survived, despite being more damaged than he'd been before. Still, she couldn't bring herself to do it. At the time her son was in no condition to help her and she simply couldn't finish what she'd started. So she rushed to her secret lover. While he was comforting her with his penis, his wife brought the children here, one by one, and held their heads under the water until they stopped wiggling."

Amelia gasped. Bobbie held on to her, keeping her close behind her when her knees tried to buckle. Rage blasted Bobbie. She wanted so badly to end this son of a bitch's existence.

"The kindly veterinarian spent the rest of his pathetic life trying to make up for what his negligence had allowed to happen to the poor children."

"There's just one fatal flaw in your story, Weller. Treat Bonner is dead," Bobbie argued. "His remains were found yesterday."

"I'm sure Savannah's finest are aware by now that the remains they discovered are unequivocally *not* the boy's."

Weller was a lot of things but he rarely overplayed his hand. If he said the bones weren't Bonner's, then he damned well knew that to be the case.

"If Treat is alive, why did she keep him chained in the basement? What kind of mother does that?"

"You see," Weller explained, "the beating and then the lack of oxygen from almost drowning did even more damage to the poor boy. He could no longer control his violent outbursts. Lucille was, in truth, terrified of him. But he was her child, she loved him. It was all quite tragic."

Weller dared to move closer. Bobbie took a step back, ushering Amelia along with her.

"Where is my son?" the older woman cried. "You said she could tell me where he is."

"As I told you," Weller said, "Bobbie knows your son very well. For that reason, I had to bring her here to meet you."

"You said he lied," Amelia accused, struggling to draw away from Bobbie.

Movement in her peripheral vision snapped Bobbie's attention to the right.

Kessler.

"I thought you'd never catch up." Weller turned to the agent. "It's your move, Janet. I've set everything up nicely for you."

Kessler took a bead on Bobbie. "You've been a pain in my ass, Detective."

Bobbie pulled Amelia behind her once more. "The pleasure was all mine."

"What're you waiting for, Janet?" Weller snarled. "Finish this. Let's see if the lovely detective is willing to sacrifice herself this fine day."

Kessler shifted her aim to him. "You son of a bitch," she growled. "Did you think I'd come here and do your bidding after what you've done? You almost cost me everything."

Weller laughed. "Since I gave it to you, I certainly had the right to take it back. You would still be sucking hind tit, as they say, had I not secured your current position for you. Eliminating the competition gave you the edge you needed. You and Rodney owe me a great deal. I made both your careers and asked so little in return."

"Shut the fuck up." Kessler took the shot, the blast echoed in the air.

Weller stumbled back.

Bobbie pushed Amelia toward the woods to her left. "Run." She lunged forward, ushering the older woman away from the threat.

A bullet whizzed past Bobbie's head. *Shit!*

Bobbie pushed harder, urging Amelia forward. They had to reach the cover of the trees.

Another shot rang in the air.

Amelia's body jerked and she tumbled to the ground.

Bobbie grabbed her under the shoulders and pulled her to her feet. "We have to run!"

Amelia stumbled forward.

Kessler was coming.

They reached the tree line.

Bobbie looked back. Didn't see Kessler. She zigzagged, taking Amelia with her. Another backward glance.

The ground disappeared from under her feet.

Bobbie swallowed her scream as she went down, Amelia held tight to her side.

The cold water swallowed them.

They were sinking, sinking, sinking.

Bobbie's feet hit the river bottom. She bent her knees and pushed upward with all her might. Up… up…up!

Suddenly their faces broke the surface of the water. Bobbie gasped for air. Amelia coughed and gagged.

Holding tight on to Amelia and treading water for both of them, Bobbie looked back to where the ground had run out. Nothing. She turned to Amelia. "Where are you hit?"

Amelia blinked. Her body was shaking hard in the icy water. "I'm sorry. This is my fault. Save yourself…" Suddenly she went limp and sank, her weight tugging Bobbie down with her.

As their heads disappeared under the surface, Bobbie watched the bright red blood float up around them.

Forty

Cold, dark fear had started to thicken in Nick's veins. Bobbie was in trouble. He could feel it. They'd found nothing at the Potter woman's shop. No one on the block had seen Potter or Bobbie. Durham had issued an APB on Bobbie and her Challenger. Every cop in the city was looking for her.

It wasn't enough.

Durham was on the phone again. Nick walked back into the shop and climbed the stairs to Potter's apartment. He moved through the small space. "Where would you go, Amelia Potter?"

He and Durham had been through the place once already. This time he paused at the mantel and studied the framed photos there. Voices whispered through him. Potter's voice was among them. Nick frowned. They had never met before their brief encounter on the street. He stared at the photo of a younger Potter and her little boy. Smiling. Cuddling. Searching for seashells in the sand.

An ache started deep in Nick's gut as the photo

came to life in his mind. He could see the boy running toward the water that rushed across the sand...he could feel the warmth of the sun on his face and the sand between his toes. *Wait for Mommy!*

"Shade!"

Nick shook off the haunting images and turned away from the photos. He rushed to the stairs and down. Durham stood in the entrance to the shop. "Have they been found?"

"We just got a report of shots fired near the river off Greenwich Road. Not far from where the children's remains were found."

Gunshots. His soul aching, Nick raced after Durham. They loaded into his SUV and rocketed away from the curb.

Not once in his adult life had Nick ever prayed. He no longer believed in God. The only thing he believed in was himself.

And Bobbie. He believed in Bobbie.

He didn't want Weller to take her from him. The bastard had taken everything else that mattered in Nick's life.

He closed his eyes and prayed for her safety. He prayed for the other woman, too.

"Yeah."

Nick opened his eyes at the sound of Durham's voice. He'd answered a call. Nick hoped it was Bobbie. The trees whizzed past as Durham sped along the street.

"Okay, patch her through." Durham handed

his phone to Nick. "Put it on Speaker. Some lady called in and said she needs to speak with me." Their eyes met for a second. "It's not Bobbie or Potter."

"Hello?" The aged voice coming across the line cracked with uncertainty.

"This is Lieutenant Troy Durham, ma'am."

"This is Camille Balfour. I had a vision about Mia."

Nick's hopes sank.

"Ma'am, who is Mia?" Durham asked.

"Why Amelia Potter, of course." She cleared her throat. "Now you listen up, Lieutenant. Mia is with the dark-haired woman. One of them is badly hurt. They need help right now. Right now, do you hear?"

"Yes, ma'am. Do you know where they are?"

"They're in the water by the cemetery," she said. "It's cold. So cold."

"Which cemetery?"

"Bonaventure. Hurry, please hurry. There isn't much time."

The call ended.

Nick's body felt ice-cold. The caller was right. Bobbie was in trouble. He could feel the danger around her.

"Yeah."

Durham had another call. Nick stared at the man's profile and prayed this was better news. Bobbie was strong. She would not go down easy.

"Text it to me. Thanks, Ellis."

Nick waited for him to explain the call. He thought he might lose his mind before Durham spoke.

"That was Agent Ellis. He had an age progression done on Treat Bonner and Noah Potter."

Nick had no idea how that was relevant at the moment. They needed to get to Bobbie. Durham hit an intersection. Traffic forced him to stop.

Another blast of tension ricocheted through Nick. *Hurry!*

"Holy shit."

Nick turned back to Durham. He was staring at the screen on his phone. "What?"

Durham handed him the phone. "That's the photo of the Potter boy—of what he would look like now."

Nick stared at the screen.

"It's you, man," Durham said, "it's *you*."

Forty-One

Randolph stood very still.

He could hear the bitch stumbling around in the darkness. The sun had set and the meager moonlight couldn't penetrate the trees.

But Randolph needed very little light. He'd always had the gift of seeing better than most in the darkness. That skill hadn't diminished with age.

He lifted his face and drew in deeply.

A smile slid across his face. He could smell her fear. She was so very close. It reminded him of the days when old man Thompson would take him to the meatpacking house. He closed his eyes and savored the memory. As soon as he stepped out onto the killing floor he could smell the fear in the animals there. Even now his pulse sped up.

"Goddamn it!" Kessler snarled.

Randolph opened his eyes. She was to his right.

"Fucking cell phone."

He heard the phone hit the ground.

Agent Kessler was no longer trying to find Bobbie and Amelia. She foolishly assumed they would die in the cold water and that he was already dead. Such an amateurish mistake. Now she was simply trying to find her way back to her car. Too bad she was going the wrong way. Extreme stress often muddled the critical thinking process of even the most highly trained soldier. FBI agents were not immune to the clawing panic of imminent failure.

He moved closer to his prey. His wound was no longer bleeding so freely. Not such a bad injury. It had passed through skin and muscle, leaving nothing but an annoying tear in his flesh. Nothing he couldn't bear until there was time to attend to it.

"Fuck, fuck, fuck!" she muttered.

Randolph caught a glimpse of her blond hair. The flowery scent of her perfume had faded and comingled with the sweat and musk of fear.

Closer. He could hear her warm breath in the cold air. *So very close.*

He reached out. His forearm was around her and pressing against her throat before she felt his presence.

He jerked her back against his body and she twisted, trying to get her weapon pointed at him.

He flung her to the ground. The wind burst from her lungs as he fell atop her.

"Time to die, you wretched bitch," he growled.

The weapon discharged. Hot iron tore into his belly. He laughed as the pain roared through him. He snatched the weapon from her hand and threw it. "You've always been full of surprises, Janet. I've appreciated your ambition and your resourceful-

ness. You should have let me go without a fight.
You and Rodney should have been happy with all
that I'd given you."

"Fuck you." She clawed at his face and tried to
kick her legs.

He closed his hand over her face and forced her
chin upward, slowly, slowly until her neck snapped.
Her body stilled beneath him.

Randolph pushed up onto his hands and knees.

The world spun, almost toppling him over.

Forcing back the pain, he managed to get to
his feet.

If he was going to die he damned sure wasn't
doing so next to that whore.

Wherever he died, he could just imagine how
thrilled Nicholas would be.

All those years ago, he hadn't been able to resist.
He had been so immensely fascinated by Amelia
Potter, he simply hadn't been able to allow Lucille,
the cow, to destroy the boy.

He'd taken the child for himself…something to
keep his barren wife entertained for a while.

He should have known all those years ago that
the child would be the death of him.

Forty-Two

Bobbie dragged Amelia onto the riverbank. Her body wouldn't stop shuddering. It was so damned dark Bobbie couldn't see her hand in front of her face. She shook the other woman.

"Amelia." Her lips would hardly work. "Stay with me." She put her face close to the other woman's nose. She was breathing. Barely.

It was too dark to see where the blood had been coming from.

She had to get up and find help. She would carry or drag Amelia with her. They hadn't gone far. The car had to be close. Her head was still spinning with the idea that Weller was not Nick's father. What else could he have meant when he told Amelia over and over that Bobbie knew her son well. At some point in the water, Bobbie had realized why... *Nick* was Amelia's son.

Weller had wanted Bobbie to have to choose... her life or Nick's mother's.

Bastard. Well, she had shown him. They had both gotten out of the damned water alive.

Bobbie just had to keep Amelia alive until she reached help.

Light passed through the woods.

Bobbie ducked down. She pulled Amelia's body close to hers.

What if it was Weller or Kessler? If the world was lucky Kessler had managed a lethal shot.

Bobbie tried with all her might to stop her teeth from chattering.

Listen. She had to listen.

"We've got a body over here!" a voice shouted. "Female."

Bobbie shook herself and listened again to make sure she hadn't imagined it.

More shouting. More lights.

Cops.

"Help!" The word ripped out of Bobbie's throat like a wad of barbed wire. "Over here!"

She could hear the rushing footfalls in the underbrush.

"Here!" a voice shouted.

A flashlight passed over her face. Bobbie put up a hand to protect her eyes.

The flashlight hit the ground. Steady hands were suddenly on her, pulling her into strong arms.

Nick.

"Are you hurt?"

Bobbie tried to shake her head but her muscles weren't working so well. "Amelia Potter. Kessler shot her."

Lights and people were suddenly all around

them. Paramedics swarmed around Amelia. Nick pulled Bobbie away from the fray.

"Are you certain you're unharmed?"

Bobbie nodded. "You should make sure Amelia is okay." Bobbie drew in a big breath. "I think Weller stole you when you were three years old. I think you're Noah Potter."

"I know." The dismay on Nick's face made her knees weak.

"Got another body over here! Wait…this one's alive."

"It's Weller," another voice shouted.

Nick turned toward the shouted voices.

The gurney carrying Amelia rushed past.

Bobbie tugged Nick's sleeve. "We should go, too."

He nodded.

Bobbie expected to walk beside him to the nearest official vehicle, but he scooped her up and carried her against his chest. She rested her head there. She was tired. So damned tired.

Whatever happened tomorrow, they had survived today.

Forty-Three

Amelia Potter would be okay. The surgeon had assured Bobbie that she would fully recover, but she was fairly certain a deep breath wouldn't be possible until she heard Amelia's voice. Special Agent Ellis had taken Bobbie downtown to get dry clothes and for a debriefing, then he'd come back for Nick. One of them had needed to be here for Amelia.

Amelia was his mother. The reality hadn't entirely sunk in but Bobbie was getting there. Weller had taken Amelia's son and raised him as his own—which meant the woman who'd brought Nick up had known. She had lied to him over and over. Everything that he knew as a child...as an adult... was a lie.

Nick had kept his feelings to himself as Bobbie recounted all that Weller had said before Kessler shot him. The FBI hadn't allowed anyone to see

Weller since he came out of surgery. On some level Bobbie wanted to see him. She wanted to know why he had taken Nick. Was his wife unable to have a child? Was it just because he was intrigued by Amelia Potter's special gift?

Kessler was dead. Bobbie would be lying if she didn't admit that a part of her wished Weller had died, too. As much as those questions about Weller's decision to steal Nick from his mother nagged at her, she could only imagine the shock and dismay Nick had experienced. On the other hand, Nick surely felt a tremendous relief knowing that he was not genetically connected to Randolph Weller.

Troy joined her in the small lobby designated for the families of surgical patients. He'd been in and out since she, Nick, Amelia and Weller were brought here. Kessler's body had been claimed by the coroner. Troy looked as tired as she felt. According to Agent Ellis, Supervisory Special Agent Rodney Pitts was already in custody at Quantico.

"We found that other FBI agent," Troy said, "Anthony LeDoux."

Bobbie's breath caught. No matter that she and LeDoux had their differences, he hadn't let her down when it counted. "Is he injured?" *Please don't let him be dead.*

"He's fine. Kessler drugged him and put him in her trunk. LeDoux claims she intended to use him as the scapegoat for what Pitts had been doing. But first she had to see that you, Potter and Weller were taken out of the picture."

Frankly, the crazy woman had come far too close to making that happen in Bobbie's opinion. "Is LeDoux here?"

Troy shook his head. "Paramedics checked him out and a couple of agents I haven't seen before whisked him away."

The FBI had some serious explaining to do. Most likely they were scrambling to do damage control. The idea of how many people had died because of Weller's free rein from prison shook Bobbie to the core. No amount of damage control would bring those people back.

The children were all accounted for, except the Bonner boy. Weller had insisted he was alive, but, at this point, they had no way of confirming his assertion. They might never find him. Other questions remained but the answers had died with the adults who'd long ago set this shocking tragedy in motion. How sad for the survivors.

"Deidre Wilson and Shelia Cotton came forward and admitted they'd killed Edward Cortland and their husbands."

Bobbie wasn't really surprised at that news. They'd basically run out of suspects beyond those two. "Nothing on Treat Bonner yet?"

"Not yet. We'll keep searching until we find him or his remains."

"His father is still here?" Sadly there was no one left to take care of the father. As soon as the nursing home was able to take him, he would spend the rest of his life there. So sad. No one should be that alone.

"One floor down." Troy gave Bobbie the room number. "Delores spoke to the nursing home director again. They should have a place for him by the first of the week."

"Maybe I'll check on him." Since Nick was with Amelia now, Bobbie could take a few minutes away.

"I'll go with you." Troy gestured for her to lead the way. "Have you spoken to your chief?"

"I have." Bobbie smiled. Her Uncle Teddy was out of the hospital and ready to go back to work long enough to get his affairs there in order so he could retire. She couldn't believe he was actually going to do it. As surprising as his decision was, she was happy for him and for Lieutenant Owens. The two were already planning their wedding. She had definitely missed a lot this week.

Including Bauer's funeral. Bobbie was pretty sure Sergeant Lynette Holt would never forgive her. Another mountain to climb…*another day*.

"So you'll be going back home soon." Troy opened the door to the stairwell. "I'm sure your unit is looking forward to having you back."

"I told the chief I'd be back in time for roll call Monday morning. We have a lot of work to do rebuilding our unit."

As they descended the final step down to the next floor, Troy hesitated. "If you ever want a change of scenery, I could use you on my team."

Bobbie smiled. "I take that as a tremendous compliment, Troy. Thank you."

He pulled her against his chest and wrapped his arms around her. "Thank you for coming, Bobbie." He drew back and smiled down at her. "I'm pretty sure I would have had a tough time getting through this without you."

"You had my back as much as I had yours."

"We make a good team."

Bobbie smiled.

"Okay, so I guess I'm not going to be able to talk you into staying."

"Afraid not."

He gave her a nod. "I had to try."

As they walked down the long white corridor toward Bonner's room, Bobbie knew she couldn't leave without asking about his family. "What about your father?"

They paused at the door. "He offered to make a full confession. His decision to not pursue what he suspected makes him guilty of a number of crimes."

"Your father couldn't have known Weller took Noah Potter. Nothing he could have done would have changed the course of that particular event."

"I'm leaving that between him and the district attorney. As for our personal relationship, I told him we're not looking back. We're moving forward."

"I'm glad to hear it." Bobbie pushed open the door to Mr. Bonner's room. She stalled.

The man huddled in the chair next to Bonner's

bed was dirty, his face was scratched. His clothes, jeans and sweatshirt were torn and bloody. His sneakers were muddy.

Treat Bonner wasn't the sixteen-year-old boy who'd disappeared thirty-two years ago. He was a scared, gray-haired man who had been chained in a cellar like an animal for most of his life.

"Treat." Troy put himself between Bobbie and any potential threat the man might represent and approached him cautiously. "I'm Lieutenant Troy Durham from the Savannah-Chatham Metro Police. We need to talk."

Bobbie had already reached behind her back, her fingers stretching toward...nothing. She grimaced. Her weapon was lost in that damned river.

"Why don't you say good-night to your daddy," Troy suggested, "and we'll get you taken care of and the rest of this mess straightened out."

Troy talked Bonner out of the room. He assured the man that everything would be fine.

So it was over.

The cold, cold fear of becoming like his father that had haunted Nick was gone. Amelia Potter had her son back. Troy Durham was a part of his family once more.

Weller was going back to prison.

What about you, Bobbie?

She took a deep breath. Whatever happened next, she was pretty sure she would be okay.

Forty-Four

Nick stared at the woman sleeping. She was his mother. Not the woman he'd thought of as his mother for his entire life—at least for all that he could remember. How had he forgotten her? It wasn't until he picked up that photograph in her apartment that he experienced a true memory. Had Weller somehow erased any memories that should have been imprinted?

Fury burned through Nick. As grateful as he was not to share DNA with the son of a bitch, he was still shaken by the revelation.

Amelia Potter's eyes opened and she stared at him for several seconds. Finally she blinked. "Bobbie told me who you are. I want you to know that I never stopped praying you'd come back."

She reached a pale hand from beneath the sheet. He accepted the gesture, allowing his much larger fingers to wrap around hers.

"For years I searched for you. I didn't care what

anyone else said. Whenever I saw a dark-haired boy about your age I'd hurry to see his face just to make sure it wasn't you. Eventually I stopped, but I never stopped hoping."

Her chapped lips spread into a remarkably beautiful smile. "You're so handsome. And so strong."

"There is much I need to tell you. I've done things," he said, his heart heavy, "I'm certain you wouldn't be proud of."

"We all do what we have to do." She squeezed his hand. "I'm so glad you found me."

"Me, too."

They talked for more than an hour. The sound of her voice grew as familiar as his own, it flowed around him, making him feel something he had not felt even once for as far back as he could recall: *safe*. She told him about his father. A good man who had died before Nick was born. She promised to show him pictures.

When Amelia drifted back to sleep, Nick stood and stretched his legs. He wanted to find Bobbie. They needed to talk.

Outside the room LeDoux waited for him.

"I thought you were on your way back to Virginia."

LeDoux shrugged. "I told them I wasn't leaving until Weller was on his way back to Atlanta."

Nick would have preferred never to have to hear that name again. "When are they transporting him?"

The sooner the better.

"They're leaving in half an hour." LeDoux stared at the floor as if he wasn't looking forward to what he had to say next. "He wants to see you before he goes. Are you interested?"

No shot to the tip of his tongue. Nick bit it back. Instead he nodded. It would be the last time the bastard ever laid eyes on Nick.

LeDoux led the way to the room where Weller was shackled to a bed. Four guards waited outside the room. There were two more inside.

A jerk of the head from LeDoux and the two inside followed him back into the corridor.

Weller stared at Nick as if trying to memorize every detail. "One day you'll appreciate what I did for you."

Nick stared at the defeated old man who had destroyed so many lives. "You're right. I will truly appreciate the day you take your last breath."

He turned his back and walked away.

Weller called after him but Nick never looked back.

Forty-Five

Thursday, November 3, 2:00 a.m.

The night air was cold but Bobbie had needed to be away from the medicinal smells of the hospital for a minute. She'd spent way too much time in hospitals and rehabs this year.

She felt at peace for the first time in a very long time.

Her life was different now, but she was alive and she had an obligation to appreciate what others had sacrificed so much for. James, Jamie, Newt and Bauer, just to name those closest to her.

She smiled. "We got him, Asher."

Her cell vibrated and she grabbed it, hoping it might be Nick. *Holt.* Bobbie took a breath and answered. "Hey."

"Owens told me what you did."

Bobbie held back the tears that burned in her eyes. "I did what I had to do."

The long pause that followed pressed hard against Bobbie's sternum. She didn't want to lose her relationship with Holt. The two of them were all that was left of their unit. They needed each other.

"Thank you." Holt's voice trembled on the words. "Now get your ass back up here. We have work to do."

Bobbie laughed and assured her she would see her on Monday.

She put her phone away, a tremendous weight off her shoulders. Whatever happened from this moment forward, she was comfortable with her place in the scheme of things. Her world might never be the way it used to be, but it was hers.

She turned to head back to the hospital. Nick exited the front entrance and walked toward her.

Had something happened? Had Amelia taken a turn for the worse? She hurried to meet him. "Is everything okay?"

He nodded. "Almost."

She wasn't sure how long it had been since she'd had any sleep, maybe twenty-four hours. There was a good possibility that she was getting a little giddy.

"We could grab a cup of coffee or find a quiet place to get some sleep if you want to stay close to Amelia."

"She told me to get some sleep. I think maybe she needed some time to process the idea that her little boy isn't a little boy anymore."

Bobbie's heart squeezed. "Guess so."

He nodded. "If you don't have some other place to be, can you come with me?"

That extra beat that bumped against her sternum had her holding her breath. "I'd love to."

They walked side by side across the parking lot. She was surprised to find her Challenger.

"Durham had an officer bring it over for you. Your purse is still inside." He produced the fob and tossed it to her.

"Do you want me to drop you off at your room?" Again she held her breath.

He didn't answer. Instead he closed the small distance between them, trapping her between his body and the car. "No. I'm going with you."

She moistened her lips. She had to know what that meant. "I should leave in a couple of days and head back to Montgomery."

"You have room for a passenger?"

Surprised, she shrugged. "Sure. You know someone who needs a ride?" She needed him to spell out his intentions.

"Wherever you go, *I* go."

Bobbie nodded slowly. "If you're sure that's what you want."

"That's what I want. You?"

She nodded again. "It is."

"Good. You want me to drive?"

She tossed the fob back to him. "I would love for you to drive."

When they were settled in the car and he'd started the engine, she asked, "What about Amelia?"

"I told her I had to get you back home as soon as she's released—day after tomorrow according to her doctor—and that we'd both be back to visit for the holidays."

"I like that plan."

He reached across the console and took her hand in his. "Good."

Nick drove away from the hospital parking lot. Bobbie relaxed into the cool leather and closed her eyes.

She was definitely ready for whatever came next.

* * * * *

talk about it

Let's talk about books.

Join the conversation:

 on facebook.com/harlequinaustralia

on Twitter @harlequinaus

www.harlequinbooks.com.au

If you love reading and want to know about our
authors and titles, then let's talk about it.